"Your brother has destroyed my sister's good name and I, in turn, shall ruin yours."

**

"You're a fool, Lord Cavendish," Mina stated in a whisper, for she knew that nothing he might do could ruin her. Long ago Society had deemed Mina beneath its notice.

"A fool?" Cavendish grabbed her chin, lifting her face to his inspection. "You'd best obey me, Miss O'Kieffe."

An impulse seized Cavendish and as a carriage turned the bend, offering its occupants a perfect view of himself and Miss O'Kieffe, he pulled her body against his and his mouth descended to cover hers.

The earl had merely intended to offer the passing spectators the impression of a passionate embrace, but his quick touch lengthened and soon he was kissing her in earnest, intoxicated by her hesitant, yet undeniable response.

Mina heard nothing save the pounding of her heart...

MAYFAIR SEASON

∽THE∽
MAYFAIR SEASON

Nancy Richards-Akers

WARNER BOOKS

A Warner Communications Company

WARNER BOOKS EDITION

Warner Books, Inc.
666 Fifth Avenue
New York, N.Y. 10103

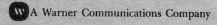A Warner Communications Company

Printed in the United States of America

First Printing: November, 1987

10 9 8 7 6 5 4 3 2 1

To the memory of my grandfather, John Rehm, with my love. And in gratitude to Pam Regis, Kathy Seidel, Myra Engers, Barbara Livingston, Diann Litvin, and Mary Kilchenstein with my thanks.

Chapter
One

1816

"Unseasonably warm," Nanny Saltmarsh grumbled into her third cup of chocolate. She was a slight woman, all grays and white, and quick to complain about a change in the weather. Her pinched expression spoke of annoyance as she glared in the direction of the oriel windows. It was the aged nurse's silent signal to pull the drapes closed, and no one challenged the wishes of Nanny Saltmarsh, for she had been at Thornhill Park since the last marquess was in leading strings. She was the oldest inhabitant of the Tudor manor house, and as such her every whim was indulged.

A liveried footman rushed to do her bidding. Crewel-worked hangings fell into place and the oak-paneled dining room was shrouded in darkness, which suited Nanny to a tee. But across the mahoghany table a pretty girl dared to challenge the elderly woman.

"How can you say that? Why the weather's positively magnificent. I love the fair days. 'Tis a most welcome change from the past dreary weeks." In a simple corded muslin frock of pale blue with white stripes, she was fresh as the violets that decorated the massive table. Everything about the girl was alive. Her eyes glinted merrily, her voice rang dulcet, schoolroom enthusiasm laced with the hint of an Irish brogue. "Come, Nanny, admit it. Weren't you the slightest bit tired of April's showers?"

It was as if Nanny had not heard a word. She stared at nothing in particular. With her free hand, she tucked a stray wisp of gray hair beneath her mobcap before she proceeded, slowly, to drain the porcelain cup.

"A little sunshine would do wonders for you. Why don't you spend the afternoon on the south terrace?" encouraged the girl.

Nanny's Wedgwood cup met its saucer with a clatter. "Stuff and nonsense, Miss Mina. I'm not a peony to be set out each time the weather turns. Mark my words, sunshine does more harm than good. Ruins your skin. I know you'll be going out, nothing I can do about that. Never could stop you. But watch out for that sun. Don't forget your bonnet."

"Yes, Nanny."

"Remember, your mother always took care of her looks. She was a beauty." Nanny smiled, a faraway look settling on her countenance at the memory of Lady Elaine. "Did I ever tell you about your mother's first season? A nonpareil the year of her come-out, and she always took care of her skin." In the next instant Nanny somehow remembered what she had been talking about before her digression to Lady Elaine, and she continued her scold. "And your gloves. Remember your gloves. Sun damages a woman's hands as surely as it does her complexion."

But gloves were a hindrance, and Mina had no intention of wearing them. Beneath the table, she crossed her fingers. "Yes, Nanny." She was not lying precisely. Her promise proceeded from goodness of heart. It was merely a way to keep Nanny happy, and the elderly woman was happiest when she believed Miss Mina was suitably protected against the elements.

It was wise to change the subject, Mina decided. But what topic to steer Nanny towards? It could not be her mother, for recollections of Mama made her yearning for Lady Elaine near unbearable, and so she ventured to inquire, "Do you know where Liam is?" Her favorite sibling, Liam, at four and twenty was seven years Mina's senior.

Like the other O'Kieffe brothers, he was frequently gone from Thornhill Park, which held few attractions for bachelors.

"Heh?" Nanny started awake from a brief doze. "Were you saying something, m'dear?"

"Liam? Do you know where he's been these past two days?"

"No, can't say as I do." Nanny yawned. Although it was early morning, she needed a nap. It was often like that; Nanny hardly possessed sufficient energy to make it through the day. No one knew precisely how old Amanda Saltmarsh was. Some said eighty-six; others claimed she was nearer to ninety-four. Whatever her years, their weight was beginning to take its toll. It was for this reason that Mina endeavored to make Nanny's lucid moments as pleasant as possible, for she loved the old woman fiercely.

Another yawn overcame Nanny. It passed and she continued, "Heard the twins talking. Liam's been seeing a local girl. Got an attachment for some country chit."

"Oh, how wonderful." Mina was delighted with this news and she laughed, the light sound tinkling through the darkened room. Her romantic imagination knew no moderation, and she began to picture Liam with a beautiful wife living happily ever after in a vine-covered cottage on a cliff overlooking the sea.

"Farradiddle!" Nanny exclaimed. She well knew Mina's weakness. The girl's sensibilities were admirable, but her propensity to daydream was impractical. She was forever spinning fantasies, a worthless occupation, and Nanny cast a chastising eye at her. Her words were sharp. "Don't know what's so wonderful. He'll end up leg-shackled to some farmer's daughter, or worse, he'll stir up a hornet's nest dangling after some puffed-up squire's lass."

"Neither will happen. I'm certain of it," declared Mina on a long, heartfelt sigh. It went against every notion she cherished that any man and woman who enjoyed the graze of Cupid's arrow might be kept asunder.

On the other hand, Nanny knew there was no such thing as a love match and it was, she considered, high time Miss Mina realized that. The nurse frowned. Had she been wrong

to encourage the girl's dreams since Lady Elaine's death?
No, never. Nanny would do it again, the very same way.
She would allow anything to keep that elfin smile on Miss
Mina's face. No, there was no sense in destroying the girl's
illusions. No reason at all.

"Perhaps you're right, Miss Mina. Perhaps Liam will
settle down with a nice gel." Her voice weakened, and she
signaled to the footman. It was time for a nap. Her final
words, "Remember your gloves; sun ruins the complexion," were barely audible as she exited the dining room.

Mina strolled to a window, pulled back the curtains, and
gazed outside. Yes, it was a perfect day despite Nanny's
grumblings, and Miss Mina O'Kieffe of Thornhill Park,
Kent, intended to enjoy it to the fullest. It was a perfect day
for sitting in the sun and reading, and that was precisely
what she set out to do as the midday sun neared its zenith in
the delft-blue sky.

Bare arms laden with pillows, a practical chip bonnet
perched atop her head, and carrying a satchel filled with
books and edibles, Mina fairly flew over the pebbled path
that led to the lake pavilion. The sky was clear and the
winds gentle; only an occasional breeze rustled the pink and
white blossoms of cherry trees which dotted the rolling
countryside. Honeybees droned in the field of jonquils
which rose beyond the lake, and as Mina skipped up the
pavilion steps, she heard the cooing of larks in the shrubberies
surrounding the lakeside structure.

At the opposite side of the pavilion lay a small rowboat,
motionless on the glassy water of the man-made lake. Mina
set the satchel in the bottom of the boat. The pillows came
next, being tossed in a large pile at the bow. Next she
removed her Grecian sandals of blue kid, placing them
beneath a bench for safekeeping. When her bare toes met
the cool marble floor, Mina shivered and then grinned at the
thought of Nanny should the woman ever learn that Mina
had left behind more than her gloves. But there was no one
to see what Mina did. The lake was hidden behind a hillock.
No one could be offended by her daring and there was,
Mina justified, no harm in being as comfortable as possible.

Ready to embark, Mina lowered her slender form into the boat and shoved away from the pavilion. Tiny waves lapped at the hull; the vessel rocked with Mina's movement and then subsided as she settled into the nest of pillows, pulling a slim novel from the depths of the satchel.

A Maiden's Plight. It was the latest romance from the Minerva Press and Mina sighed, her heart heavy at the predicament that confronted the lovely lady Lydia de Lisle. But, of course, love would triumph. It always did, Mina's inner voice consoled, although Lydia had, only pages before, been cruelly torn from the arms of her betrothed. Lord Ranald was off to the Holy Land, and the despicable Black Earl took Lydia into his keep. True love must be victorious, Mina's romantic soul declared, and naturally, three chapters hence, Lydia's plight began to abate, for Lord Ranald was heading home from the Crusades to claim his beloved.

Absorbed in the unfolding drama, Mina hooked her legs over the prow to dangle bare toes in the cool water. She sighed again. Then she smiled with delight when Ranald, astride his white steed, rode into the Black Earl's bailey to sweep the lovely Lydia off her feet.

Mina closed her eyes and nestled deeper into the pillows. A breeze blew the skirt of her dress about her knees, but she did not notice. Her heart swelled with satisfaction. True love had triumphed, and the world was at peace once more. The sun warmed Mina, a gust of wind rocked the boat, and within moments she was asleep.

On a hill beyond the blanket of jonquils was a man on horseback. He was lithe and fair-haired, his riding garb heralding him a Corinthian of the first stare. A coat of royal blue superfine fit his athletic form to perfection, and seated as he was, atop the finest piece of horseflesh in the county, he appeared larger than life, a veritable Atlas looming on the horizon.

Lord Compton Cavendish's gaze rested on the female figure in the rowboat. An expression of utter disgust shadowed his aristocratic face.

The girl was a trollop. Certainly she was no better than

her brothers, an O'Kieffe through and through. In his judgment, Miss Mina O'Kieffe was a common Irish chit whose lack of breeding was revealed in the abandoned fashion with which she displayed her ankles and calves to any passerby.

His mount ambled closer while the boat drifted towards the shore, affording a closer view of its passenger. Her ankles were slender, her legs delicately curved and creamy. Mina's bonnet had fallen back to reveal her piquant face, cheeks rouged by the sun, honey curls tumbling about her chin. She stretched, catlike in her dreams, the fabric of her gown pulling against her delightful figure.

For an instant, the man's gaze lingered on the appealing curves. His eyes traveled upward from her tiny waist as he endeavored to recall the color of her eyes. Were they blue? he wondered. Or green? He had always had a penchant for emerald-eyed lightskirts, he considered with a low chuckle. And her lips? Were they as enticing as the rest of her?

But it was ages since he had set eyes on the chit, and he sighed with disappointment. His recollection was too vague to complete the sultry picture before him. Cursing his foolishness, he gave the reins an angry jerk. There were far more important matters that demanded his attention than gaping moon-eyed at a girl who was beneath his notice.

Looking the very devil, Lord Cavendish, the seventh Earl of Brierly, gave the stallion's flanks an angry slap and cantered off in a northeasterly direction.

An hour later the little boat punted against the marble pavilion, awakening its occupant. Mina yawned and rubbed her eyes as a high-pitched female voice pierced the silence.

"La! At last I've found you." A plump woman, her frizzed hair dyed an astounding red, puffed up the steps of the pavilion. "Been looking high and low for you nigh on thirty minutes. Never imagined a soul would traipse all this distance just to look between the pages of a book," stated the redhead between gasps. Her elaborate Coburg walking dress and immense bonnet from which a Zebra plume of lilac extended were the height of fashion. London fashion, that is, and she was better suited for a carriage ride through Hyde Park than a stroll through the gardens at Thornhill.

Mina looked up from the nest of pillows, and as she pushed a thick, honey-colored tress from her sea-green eyes, she managed a smile of greeting. She had no more affection for Eugenia Grevey than for the other women her brothers brought home from London. Miss Grevey was too garish, not at all like the elegant ladies Mina emulated from the pages of *La Belle Assemblée*. But Mina was never rude, so she inquired politely, "Am I wanted at the house, Miss Grevey?"

"Miss Grevey, indeed. Come now, lambie, let's not be so formal. My friends at Drury Lane call me Genie, and Genie it should be, for I'm certain you and I are going to be very good friends." Eugenia Grevey plopped her generous form on an alabaster bench and, patting the empty space beside her, she gave Mina a friendly grin. "Wanted at the house, you ask? Why no, I don't believe so. Truth to tell, I was hoping for a friendly coze, just the two of us."

It was the same as always, Mina mused with a sad sigh. One of her brothers would bring his latest *chère amie* to Thornhill, and immediately the woman would decide that the way to the O'Kieffe fortune and a wedding band about her finger was through Mina. This very scene had occurred countless times before, but with slight variations; Sean, the eldest O'Kieffe, had a liking for second-rate actresses like Miss Grevey, while the twins, Kevin and Michael, preferred fallen ladies of the *ton*. Only Liam had never entertained a ladyfriend at Thornhill. It was an odd thing, that, for Mina was certain a man so handsome and kind must be prodigious popular with the ladies; yet he had never brought any home. Often Mina wished it was not so, for she fancied Liam's friends might be to her liking, and above all else, Mina longed for friends.

Once Mina had enjoyed a certain friendship with a girl in the neighborhood. Lady Catherine Cavendish of Brierly Castle had often visited Mina while Mama was alive. Mina fondly recalled the lighthearted girl who had chatted with her on winter afternoons in the schoolroom. Catherine was fun-loving, filled with laughter and a contagious merriment, and the two girls had giggled about their brothers, loathing the approach of spring, when the lads would taunt their frailer siblings with buckets of minnows. There were beautiful memories of rides in the pony cart and trips to the village of Sutton Valence when the girls were permitted to select their own hair ribands and scented soaps.

But all that had ended shortly after Mina's eleventh birthday. Mama had died then, leaving her alone in a household of O'Kieffe men, four older brothers whose presence was not welcomed in any decent home. They were not bad men precisely. Irishmen, indeed, their father's sons, rough and ready for a mill, eager for a cockfight and a night of drink, gambling, and friendly women.

In her innocence, Mina did not realize that she had been welcomed into Society merely out of sympathy for her mother. Mama, gay and beautiful, had been the only child of the Marquess of Thornbury, a thoroughly dissolute nobleman who, having gambled away the family fortune, bartered his daughter to a wealthy Irish merchant. Before her marriage to Ryan O'Kieffe, Lady Elaine had been well loved by her neighbors, and for that reason alone her daughter had been received in Kent. But after Lady Elaine was gone, Society forgot Mina. They saw only the O'Kieffe brothers, loud and laughing heartily, racing their cattle through the village streets and supplying the gossips with a surfeit of scandal.

It was simply, Mina often told herself, that her brothers knew how to enjoy life. They were happy and satisfied, unlike the gentry who disdained their company. It was jealousy, plain and simple, jealousy of their exuberance and spirit. But that thought did little to assuage the profound hurt Mina experienced when afternoon visitors no longer came to tea and when invitations no longer arrived at Thornhill.

Even Catherine had ceased coming, but Mina did not blame her. In her heart of hearts, Mina knew that if it were not for Catherine's odious brother, her dear friend would have stood by her side. But Cavendish, the earl, ruled

Brierly Castle with an iron hand. His word was law and Catherine, who had defied him by secretly meeting Mina in the village churchyard, had, upon discovery, been promptly sent to Miss Hedgecombe's Institute for Young Ladies in Bath.

So it was that the past six years had been lonely. But all was not lost, for in those years she had turned to books, reading and dreaming, dreaming and reading. There were a myriad of friends to be found between the pages of a novel. There were adventures and romances aplenty, and so while other girls were preparing to make their come-outs, Mina was traveling to far-off places, worlds replete with kings and pharaohs, sultans and princes.

"Ah-hem." Eugenia Grevey coughed and repeated herself. "Been reading one of them Minervas again?"

"Yes. It was such a glorious day I couldn't resist going out on the lake." Mina climbed from the boat, smoothed down her dress, and retrieved the kid sandals from beneath the bench. She sat down to retie the delicate shoes as Miss Grevey continued. "Sean says you read a lot. Bright, too, he told me, and I daresay he was bragging. Now, lambie, books may be nice for an afternoon, but don't you ever wish for the real thing?" Her voice lowered to a theatrical whisper and she gave Mina a wink. "Ain't you ever wondered what it would be like to waltz with a real man?"

A blush heightened the natural pink in Mina's cheeks. Judging from the descriptions in the *Times*, the waltz seemed a shockingly intimate dance. Of course, Mina dreamed of dancing with a man whose handsomeness surpassed that of the Minerva heroes, but she was not certain she wished to be held quite so tightly as the waltz dictated.

"Not up to the waltz, eh?" Miss Grevey stated with earthy perceptiveness. "Well, not to worry, there's something for everyone in London. I'm sure you'd enjoy Astley's Circus and Covent Garden and carriage rides in the Park. Wouldn't that be nice?"

"Yes, it would be lovely," Mina admitted in a faint, noncommittal tone. Yes, Mina longed to visit London. But she wanted to be a part of her mother's world, not a part of

Eugenia Grevey's, and that was simply not possible. The
O'Kieffes might be as wealthy as Midas and she might be
the granddaughter of a marquess, but Mina did not doubt
that she would be no more welcomed at Almack's than at
the assembly rooms in Sutton Valence. She could not bring
herself to explain this. It hurt far too much to voice the
truth. A tear formed in the corner of one shamrock-green
eye, but she held it back. Above all, Mina did not want
anyone's pity.

"Well, lambie, then it's up to you and me to be doing
something about it. Can't sit back and wait for your brothers, you know. Men ain't always in the know when it comes
to what's right and proper for a young lady like yourself."
There was a warmth in her voice that touched Mina.
Eugenia Grevey honestly meant to be kind, and Mina could
not resist smiling at the the blowsy woman as she reassured,
"Now, don't worry. I'll be speaking to Sean tonight, and
we'll be seeing you in London in no time."

Mina's smile broadened. This was another familiar scene.
It was inevitable that her brother's ladyfriend would have
decided to embark on this grand plan: the introduction of
Miss Mina O'Kieffe to London. Similar schemes had been
concocted before and, as in the past, the same outcome
would ensue. Sean would tire of his houseguest; the woman
in question would tearfully return to London, all thoughts of
aiding Mina abandoned; and Mina would remain at Thornhill
awaiting the next installment of romances in the morning
post.

"That's very kind of you, Miss Grevey."

"Nonsense! There's nothing kind about it at all. I'd only
be doing what you deserve. And don't be forgetting, I told
you to call me Genie." With a smile, she linked her arm
through Mina's, and they walked back towards the manor
house.

Mina felt a stab of sadness for Eugenia Grevey. She was
different from the others. Of a certainty, she was coarse and
ill-bred, but she was sincere, and Mina wished that her
brother would not hurt this kindhearted woman.

It would be lovely, she thought with a little sigh, if Sean

were to fall in love. Why, then he would stay home and Miss Grevey might have children and Mina would be an aunt and Thornhill would be filled with goings on and she would never lack for company.

This happy fantasy so preoccupied Mina that she did not hear the approach of horses.

"Lawks!" Eugenia Grevey shrieked and yanked Mina out of harm's way as three O'Kieffe brothers, Sean, Michael, and Kevin, galloped down the drive towards the open road. Dust rose, encircling the pedestrians in a choking cloud and leaving them to wonder what prank the men were about this time.

It was past eight in the evening before the men returned, and their entrance was no less dramatic than their departure; the echo of heavy boots and angry voices resounding in the great hall heralded their arrival. They marched into the lounge, where they unceremoniously dumped Liam, his lower lip bloodied and both eyes swelling purple, on a damask-covered settee.

"See what you can do for him," Sean said to Miss Grevey, and then he noticed Mina, who had jumped up from a cushioned seat in the window bay. Her face was white with alarm, the book she had been reading fell to the floor, and she called her favorite brother's name as she crossed the room to kneel on the Aubusson carpet. She reached for Liam's hand, her worried glance alternating between his injured face and Sean's.

"It's not as bad as it looks. All he needs is a bit of washing," Sean said all too matter-of-factly.

Mina bit back a retort; it was futile to argue with Sean. If he said it was not bad, he expected his family to accept that statement. Oblivious to Mina's distress, Sean crossed the lounge and poured a healthy dose of brandy into a balloon-shaped snifter which he emptied in a single swallow. "How about it, lads?" he said to the twins.

"Don't you worry, lambie," Eugenia Grevey consoled Mina in a quiet voice, too low to be heard by Sean. "He's right, you know. Likely this is no more than a scratch. Simply looks worse than it is. Besides, you know how men are." There was a faintly caustic note in her voice.

"Oh, yes, I know how my brothers are," Mina answered, and she tossed Sean a look that carried both affection and a sisterly reprimand. "And if they aren't careful, they'll all meet dire ends before their time." This she spoke in a voice loud enough to be carried across the room. Sean acknowledged her warning with a nod and a cryptic grin.

Raising his second glass, he toasted, "*S'rioghal mo dhream.*" It was an ancient Celtic battle cry. "My blood is royal." Passed from father to son by generations of O'Kieffe men and, these days, generally reserved for those times when the O'Kieffe men experienced a certain victory over their English neighbors.

"*S'rioghal mo dhream,*" echoed Kevin and Michael.

Three miles to the northeast at Brierly Castle, Lady Catherine Cavendish was crying bitterly. The lady, only that morning having been returned by force to the castle, was a prisoner in her own home. The earl had actually ordered the servants to lock Catherine in her room and she cried at the hopelessness of her predicament.

There was also a touch of fear in those tears. That Catherine had been unable to discover Liam's fate was frightening, for she never imagined her brother could display such anger as he had shown at the coaching inn outside Gretna Green. The earl clearly intended to punish Liam, and Catherine cried harder at the thought of what might befall her beloved.

"Oh, Liam, my darling," she managed to whisper between sobs. "I never meant for it to happen like this. Please believe me. I never meant to hurt you." Like a small child, she curled her body inward, exhaustion pressing her into a blessed, mindless sleep.

Downstairs, the silhouetted figure of Lord Cavendish, Earl of Brierly, paced before the library hearth. The high-ceilinged room was black save for what little light came from the dying fire, but not so dark as to hide the tightness in his shoulders, the frustration in his step. The man was angry, and in the firelight he appeared demonic. Orange flames flickered higher, a sudden burst revealing a bruised jaw. A thin line of broken flesh flared scarlike across his right cheekbone. He raised a hand to touch the tender skin, cursing aloud the folly of his confrontation with Liam O'Kieffe.

He had behaved no better than that half-breed Irishman, and the earl experienced a profound sense of self-loathing. It was unthinkable that he had displayed such emotion, resorted to such physical means, but then his behavior was well founded. Never before had the Cavendish name been so despoiled.

The library door opened, and a statuesque woman appeared on the threshold. Dressed in an elaborate satin gown, her hair piled high in an abundance of intricately arranged curls, there was no doubting that she had been a beauty in her youth. When she spoke, her voice retained the same sensual quality that had made her irresistible to men. "Is that you, Compton?" She did not wait for an answer, entering without an invitation.

"As you can plainly see, the answer to your question, Grandmère, is yes."

"No need to be rude," she responded in a quelling tone.

"You're right. Please excuse me." He threaded his fingers through his fair hair, frustration evident in the repeated and unnecessary movement.

Satisfied that her grandson was appropriately contrite, Grandmère softened her voice to ask, "Don't you think you were a bit harsh on your sister?"

"Harsh?" The single word spoke of the earl's extreme weariness. "I think I showed remarkable restraint. As for O'Kieffe, he deserved far worse than he got. That he dared to court Catherine is beyond belief. Any other man would be dead for having done less."

Grandmère did not respond immediately; instead she took a few moments to light a multi-tiered candelabra. The freshly lit candles sputtered and then, once bathed in the white circle of light, her mood became evident. She was deeply concerned. Delicate lines marred her brow, and she was frowning as she sat down, her eyes locked on the figure of her grandson.

When she spoke, it was gently. "He wasn't trifling with her affections. They're truly in love, Compton, and sometimes that counts for a great deal more than bloodlines."

"Love." The earl made the word sound like a curse. He walked away from the hearth and leaned over a writing desk. Resting his palms on the table, he closed his eyes and scowled at the memory of Liam O'Kieffe and Catherine at the inn near the Scottish border. Cavendish had not known what to expect when he caught up with his runaway sister. Certainly, it would have been easier to discover she had been forced to accompany O'Kieffe. That, of course, was not the case. She had gone willingly, an accomplice in the secretly planned elopement. Worse, he had been unprepared to discover himself cast in the role of villain. As if Catherine had needed protection from him, the Irishman had wrapped a protective arm about her waist. With that single gesture, the earl became an outsider in his own family. If that was love, it filled him with anger.

"Don't gammon me with talk of love, Grandmère. If Liam O'Kieffe truly loved Catherine, he would never have entertained the notion of marriage. Any decent man would have realized the damage such a connection would wreak on a lady's reputation." The earl's eyebrows were several shades darker than his hair, arching cynically above deep-set eyes, and in the firelight they heightened the sense of barely leashed fury which he held in check.

"Compton, Compton, my boy. And what do you know of love? To you, marriage is a business arrangement. That's all the matches were that you arranged for Elise and Cassandra. Nothing more. Though your sisters have been happy, they were lucky, and if you set out to do the same for Catherine, you might not be so fortunate. She's a different gel than her sisters. Not quite so patient. She wants all of life at once." She paused and squinted through the half-light at her grandson. He was so serious, so distant, and so different from the rest of the Cavendish family.

"Have you ever known true love, I wonder? Compton, Compton." She repeated his Christian name very slowly. "You're like a horse with blinders when it comes to propriety.

You want everything to be safe and predictable, which is merely a way of justifying the emptiness of your life. Ten years ago, when you assumed the title, I knew it would come to this. You were too young for such a burden— myself and three younger sisters to care for. Look at you, pacing and muttering. All your spirit wasted on defending the family honor.''

''Wasted!'' was the reply, and with a tinge of dismay.

''*Certainement*. Loyalty is expected in a gentleman of rank. That I admit. But what about yourself, Compton? Did it never once occur to you that this devotion has been at the expense of your own youth? Sometimes I think you're older than I and *that*, dear boy, would be ancient indeed.'' She paused to measure the effect of her words, but the earl guarded his reaction closely. He did not move away from his position over the desk. When Grandmère continued, her tone was grave once more. ''It saddens me deeply to see you so serious and to watch you ruin Catherine's chance for true happiness.''

''You blame me, Grandmère?'' The earl was truly shocked. ''Who else?''

''O'Kieffe, of course. Catherine's a decent girl, but she's far too impetuous for her own good. Needs a firm hand to prevent her behavior from listing on the rackety side. Look at this mess. And it's too late now to undo the damage. She's ruined, and in no time her disgrace will be the latest *on-dit*.''

''That's doing it up a tad brown. A few tongues will wag, but it's hardly the end of the world.''

''Not the end of the world, you say? It's a veritable disaster, and why you refuse to see that is beyond my ken. 'Tis your French blood, I suppose, and I forgive you for that.''

''Forgive me? You'll do no such thing.'' Here, Grandmère affected a heavy Parisian accent. Although she had been living in England for more than fifty years, Elise de Montaigne Cavendish, Dowager Countess of Brierly, could sound like a newly arrived emigré if she wished. ''*Mais, naturellement*, it is my French blood, and I am very proud. It is you who must be pardoned, monsieur. For do you not know, 'tis *l'amour* which makes the world go round?''

''Egad, Grandmère, you're as birdwitted as Catherine.

Next I suppose you'll tell me you condone her plans to elope with O'Kieffe.''

''I do.''

''That's a ramshackle notion, if I ever heard one. O'Kieffe's scarcely a suitable match for Catherine. Consider his family. All of them beneath our notice. Three brothers who've never spent a moment's time in the company of a decent woman, a sister who's been unchaperoned for nigh on six years, and, if the stories are only half true, a father who made his fortune in the slave trade and died a traitor, running blockades for the Colonies. Why, even his mother's family was no better. Old Thornbury gambled away his estates until all he had left was his daughter. Hardly suitable in-laws.''

''I'm surprised at you, Compton. Surely you don't hold the deeds of others against a man. Liam O'Kieffe should be judged as his own man.''

Silence descended on the room.

The earl peered sharply at his grandmother. Soft candle-light framed her, endowing her with a fragile, almost ethereal quality, an impression that was highly deceptive. The Dowager Countess of Brierly was no trembling barque of frailty. She was a formidable woman with definite notions, and the earl was fast regretting the message he had sent to her. Grandmère was not usually at Brierly. It had been more than five years since she had been in residence at the castle, preferring instead the gay round of parties that Town life offered. Sheer frustration on the earl's part had led him to summon Grandmère, hoping she might be able to make Catherine see the error of her ways. But Grandmère was not the ally he anticipated.

She continued. ''Yes, Liam O'Kieffe ought to be judged as his own man. He's done a most remarkable job in increasing the income at Thornhill Park. Been experimenting with modern agrarian systems, something to do with irrigation, I understand.''

''You appear to know a great deal about Liam O'Kieffe,'' the earl remarked with as much patience as he could muster.

''His grandmother and I were old friends. Lady Letitia was the first member of the *beau monde* to welcome me when your grandfather brought me here from France."

"You're evading the issue, Grandmère. Truth to tell, I get the distinct impression you've been going about behind my back."

Grandmère was not one to be intimidated by the earl, and she laughed aloud at his accusation. "What I do with my life, young man, is none of your affair."

"But," Cavendish amended seriously, "what you do with Catherine's life is very much my affair. I never should have let the girl stay with you last Season. Should have sent her off to Northumberland for Cassandra's lying-in. I believe the two of you have landed us in this muddle."

"Muddle? I see no muddle. If you'd only let O'Kieffe court Catherine when he first approached her in London, then they wouldn't have resorted to going behind your back and there would be no grist for the gossip mill."

The earl's anger rose anew at the thought of his beloved sister becoming the subject of gossips. She deserved far better than that. His hand closed about the letter opener which lay on the desk and as the grip tightened, razor-sharp edges sliced the skin. He dropped the opener, unfolded his hand and, mesmerized, he stared at the deep red blood that streaked the palm.

Revenge. The thought sprang forth like the blood that dripped down his wrist. Although he did not know how he would do so, Compton Cavendish, Earl of Brierly, knew that he would never be at peace until he had his revenge on Liam O'Kieffe.

Chapter Two

"Back off, Mina darlin', or you'll kill me with your fussing." Liam's crisp blue eyes danced with affection at the sight of his sister, who was busily tucking a wool tartan about his legs. He loved to tease Mina and he knew that in the next instant she would jump back, place her hands on her hips, and glare daggers at him with pure indignation.

As predicted, she did precisely that.

Leaving the plaid where it lay, she backed away from her patient. Honey curls bobbing about her elfin face, Mina appeared the very picture of righteous outrage. Her apple-green morning dress set off the sparkle in her eyes, and there was no hiding the asperity in her lilting voice.

"Kill you with my fussing." An incensed scowl creased her forehead. "Why you ungrateful wretch! I ought to leave you to fend for yourself." Arms akimbo, she began to lecture her brother, who by the look of the lines about his injured eyes and mouth was either in extreme pain or on the verge of laughter. It was the latter, and his eyes watered with mirth, fueling Mina's indignation.

"Sick men ought not to enjoy themselves quite so much, especially not men who are responsible for their own condition. It strikes me they ought to give some thought to the efficacy of their actions." She sounded ever so much like Nanny Saltmarsh.

"*Efficacy*, is it, now?" he needled. "And where would you be picking up such big words?"

Mina stomped her foot in frustration. "Oooh! Don't you mock me, Liam O'Kieffe."

It was no use. Her words only served to make matters worse, and by this time Liam was roaring with laughter. Then, seeing Mina's injured expression, her lips pursed in a delicate pout, he quickly doused his merriment. Although his sister was a delight to tease, it was, he admitted, poor game when she did not join in the fun, and today Mina was clearly in no mood for revelry.

"Mina, what's overset you so?"

"Need you ask? Look at you. Black and blue from head to toe. Your beautiful face beaten dreadfully. Oh, Liam, whatever have you done this time?" she worried aloud.

"Ain't all that bad, m'dear." He offered a tentative smile. "Appears one of our neighbors has developed a serious disagreement with me, and we merely chose to air our differences with a healthy round of fisticuffs.''

This was not precisely what Mina wished to hear, and recalling what Nanny had said yesterday, she quietly asked, ''Was it a girl?''

Liam's smile faded, and after a few moments' silence he parried, ''A girl? Now, what would you know about things like that? An unmarried maid even considering such a matter. Won't do atall.'' He rallied with a wink.

''Can't you be serious? I care about you. That's the only reason I'm asking—not to pry. And if you don't want to talk, then that's fine, but don't make light of it when it's obvious your injuries aren't only on the outside.''

He quirked a dark eyebrow. ''That obvious, eh?''

''Well, not really,'' she consoled. ''I'm sure Sean and the twins haven't noticed a thing. But I remember the time Da took Sean on board the *Seawitch* to the Indies and left you behind with the twins. Said you weren't old enough for an ocean crossing.'' Mina tilted her head sideways and her smile softened, as did her voice. ''I daresay, it was the worst thing ever to have happened in your eleven years. I was but four or five then, but I clearly recall the brave way you pretended not to care when, in truth, your heart was breaking. You stood ever so tall as the carriage with Da and Sean disappeared down the drive, and I wanted ever so much to run up to you and hug your disappointment away. But even then, I knew you'd deny it all and so I simply watched. You concentrated so hard that your eyebrows pushed together. They formed one long, bushy brow, and since then it's been easy to tell when you're hiding something. In fact, you're squinting ever so dreadfully right now.''

His reaction was immediate. Liam's facial expression relaxed and on a sigh he remarked, ''Clever puss.''

Mina returned to the settee where Liam rested, and carefully she sat on the corner. She reached out and took hold of his hand. ''I'd be more than happy to listen. And if you didn't fancy yourself too old for it, I'd be happy to hug the hurt away, too.'' Mina's words softened Liam's resistance. Too, her sweet smile raised his spirits.

"There's not much to tell. In the simplest terms, I was harebrained enough to think my dreams might come true. But it proved a mistake. That's all.''

"A mistake?'' Mina could scarce imagine that following one's dreams could be wrong.

Before Liam had the opportunity to respond, Nanny shuffled into the makeshift sickroom. She exclaimed, "Knew it would come to this! Didn't I tell you he'd stir up a hornet's nest?''

Their eyes met, sister's and brother's, and Mina's heart went out to Liam, for in that instant she recognized his sadness. It was something she well understood, the dashing of one's dreams. For dreams of a friend, romance, and a Season in London were all that Mina possessed, and she knew it would be devastating to part with them. Her nose burned, and she quickly turned away to hide the tears that shimmered in her eyes.

"Don't cry for me, puss. I'm not worth it. I've got a heart of stone.''

But Mina knew it was not so. Liam was not like Da or her other brothers. He did not revel his way through life, never pausing to take stock of the consequences of his actions. Liam cared about the people he knew and about the outcome of his deeds. He was committed to a life that bound his choices to the lives of others, and be it with the home farm or its tenants he put his heart and soul into everything he did. No, Liam did not have a heart of stone; he possessed a very human and vulnerable one. Nevertheless she forced a smile and bent down to kiss his brow.

In response he urged, "Go on now, puss. Nanny will sit with me. It's another glorious day, and you ought to be outside enjoying it.''

"All right, but promise to wait luncheon for me. I'll take a quick gallop across the meadows and be home by noon.''

"An engagement it is. We'll dine at noon.''

*   *   *

After changing into her riding costume, Mina hurried to the stables, where Thistle, her bay mare, pranced in waiting. The horse was eager for a gallop, and when her mistress approached, the animal whinnied in anticipation. Mina mounted without delay, her split skirt of bishop's blue merino (an invention that had caused Nanny a severe bout of the megrim) draping over the mare's gleaming flanks. She did not use a crop, believing love was the most persuasive force between mistress and beast, and with a gentle click of her tongue, horse and rider were soon beyond the formal gardens and into the open meadow, where Mina allowed Thistle free rein. Leaning low over the mare's neck, she laughed aloud at the exhilaration derived from racing through the tall grass and over the hills.

This was Mina's wild streak, the legacy of her Celtic heritage.

Books filled her world, but when the confines of that world closed in on her, Mina enjoyed nothing more than a wild gallop. She loved horses, especially the feisty Thistle, and her father had taught Mina to ride astride almost before she could walk. That was her most vivid memory of Da, a ruddy-faced man who had set her atop his stallion, a man who had been delighted with the spirit his only daughter displayed. Mina often remembered Mama, but it was when she was riding that she best recalled Da. Then she could even hear his heavy Irish accent, which he had passed on to his children, exclaiming, "Praise be, me darlin' Mina's got the pluck of the leprechaun in her blarney green eyes."

All across the rolling Kent hills, the sweet scent of apple blossoms clung to the air. Mina inhaled and laughed aloud, reining Thistle to a walk as they passed a small pond. Geese scattered at their approach, honking at the invasion of their territory, and Mina giggled at the sight of one gander who had dared to linger and hiss at the invaders. Horse and rider meandered down a lane that bordered an orchard, and Mina's thoughts turned to Liam. As often was her practice on these rides, she began to talk to Thistle.

"There must be something we can do for Liam. Perhaps we might discover the name of the girl. I'm sure she must love him, and perhaps she would tell us what went wrong.''

The horse inclined one dark ear towards her mistress, as if understanding every word. Satisfied that the horse was listening, Mina continued, "Do you think it was her father, Thistle? Perhaps he misunderstood Liam's intentions? Why, we could find this girl's father and talk to him. Surely he would listen to reason, for there's no man alive so hard and unfeeling that he would deny true love once the facts were presented.''

"Now, who could it be? Some local girl, Nanny said. Well, one thing I know for certain, Thistle. She'd have to be exceedingly special to catch Liam's eye. Exceedingly special, indeed.''

By this time, they had come nearly to the boundary between Thornhill Park and Brierly Castle. The sun was high and it was time to be turning back. Liam would be waiting for her.

Mina nudged the mare forward, clicked her tongue, and breaking into a canter, they were homeward bound. Over a hedgerow, neatly taken, the next obstacle was a narrow stream with a stone wall on the far bank. The wall was low, and Mina was certain Thistle could make both stream and wall. She urged the mare forward, and only too late did she sense the horse's hesitation. The stream was wider than she remembered, swollen by the recent rains. Thistle refused the jump, stopping dead in her tracks and propelling Mina, head first, through the air as if shot from a cannon.

There was no time to protect herself, and Mina let out a helpless yelp only seconds before her head hit a very large bolder. She felt no pain, heard only a loud crack, and then crumpled in the water, conscious but unable to open her eyes, a terrible ringing in her ears.

From the pink orchard on Brierly land, a man had observed the entire incident, and he was quick to respond. Sliding off his stallion, the earl leapt over the stone wall and waded to the middle of the stream.

Thank God, she was still moving, although how so frail a creature might have survived such a tumble was quite miraculous. Her head rested on the boulder, thrown backwards at a horrendous angle as if her neck might have snapped; the lower portion of her body was submerged in the rushing water, skirts billowing about her, and she looked for all the world like a drowned rat.

The girl moaned, and Cavendish did not hesitate to kneel in the chilly waters and gather her into his arms. Golden brown hair was plastered across her face; her bonnet, bedraggled and ruined, dangled carelessly by its ribands across her shoulder. In such a state, there was nothing appealing or attractive about this girl, and yet Cavendish was drawn to her. Gently he removed the bonnet. The girl winced, and his grip about her tiny waist tightened.

"'Tis all right, m'dear," was his deep, mellow whisper, his lips lingering at the spot below her ear. The scent of rose water assailed his senses and he shuddered, realizing the river had soaked through his butternut trousers.

His words comforted Mina, and her small hand reached out, grabbing hold of her rescuer's linen shirt. The grip was surprisingly strong; slender fingers tugged at him, pulling him closer, and that simple gesture had a devastating effect on the earl. Gazing down at her hand resting against him he felt a stirring within his chest, and he longed to have this girl, but it was not the same longing he had felt toward any of his mistresses. This was not a transitory desire, yet its source was unfathomable, something Cavendish could not quite identify.

Who was she? he wondered. Which one of his neighbors had visitors? He did not recognize the girl and he knew that if he had enjoyed the pleasure of meeting her, he would not have forgotten her name.

Then she moaned anew, and the earl jerked upright. "M'dear, hold still while I check for broken bones. I promise to be as gentle as possible." The husky tenderness in his voice matched that of his touch. He examined her and decided that she had merely had the wind knocked from her. "Don't think anything's broken, although I vow you'll be extremely uncomfortable for the next few days."

As the ringing in Mina's ears subsided, she slowly became aware of her surroundings. She was being held by a man, and it was as delightful an experience as any novel had described. Eyes still closed, she felt his arms about her, strong arms like the ones that had cherished Lydia de Lisle. Only moments before, his lips had hovered above her neck, and the bare skin there still tingled as she recalled the comforting warmth of his breath. Someone very caring and kind was tending to her. There was nothing to fear, and the beginning of a tiny smile tugged at her mouth. It was odd, but despite her fall she was content, and she snuggled against the firm chest. A sharp, distinctly male scent enveloped her. Images of Da and Liam floated about her, and caressed by a sense of well-being, she longed to remain where she was forever.

It was a silly notion, but Mina's imagination took command and she pictured her rescuer. He would be a tall man with fair hair and blue eyes like the endless sky; a handsome man whose strength and compassion, loyalty and, of course, love would be reflected in his every glance. Yes, her groggy mind confessed, it was prodigious silly fancy, but she imagined herself to be in love and loved in return, and that was quite the most wondrous thing that had ever happened to Mina.

When Mina rested her head against the earl's chest, his hold tightened instinctively. She was so delicate, so helpless, and with an impulse he did not understand, he let the very tips of his fingers brush against her cheek. Her eyes opened—they were luxuriantly lashed, and his breath caught at the sight of the most beautiful green eyes he had ever beheld. As green as the Saxon forests of primeval England, reminding the earl of something rarely found in one's lifetime.

"Thank you, sir." Her breathless whisper was captivating to the earl's ear. "If you could help me to the bank, I would like to rest against the wall for a few moments, please."

"Of course." The earl offered the enchanting girl his arm and helped her stand. He smiled down at the top of her head, and when she swayed slightly, he wrapped a supporting arm about her slender waist. "Thank you," she murmured. Her voice was as soft as a May breeze, but there was something more there. Mina spoke with the hint of her father's homeland and as Cavendish stared down at her, an awful recognition washed over him.

This girl was no angel, no innocent miss to be protected. Irish-accented and riding like hellfire on the lands adjacent to Brierly Castle, she could be none other than the O'Kieffe chit.

"Provocative wench," he swore between clenched teeth. No wonder she had pressed up to him with such abandon. Only a wanton would have eyes so verdant that their color alone could seduce.

There was no mistaking the scorn in his words, his scathing glance. It caused Mina to feel quite wretched, and she tilted her head to focus a questioning gaze on her rescuer. Yes, his hair was fair. It was styled elegantly but simply. No foppish curls for this man—it was trimmed precisely at the collar of his shirt. His face was a strong one, and he appeared a man of conviction, with a firm jaw, an aquiline nose, and a well-shaped mouth. And yes, his eyes were as blue as the sky when a storm has passed and the clouds lift to reveal a vast sapphire expanse. He was so beautiful. Why did he sound so angry?

"Who—who are you?" she asked.

"Brierly," came the harsh and unexpected answer.

Then she saw the fresh scar across his cheekbone and the bruised jaw. Immediately, her mind flew back to Liam. In that second, she understood everything she needed to know about this man: he was Compton Cavendish, the Earl of Brierly. The other pieces fell into place: Mina guessed somehow that it was her childhood friend, Lady Catherine, whom Liam loved, and it was the earl whom Liam had fought.

Tears misted her eyes, and a great sadness descended on Mina. Her heart broke for Catherine and Liam and, she admitted somewhat reluctantly, it broke for herself, for she had to accept that her rescuer was no knight on a charging white steed. He was merely a man—and a despicable one at that.

"You!" Mina accused, wrenching free of the arm he had

wrapped about her. "I don't need any help from the likes of you! A person with no soul, no compassion!"

This was certainly not the reaction Cavendish had expected, and he was momentarily at a loss for words. He watched open-mouthed as she backed away from him, moving one tiny step with each word.

"Never in a thousand years would I have suspected you were the culprit, my lord Cavendish!" Mina pointed a condemning finger at the earl, who remained motionless by the boulder.

Culprit? He arched an eyebrow. What in God's name was the chit babbling about?

"But, of course, it makes perfect sense. There isn't anyone more insensitive in the county, perhaps in Sussex as well." The sodden double skirt clung to her legs, forcing a momentary halt in her retreat. With as much dignity as possible she reached down and lifted the drenched fabric about her knees, and unaware of the indecorous picture she presented to the earl, she took another, larger step away from him.

The earl stared at this astonishing creature, hardly believing his own eyes and ears. Why was she so offended? And was she truly talking about him? He ran fingers through his hair, disconcerted to discover his hand was trembling.

"Oh, don't stand there looking so bamboozled. I know perfectly well it was you, and there's no way to deny it. The evidence is written all over your face!"

His face? Cavendish raised a shaking hand; the flesh was still tender and he winced, memory returning. "Ah, I believe I now comprehend the direction of your unladylike tirade, Miss O'Kieffe." He stepped towards her.

Mina moved another step backwards, stumbling slightly, but she did not miss a beat. She was well into her crusade, intending to right injustice and guarantee that true love triumph. In a clear voice, she informed him, "Whether or not my tirade is ladylike is of no consequence, my lord. 'Tis your behavior I am addressing." And with that she reached the muddy bank, stopped, and glared daggers at the earl.

That this chit would dare to address the earl in so forward

a manner was the outside of believable. He studied her, slender arms akimbo, still clutching the skirts about her knees. He wondered briefly if she was touched in the upper region, for no one had seen Mina O'Kieffe in many years, and perhaps the girl was a candidate for Bedlam. Admittedly, she was in high dudgeon, but probably not insane, so he ventured, "My behaviour is not a matter for your concern, Miss O'Kieffe." His condescending tone was edged with annoyance.

Oblivious to the earl's displeasure, Mina perceived this moment as her golden opportunity to champion the cause of true love. "How could you be so heartless?"

"If you are referring to the thwarted romance between your brother and my sister, let me assure you that heart or the lack thereof has nothing to do with it," said the cool aristocrat.

"Balderdash! Of course it does. Whyever else would anyone marry?" she demanded with a punctuating nod, her tenacious gaze blazing with zeal.

To her horror, the earl threw back his head to emit an unrestrained guffaw. "Whyever indeed, Miss O'Kieffe." While his blue eyes twinkled with amusement, a cruel mockery laced his words.

She pursed her lips. His laughter was most discomposing. In an uncharacteristically missish gesture, Mina self-consciously patted her disarrayed hair. Wet tendrils clung to her neck, snaking down the bodice of her sodden blouse. The earl's laughing eyes were bold upon her as he moved towards her, crossing the stream in two long strides. Mina gasped at his approach, fear mingled with an odd little excitement that made her heart skip a beat. Suddenly shy, Mina lowered her glance and then from beneath thick lashes she peered up at him, seeing a man who would laugh at love, a man who would fight to keep lovers apart.

"What a poor creature you are," she said, a sad, somewhat wistful, tone cloaking her words.

Perhaps if she had merely championed romance, the earl would have better tolerated Mina, for he was bemused by her impassioned speech and ingenuous defiance. But insults were unacceptable to his lordship, and calling him a poor creature was certainly a slap in the face. Although Cavendish did not fully comprehend her meaning, Mina's words pushed him that final inch from anger into full fury. First, it had been that rakehell O'Kieffe daring to challenge his rights as Catherine's brother, then Catherine ranting at him during the whole of the carriage ride south and Grandmère disagreeing with him the night before, and now it was this chit of a girl who was lecturing him as if he were a naughty tenant farmer's son. Words escaped him. He grabbed hold of Mina's wrist and gave her arm an angry yank as if he had caught her raiding the pantry.

"No one, Miss O'Kieffe—I repeat, no one—talks to me like that." He was deadly serious.

She quelled a surge of panic and met his gaze unflinchingly. "Unhand me, my lord. I have no desire to pursue this conversation. I had hoped to assist my brother, but clearly pursuit of this topic is fruitless with so unreasonable and unfeeling a man. So I shall bid you good day. I wish to go home."

An inexplicable glimmer flickered from the depths of his eyes while Mina observed them, and foreboding assailed her. When he spoke, his words confirmed her worst fears. "Home? Why, no, I don't believe you'll be going home, Miss O'Kieffe. You see, m'dear, you're my prisoner." His own words shocked him. What folly was he contemplating? Kidnapping? What devil was plotting in his subconscious? It was he, not Miss O'Kieffe, who was behaving like a Bedlamite, he decided as he turned the barely formed notion of her captivity over in his mind.

"You see, Miss O'Kieffe, only last evening I swore revenge for the shame your brother Liam has brought on my sister and the Cavendish family name. And although I had not considered how I might accomplish that end, you've obligingly worked out that detail for me."

Realizing the direction of his plan, she charged, "You not only lack compassion, my lord, you're insane." This accusation was punctuated with heartfelt conviction which was uniquely Mina's.

His grip tightened about her wrist and he drawled, "Perhaps. But if you've never shouldered the burden of family honor, then I doubt you'll understand my motivations. Let me explain. By his actions, your brother has destroyed my sister's good name and I, in turn, shall ruin yours." The words flowed smoothly and frigidly.

"You're a fool, Lord Cavendish," she stated on a whisper, for she knew that nothing he might do could ruin her. Long ago Society had deemed Mina beneath its notice; there was nothing the earl could do to distance her further from its good regard. She was already an outsider.

A large tear formed at the corner of her eye. She tried to blink it away but failed, and it slid down her cheek. Another followed and then another, and she bowed her head, overwhelmed by immeasurable sadness. If he had intended to hurt Mina, Lord Cavendish had accomplished that goal, for the futility of his plan was punishment enough for her. He had touched a terribly vulnerable spot—he had touched her dreams. How she longed to be a part of Society; the joy of company would be utterly delightful.

"A fool?" Cavendish echoed her accusation in an altogether expressionless tone. He grabbed her chin lifting her tear-stained face to his inspection. "You'd best obey me, Miss O'Kieffe."

In truth, the earl was not certain what to do with Mina. Yes, he had threatened her, but he did not want to hurt her physically, merely to dishonor her as Catherine had been dishonored. He was at a loss as to what his next step might be when the sound of an approaching carriage met his ears.

Once more, impulse seized Cavendish, and as the carriage turned the bend, offering its occupants a perfect view of himself and Miss O'Kieffe, he pulled her body against his and his mouth descended to cover hers.

The earl had merely intended to offer the passing spectators the impression of a passionate embrace, enough of a glimpse of impropriety that word would spread through Kent condemning Mina O'Kieffe for the tart that she must surely be. But that was not what transpired. Beneath his lips, Mina's mouth tasted of tears. Slightly salty, it was soft

and tender, and her lips trembled as his arms circled her
waist. One hand moved upward to cup the back of her head
as his lips feathered kisses across her mouth. The quick
touches lengthened, and soon he was kissing her in earnest,
intoxicated by her hesitant yet undeniable response.

A sigh escaped Mina. His was not a harsh or unkind kiss.
What began as teasing caresses quickened as if he were
seeking something within, and Mina experienced a tingling
throughout her limbs at the demanding pressure of his lips.
The sound of the stream dimmed. She heard nothing save
the pounding of her heart as a languid warmth spread
through her. Her arms moved upward, her fingers meshing
at the nape of his neck.

This kiss was luscious; it was divine. It was precisely as
the books described, and Mina was not afraid. She longed
to lose herself in the sensations it aroused, to surrender to its
love as did the Minerva heroines.

Love. That was the key, and with a start Mina realized
there was no love in this kiss. A man like the Earl of Brierly
knew nothing of love. Mina stiffened in his embrace. She
twisted her head from side to side. "Please, my lord.
Please, stop."

The earl heard Mina's plea and, confused by it, he did as
asked. He ended the kiss but did not let go of her. He
searched her flushed face and what he saw there stunned
him. Hers was the countenance of a green girl newly
awakened to passion. Bizarre as it might be, he had to admit
that she was as pristine as the crystal waters of the stream.
Her cheeks were a delicate shade of pink, her emerald eyes
glistened with excitement, her mouth quavered with uncertainty, and Cavendish knew only too well what he had done.
She had not been provocative, merely stunned and frightened; she had turned to him for help, and he had abused the
trust she offered him. Pain was clearly etched on her
delicate features, and it was all his doing.

It had been a stupid thing to imagine satisfaction might be
gained in vengeance. Cruel, too, for his quarrel was not
with this untried girl. It was with Liam O'Kieffe, and his
sister should not be made to pay his debts.

The magnitude of his misdeed overwhelmed the earl. He shook his head and in a weary voice said, "You were right. I am a fool. A very great fool, indeed. Please accept my apologies, Miss O'Kieffe." Again, he reacted on impulse, his right hand rising to trace her slightly swollen lips. Then he closed his eyes and sighed, a melancholy sound, as he let his arms drop away from Mina.

A panoply of noise assaulted Mina. She heard everything that only moments before had been muted by other senses. Ravens cawed in the orchard, water gurgled by, and at the overwhelming sensation of her heart beating a staccato rhythm against her rib cage, Mina wobbled at the edge of the stream. She did not acknowledge the earl's apology, for she could not speak. Her throat was uncomfortably tight. His apology seemed to matter very little, for even if he had not ruined her with Society, she was betrayed and soiled for having responded to his kiss. Scarlet fanned across her face, her heart drummed louder, and she heard herself exclaim, "Oooh!" It was an exclamation of disgust and self-reproach, an outburst filled with frustration, and as she cried out a second time, Mina stamped her foot as was her habit when goaded beyond endurance, speckling the earl with dots and dashes of mud.

"Why, you little hoyden," he shouted. "That's quite enough!" He lunged for her, and she jumped out of his reach.

Just then one of the occupants of the carriage called out, "Compton!" It was a female voice.

"What the devil?" the earl shaded his eyes to better view the passenger and then swore beneath his breath. "Grandmère."

Mina's eyes flew up the bank, where an elegant woman was climbing from the carriage. With the assistance of a groom, she walked as close to them as was possible without muddying her chamois shoes.

"By the saints! I hoped against all odds my eyes were deceiving me in my dotage, but I can see 'twas futile. You were correct after all, Griffin," she said in an aside to the groom. Then she studied Mina and added incredulously,

"*Mon Dieu*, it's the O'Kieffe child. I'd recognize her anywhere. The replica of her mother. *Une belle jeune fille, n'est-ce pas?*"

Mina curtsied as best she could manage and then glanced sideways at the earl, who was evidently mad as Lucifer at the unwanted intrusion. His blue eyes had darkened to a stormy hue, and his right brow arched upward in supplication. He well knew that Grandmère slipped into French only when she was furious beyond all reason; and the earl knew he had lost to her before even stating his case.

The countess continued, "You've gone and done it, I collect. Decided to compromise the O'Kieffe chit and you've made a cake of yourself, I might add."

Mina cringed. It mattered what this woman thought of her. She longed for acceptance. Hesitantly, she said, "It's not at all what it seems, my lady. My horse refused the wall, and the earl was merely rescuing me."

"Twaddle. It may have started as you describe, but I'm no dimwit. *Maintenant*, out of that muck, the two of you. And give the gel your hand, Compton. Don't act any more the dolt than you can help."

"Come," the earl commanded, all vestige of emotion erased from his voice and face. His manner was abrupt as he guided Mina to the top of the bank.

It was a distance only of several feet, but it was endless to Mina, who was experiencing a host of extremely disconcerting emotions. On the one hand, she loathed the earl to the very core of his soul. He had intended to humiliate her and he had accomplished precisely that. On the other hand, that same languid warmth which had invaded her when he had kissed her returned to her limbs.

In a panic, Mina feared she might melt on the spot. This would not do. Not at all, she scolded herself. She had to exert more self-control. Mortified, she fixed her gaze on her boots and forced her legs to move up the bank to where the dowager countess was waiting. But there was no reason to keep her head bowed as if she were a felon destined for Tyburn hill. Mina had done nothing wrong, and so thinking, she proudly raised her head to confront the countess.

The older woman's words surprised Mina.

"Come, m'dear, let me help you. Griffin," she called to the groom, "a blanket for Miss O'Kieffe." Mindless of Mina's wet state, the countess put her arm about the girl's shoulder.

"Thank you, my lady." Mina smiled, her heart bursting at this honest display of kindness. The countess, like her grandson had earlier done, touched a sensitive spot in Mina's psyche. She forgot the glowering earl beside her. Memories of childhood flooded Mina and she longed to ask the countess about Catherine. She began to speak but was cut off by the older woman.

"Which one of you would care to explain what's been happening here?" Imperious, the dowager stared directly at the earl, demanding an answer, all the while giving Mina's shoulder gentle little pats.

The earl, for his part, was occupied with straightening his cravat. He took his own good time about completing the task and when at last he glanced up, his gaze found Mina. There was a peculiar light in his eyes as if seeing her for the very first time, and she could not help but blush beneath his scrutiny.

This interplay was observed with satisfaction by the dowager countess. It confirmed what she had deduced while observing their earlier response to each other. Taking no measures to hide her amusement, she smiled broadly as she addressed the earl. "I knew you were overset last evening, but I never imagined you would do anything as precipitous as this."

Still he said nothing; he merely continued to stare in that most disconcerting fashion at Mina. The air crackled with tension, and so Mina took a deep breath and spoke.

"I cannot deny that your earlier assumption about the earl's misintentions is correct. But I hasten to add, no harm was done, and truly, I might have drowned had he not happened along."

"Don't talk such fustian, m'dear." The countess was not truly scolding; she was concerned and merely impatient to get at the truth. She set Mina a few feet in front of her and proceeded to pull the blanket tighter about her as she continued, ''My grandson has committed a grievous error, and I intend to see that he makes amends.''

This final statement captured the earl's attention. ''What do you mean by that, Grandmère?'' he asked, wishing that he had never set out for a ride that morning.

''Nothing mysterious, Compton. You must make amends to Miss O'Kieffe.''

Both the earl and Mina spoke at once.

'' 'Tis not necessary, I assure you. If the earl would only get my horse and help me mount I'll be on my way.'' Mina was not certain that she wished to hear what the countess intended to do.

''Amends!'' He was far less civil. The icy note in his voice matched the glacier blue of his eyes. ''Surely you're not implying that I owe anything beyond an apology to an O'Kieffe?''

''*Mais oui*, Compton, amends.'' The countess was speaking her native tongue again, a clear indication that she would tolerate no argument. ''And, yes, I mean something far more than a mere apology.'' She directed her next remark to Mina alone. ''How would you like to spend the Season in London, Miss O'Kieffe?''

For an instant, Mina thought she had misunderstood. She barely squeaked, ''London?''

''London?'' the earl echoed with a tinge of apprehension, a frown forming between his eyes. This was not at all the turn of events he would have favored. As a gentleman he was, of course, willing to apologize to the girl, but that was the limit. He had already guessed the direction of his grandmother's thoughts, and he was stunned. How could Grandmère be suggesting that Mina O'Kieffe accompany her to London? It was unthinkable. If Liam O'Kieffe was not an acceptable suitor for Catherine, his sister was certainly no proper companion either. Moreover, the presence of Miss O'Kieffe in London would make the task of keeping Liam and Catherine apart impossible.

''Why, of course, I said London and I meant London. We shall take Miss O'Kieffe with us as our guest for the Season.

'Tis the least the Cavendish family can do to set right my grandson's indiscretion. Besides, as I told him only last evening, my dear, I owe a debt to your family. Your grandmother was most welcoming when I first came to this country, and I would be honored to repay that kindness.''

Visions of Almack's and Hyde Park danced through Mina's head. It was difficult to credit, but one look at the countess left no doubt of the woman's sincerity. "And Catherine? Will she be going as well?"

"Of course. In fact"—here an enigmatic glint lit her eyes—"I trust that you two young ladies will be able to help each other."

The meaning of this remark was not clear to Mina. She registered little else except the fact that she was going to London and that Catherine would be there, too. "I hardly know what to say, my lady. Your generosity is overwhelming." An almost magical aura haloed Mina's countenance. Happiness made her radiant, and the countess, pleased with the results of her plan thus far, returned the girl's smile.

"Oh, it won't be my generosity. We'll put up in Compton's town house in Berkeley Square, a much more stately establishment than mine on Curzon Street. Far better suited to entertaining."

The earl shot his grandmother a narrow glance, willing her to keep quiet, but it was useless.

To his dismay as well as to the utter surprise of Mina, the countess said, "Yes, we shall all be much indebted to Compton, for you see, m'dear, he'll be paving the way for us. Pending the consent of your eldest brother, Compton shall serve as your guardian and endeavor to contract a suitor for your hand in marriage." To thwart any argument from her grandson, she met his irate gaze and firmly concluded, "C'est finis."

Chapter
Three

A week had passed since Mina's watery encounter with the earl. After a day in bed, at Nanny's insistence, Mina was fully recovered from her plunge. The ensuing week was a delightful one spent in daily visits with Catherine, dancing lessons arranged by the countess, and general preparations for the impending trip. Even Eugenia Grevey was not to be left out, and she proved a cornucopia of advice on one exceedingly vital topic: how a lady preserves her virtue.

By week's end, Mina had learned all there was to know about Catherine's school days at Miss Hedgecombe's in Bath and how she had come to fall in love with Liam. Verily, she had heard that story countless times. The lovers had met by chance two summers earlier during the peace celebrations in Green Park. It was, Mina thought, a highly romantic tale, for Catherine, separated from her party, had been swept along with the rabble. The twilight sky had darkened and when the fireworks began, the sudden pop and bang startled the crowd that pressed about Catherine in pandemonium. Great billows of smoke rolled down the walkways, and when Catherine was in mortal danger of being trampled, Liam appeared. Standing shoulders above the crowd, he recognized his sister's childhood playmate, plowed through to wrap his arm about her, and as Catherine was wont to describe her guardian angel, he pulled her to safety beneath a leafy arbor.

The girls chatted each morning and then in the afternoon they met with Mr. Peterkin, the dance master engaged from Royal Tunbridge Wells, in the ballroom at Brierly. In a whirlwind of four lessons, Mr. Peterkin taught Mina the gavotte and minuet while Catherine accompanied on the pianoforte. Mina was an avid learner. She possessed a natural grace, Peterkin enthused, and he had oft exclaimed to Nanny that Mina was far and above the aptest pupil he had coached. He declared Miss Mina would be a lily among a meadow of posies.

From Eugenia Grevey Mina learned a few things that she suspected most young ladies of Quality did not know. It seemed highly improbable that any gentleman would dare to take the liberties Miss Grevey described. Nonetheless Mina had listened and absorbed, hoping all the while that no gentleman of her acquaintance would leave her no alternative save to deliver him a well-placed facer across the bridge of his nose.

Finally the time arrived for Mina to leave Thornhill Park. It was a fine day for traveling, clear skies and fair, and everyone was up at dawn, attending to the final preparations. Nine chimes sounded from the ormolu clock on the marble mantle in the parlor where Mina and Nanny were enjoying a last cup of chocolate. The earl's party was scheduled to arrive shortly after nine. It was time to say good-bye, and the ladies picked up their reticules and proceeded to the front hall.

Attired in a buttercup-yellow outfit reserved for precisely such a momentous occasion, Mina exited the half-timbered manor house and paused for a moment to glance at the familiar structure. She had lived seventeen years within those stucco and granite walls, and Mina dearly loved its drafty corridors, stained glass windows, and beamed ceilings. Every inch was known to her. It was home, brimming with memories of childhood and Mama, but now it paled when contrasted with the adventure that awaited her.

"This time tomorrow I shall be in London, Nanny," she mused aloud, a pensive half-smile turning up the corners of her rosebud mouth. She was going to miss Thornhill Park, but Mina fancied herself a heroine embarking on a voyage to the Indies or faraway Siam.

Nanny Saltmarsh nodded her understanding. "And a miracle it is.'' Dressed in her usual gray, Nanny clutched the trellised wrought-iron railing with one hand, an ancient handbag of cracked, black leather dangling from the other. Nanny was going to London with Mina, and although the girl had worried that the nurse was too old for the trip, Amanda Saltmarsh had declared that Miss Mina was not venturing farther afield than Sutton Valence unless she accompanied her. And that was that.

"Of a certainty, Nanny, I marvel at the drastic turnabout my life has seen in only a few days' time. Why, 'tis near impossible to credit,'' Mina said with an air of disbelief.

"Unbelievable. Miraculous. Doesn't really matter though. What matters is that you're going to Town. You're the granddaughter of the Marquess of Thornbury, gel, and you ought never to have languished in the country. Not a thing I could have done for you, but the dowager countess will see right by you. With the Countess of Brierly your sponsor, you'll be sure to make a splendid match. Had my worries, I admit. Thought you'd end up on the shelf, but 'tis all changed in less than a fortnight, and we've nothing to worry about, nothing atall.'' Nanny clucked her contentment and offered the slender girl a reassuring smile.

A knot of familiar faces, Eugenia Grevey's among them, clustered at the bottom of the granite steps. They were waiting to bid farewell. A few of the maids wiped at their eyes, for Mina would be sorely missed. Everyone belowstairs had exclaimed at the young mistress's good fortune, and high time, too, old Bedlow, the butler, had declared. It was a good thing, this strange alliance between Brierly Castle and Thornhill Park, a good thing the young Miss Mina being off to London under the protection of the dowager countess, and the servants hoped the sweet lass would find happiness.

Overdressed, as usual, Eugenia stepped forward to embrace Mina. "Aw, lambie, it's good to see this happening. Like I said to Sean, 'twas unholy odd a young girl reading and dreaming all sorts of nonsense.'' In a gesture that bordered on the maternal, she adjusted the satin bonnet ribands beneath Mina's neck and looked directly into her eyes. "You're not nervous, are you?''

"Only a little," Mina said valiantly. In truth she was more than passing nervous. She was terrified of leaving the safety of Thornhill Park, terrified of again encountering the rejection she had experienced after Mama's death, and, over and above all else, Mina was terrified of the earl. She could not fathom the precise nature of that fear, for Mina had never thought overmuch about any man—any real man, that is—having reserved her fantasies for the heroes in novels. But it nagged at her nonetheless. She tweaked at a mother-of-pearl button on the left cuff of her jacket and turned to Miss Grevey for advice, green eyes wide with apprehension which betrayed her brave words.

"A little frightened, are you? Well, not to worry. That's to be expected, and if you had said no, I'd have known you was bamming me. Now, you remember everything I told you about those town swells." Eugenia paused and sniffled a little. She was an emotional woman, a veritable watering pot, a fact to which she credited her modest success on the stage.

"I'll remember," Mina said earnestly.

The redhead nodded. "Good. That's my girl." In the past seven days, a friendship had developed between Mina and Eugenia Grevey, for it was Miss Grevey who had been instrumental in convincing Sean to accept the dowager countess's offer in lieu of charging off to Brierly murderously intent on beating the earl witless for having kissed his sister by the orchard stream. Wild Sean O'Kieffe might be, but he was as protective of his sister as any man, regardless of rank or birthright, and it was Miss Grevey who had made him see the sense of the countess's offer. Miss Grevey was as sensible as she was kind and, in her own manner, she had hoped to impart some of her hard-won knowledge of London to Mina. Life and men in particular were a bad lot, and Miss Grevey did not want to see Mina hurt. The girl had too many romantic notions and it would be criminal, Miss Grevey had lectured to Sean, if no one pointed out to Mina that one did not always find a happy ending in the real world. Mina had listened to her advice, but Miss Grevey was not certain that the younger girl truly understood the warnings she offered.

"Always remember you're a lady, and all you've got to do is make certain the coves know that. And if you ever need help, you know where to find me. Ask for Mr. Tarleton at Drury Lane, and he'll give you my direction." She hugged Mina one last time.

The clacking rhythm of metal-rimmed wheels could be heard winding down the drive, and the women glanced up to observe the earl riding alongside a splendid traveling barouche. The vehicle, drawn by a matched quartet of grays, circled the drive and halted before the front steps. The earl dismounted and handed his reins to a waiting tiger. He strode purposefully to Mina and executed a terse bow.

"Good day, ladies." The deep voice was cool, and there was no sign of any emotion whatsoever in the earl's expression. "I trust you are ready, Miss O'Kieffe."

She inclined her head in greeting but could not utter a sound. The earl, she decided, was quite dashing this morning in russet browns. He wore dark brown riding trousers, a coat of rusty superfine, and gleaming boots of an unusual mahogany shade. She had forgotten how fair his hair was, how extraordinarily tall his figure, how his blue eyes gleamed like gemstones. How was that possible? She put a hand to her lips, remembering his kiss. How strange that he remained so formal and distant while she could not control the horrid blush that crept up her neck. He behaved as if nothing intimate had ever occurred between them, and, tongue-tied, Mina concentrated on the yellow kid slippers poking from beneath her dress.

"Miss O'Kieffe?" he said impatiently. Mina blinked, then gulped, but still could not speak.

Fortunately, Mina was spared making a response by Nanny, who piped up, "Yes, my lord, we're ready." Her words sounded deceptively acquiescent, for Nanny was not a woman to be cowed by anyone, even an earl. "Our luggage can be loaded, if you would be so kind as to direct the servants." She instructed him as if she were addressing a lad barely out of knee breeches.

"Of course." With impeccable courtesy, the earl executed a second bow; then he turned on his heel and went in the direction of the huddle of coachmen.

"So that's your earl," Eugenia remarked.

Breaking from her trance, Mina corrected, "He's not *my* earl." She bridled at the insinuation. There was no special relationship between herself and the earl, but she was not really sure what their relationship was to be. Sean had given his consent that the earl act as Mina's guardian, but Mina did not know what that entailed. Would she see him daily? Would he exert control over her activities or the people she chose as friends? Would he continue to be so aloof, while his very presence reduced her to a skittish schoolgirl?

"Well, whatever you say, lambie. He's a fine figure of a man, to be sure." She grinned her special and rather worldly grin, which seemed to say "You can't pull the wool over *my* eyes, lambie" and then moved away, assisting Nanny to the gleaming black carriage.

When the door opened, Catherine hopped out and hurried to Mina's side. "Oh, my dear friend, we're on our way at last." She trilled with excitement, and for the hundredth time since their joyous reunion, the two girls hugged and then launched into a friendly chat.

"Your wardrobe is most exceptional, Mina. I daresay no one will know you've brought it from the country." Catherine critically studied Mina's smart yellow walking dress, which was edged in a contrasting cream-colored rouleau. A spencer of the same buttercup shade as the dress and a matching reticule embroidered with tiny star-shaped flowers completed Mina's ensemble. "That outfit is so modish, it might have been designed by Madame Lucille. But when do you wear all those things?" She gestured expansively toward the pyramid of bandboxes, portmanteaux, and trunks secured atop one of the three luggage wagons which would follow behind on the London road.

"I don't," Mina admitted with a rueful grin. "But I longed to have a wardrobe as beautiful as the pictures in *La Belle Assemblée*, and when I discovered that Mrs. Jenkins, our gamekeeper's wife, was a wizard at patterns, I engaged her to copy the designs." There was more than a touch of pride in Mina's voice. She was pleased with Mrs. Jenkins's handiwork, but heretofore only Nanny and her brothers had seen Mina in her finery. At last, she was going to be able to show off her clothes, and the prospect of wearing all those beautiful ball gowns and morning dresses and riding habits was most delightful indeed.

"I'm quite green with envy." Catherine had never cared for fashion. Like her grandmère, she loved parties, but, unlike Grandmère, she was perfectly content to wear the same gown several times during a single Season. What she had seen of Mina's smart wardrobe, however, made her realize for the first time how flattering was a well-selected ensemble. She was delighted by Mina's next statement.

"Well, you may certainly borrow whatever you like. We're of a like size, and although your coloring is far more exotic than mine, I'm certain several of the gowns would suit you superbly."

"You're exceedingly generous."

"Not at all. And I know the ideal dress. A deep red organza. It will highlight your dark hair to perfection." Again, Catherine expressed her gratitude, and Mina said, "Say not another word, my dearest friend. I shall forever be indebted to you and your grandmère. What I offer is very little." With their arms linked the girls began to stroll towards the carriage. Out of the blue, Mina asked, "Why do you suppose she did it, Catherine? Your grandmère, I mean. Why did she decide to bring me to London without letting anyone naysay her plans?"

"How can you ask? 'Twas the outside of enough that Compton acted as he did, but I can assure you that wasn't the only reason. She was as shocked as I to discover how appallingly isolated you've been these past years. 'Tis high time you entered the world and enjoyed yourself." She gave Mina's arm an affectionate squeeze.

"But will they accept me?" This question was no more than a whisper. It was terribly hard to vocalize her worries. The smile collapsed from Mina's face and she pursed her lips in worry as she awaited Catherine's response.

"Fustian! Of course they will when Grandmère launches you. She holds great sway in Town." The girls had reached the barouche, and before they climbed inside, Catherine turned about and anxiously peered towards the massive front door of Thornhill Park; then she glanced up and down the staircase. She was searching for someone, and when she realized Mina had observed this, she blushed slightly. In a hushed voice, she inquired, "Tell me, how is Liam?"

At this question, Mina assayed a smile for her friend's sake. She answered reassuringly, "Liam is fine. He's quite recovered from his encounter with your brother and is his devilish good-looking self once more. There's not a scar on his face, and he's resumed his estate work. He dearly wanted to see you this morning, but he, like all my brothers, decided it was wise to avoid the earl. He sends you his love and this note." Mina withdrew an envelope from her reticule.

"For me?" And when Mina pressed the letter into Catherine's hand, the dark-haired girl, giddy with joy, tittered.

"Quick. Put it away," Mina whispered, for at that moment the earl had turned and was watching the girls. The envelope disappeared up Catherine's sleeve and Mina nodded. "Save it for the ride. I don't believe your brother would be very pleased to learn I had brought you a message from Liam."

The girls eyed the earl. A dark scowl marked his lean, aristocratic features, and Catherine said, "He seldom is— pleased, that is. He's such a high stickler. Wasn't always such a prig."

"Well, perhaps," Mina suggested with a mischievous grin, "we can bring a little excitement into his life."

At this remark the girls burst into a peal of giggles, eliciting a renewal of sour glances from the earl. And as Catherine slipped into the coach to read her letter, Mina waited outside while the earl approached.

"Are we ready to leave, my lord?"

He acknowledged Mina with a curt nod, as if from very far away, and for an instant Mina imagined she caught a glimpse of discomfort in his stance, in the manner in which he held himself erect, unbending and defensive. It was as if her open nature unsettled him, and Mina felt a pang of something akin to sympathy for the earl. Most unexpectedly she wished that they might be friends, if for no other reason than for Catherine's sake. Giving him the hint of an elfin smile, she softly, almost teasingly, said, "It won't be at all pleasant if you keep this up, my lord. I know I've been foisted upon you, but might we call a truce?"

His eyes narrowed and he scrutinized Mina for several heartbeats. He had vowed to avoid her at all costs once they reached Town. He would do the necessary as Grandmère dictated, but beyond that he intended to stay as far away from Mina O'Kieffe as he could contrive. She was a bothersome piece of baggage. What did he need with a girl who spun ridiculous fantasies about love? She could only cause more trouble in his household, trouble that he certainly did not need. He would make quick work of the guardian business and find her a husband before the summer was out, disabusing her, in the process, of those silly notions she espoused about romance and love matches.

He responded evenly, "I quite agree. A truce would be in order."

At his agreement, Mina's tentative smile widened with relief. She released a pent-up breath of air, and a charming sparkle lit her emerald eyes. Talking to the earl was far easier than she had imagined it would be. He had not barked at her, and she struggled for something to say in return. She wished to share her pleasure with him. She was thrilled to be going to London, she was pleased they would not be at dagger points with one another, and she was about to speak when he gently prompted, "Into the carriage now, Miss O'Kieffe. I shall ride my stallion until we stop to water the horses, after which I plan to join you ladies for the final miles into the metropolis."

Then they were off. Mina stayed at the open window for as long as she could, waving to Eugenia Grevey and watching Thornhill Park fade from sight. Catherine, naturally, pored over her note from Liam as if committing it to memory.

Once on the main road, the carriage headed north. The earl's coachman did not drive the team at full speed as so many travelers, eager to reach their destinations in record time, did these days. They were in no hurry. Grandmère had gone on ahead to instruct the staff in Berkeley Square, and there was no need to reach Town before dusk. The carriage, followed by the three luggage wagons, wound down the country roads at a comfortable but steady pace. Nanny slept the whole while, and Catherine babbled for miles about Liam, quizzing Mina as to his every word and action; as only a young lady in love can be, she was enthralled with even the most insignificant details of his daily life.

It was an uneventful trip until they stopped to water the horses and stretch their legs at a coaching inn. The Rose and the Crown was in Bexley, only a few miles outside London. A popular establishment for travelers city bound and for those on day outings in the countryside, its yard was a jumble of wheeled conveyances, ostlers, and scruffy yardboys when Mina peered out the carriage window. There was, she heard a tiger remark, a prizefight featuring fearless Scroggins and Black Richmond in a nearby village, which accounted for the number of sporty tilburies and the circle of young bucks milling outside the taproom door. They were a gay lot, each a pink of the *ton*, garbed by the finest tailors, and Mina stared in awe, for she had never before seen such grand gentlemen.

Heads turned as the earl's party alighted from the barouche. Together, the two girls made a delightfully pretty picture; Catherine, dark and exotic, was a natural foil for Mina's fragile and honey-colored beauty. Several of the gentlemen broke away from the others, eager to renew their acquaintance with Lady Catherine and to meet her lovely companion. One of these dandies, a darkly handsome man with crisp black curls and a bronzed face, attracted Mina's attention. He was wearing an officer's uniform and as he crossed the yard, he leaned on a gold-tipped cane.

Behind a gloved hand, Mina whispered to Catherine, "The soldier. Who is he?"

"Duncan Ramsey," Catherine answered, "and a very eligible bachelor. But don't let my brother catch you glancing his way. Captain Ramsey may be a war hero and a titled Scotsman with vast holdings in the Highlands, but I overheard Compton remark that he's a rake and a gambler. Precisely the sort of man my brother detests.''

"Really," Mina remarked absentmindedly, for she was thinking how dashing a figure the captain cut in his scarlet uniform. "His leg. Was he wounded on the Continent?"

"Yes, at Waterloo."

The girls quieted, for the captain was within earshot.

"Cavendish," Captain Ramsey addressed the earl. "Fine day for traveling." He turned to Catherine and bowed. "Lady Catherine, 'tis a pleasure to see you. As always, you're looking exquisite." He cast a questioning glance at Mina, who sighed audibly beneath the handsome captain's regard.

The earl witnessed this and scowled deeply, allowing an awkward moment to pass before saying, "Permit me to introduce my neighbor, Miss Mina O'Kieffe." The earl wished that he might have avoided this introduction, but he had no choice. Etiquette dictated that as a gentleman he observe such formality.

"At your service, ma'am," the captain drawled, and he carried Mina's fingers to his lips. He glanced up and murmured in a husky whisper, "Charming. Eyes as green as a Highland pine forest. Most charming, indeed."

The earl was sharply intent on this scene. He saw Mina blush and her eyes dance with delight at this flirtatious attention. Catherine was carefully watching her brother; she was hard put to repress a giggle at the sight of his displeasure. And Mina, who had never received such a compliment before, was spellbound by the captain.

"Are you staying the Season in London, Miss O'Kieffe? Pray tell me yes, and that I will be fortunate enough to enjoy your company," the earl heard Captain Ramsey inquire with flattering interest. Mina responded in a breathless voice, and Catherine, to the earl's horror, leapt into the conversation. "We plan to stay at Cavendish House in Berkeley Square, should you wish to call on us, Captain Ramsey," she supplied, and Mina's mouth dropped open in astonishment.

"Most kind of you, Lady Catherine. I look forward to

seeing both of you ladies in Town." He clicked his heels together and gave them a sweeping bow.

In the next instant, the earl abruptly took Catherine in one arm and Mina in the other and propelled them across the yard. Mina well understood the earl's show of rage. What had possessed Catherine to say that? she wondered, especially since Catherine well knew her brother did not approve of Captain Ramsey.

"How dare you?" he demanded of his sister. Mina tilted her head and glanced between Catherine and the earl. She was smiling saucily; he was livid. "I ought to throttle you, Catherine. I don't know what got into you, but you know far better than to encourage a rogue like Ramsey."

"Did I do that?" Catherine said with deliberate flippancy, and the earl cursed as he fairly dragged the girls into a private parlor. He kicked the door closed behind them before turning around and lecturing, "I would like to make something abundantly clear before we reach London. Something which I trust both you, Miss O'Kieffe, and you, Catherine, will take seriously." He was pacing now, the thud of his riding boots punctuating every syllable. "You will both comport yourselves with the utmost decorum while residing under my roof. And neither of you will be seen in the company of fellows like Ramsey. He's a bounder, and I don't want the tattlemongers going on about either of you; nor do I wish to see your names in the books at White's. Is that understood?"

Catherine was no help at all when she said, "It's very boring, Compton, when you say the same thing over and over again."

This prompted the earl to turn his anger on Mina. He pointed an admonitory finger in her direction. "And you, Miss O'Kieffe, am I boring you?" In frustration, he ran both hands through his hair. Oh, where was Grandmère when he needed her? The next three months promised to be agonizing, shackled with two, no three, including his grandmother, birdwitted females. "Well? Answer me. Do you intend to cavort through Town like my sister here and land us all in the scandal broth?"

"Oh, Compton, I've never done such a thing, and leave Mina alone," Catherine snapped.

"It's all right, Catherine, I can speak for myself," Mina said in a quiet voice. She fidgeted with her reticule before continuing in her soft, melodic brogue, surprising both the earl and Catherine. "My lord, I can assure you that I won't land us, as you phrased it, in a scandal broth. I've already experienced the censure of Society and I have no intention of doing so again." It was an exceedingly personal statement, and twin dots of color rose in her cheeks. Mina made a bleak gesture with her hands and sat down, her face averted from him, hidden by the wide brim of her bonnet.

She looked very young and vulnerable perched on the edge of the bench, a mere lamb compared to Catherine, thought the earl, and a sober look settled on his countenance. Her words reminded him of the despair he experienced when Liam had declared his love for Catherine, that moment when he had been an outsider. He was acutely aware of the loneliness she must have experienced since her mother's death, and suddenly the earl felt as if he knew Miss O'Kieffe very well, and he did not like that at all.

He coughed nervously. "Again, Miss O'Kieffe, I find I owe you an apology. You did not deserve my anger; however, I am sincere when I say that I trust you will attend my advice and avoid the company of Captain Ramsey."

"Certainly, my lord," Mina said. She cocked her head to look at him with wide green eyes. "Although he did seem a nice fellow. I thought his manners very pretty, and he was prodigious dashing in that uniform and—"

Whatever she was going to say was cut off by the earl, who tossed his arms in the air and declared, "Romantic twaddle, Miss O'Kieffe. Nothing but romantic twaddle." Then he exited the private parlor, the sound of Catherine's giggles following him into the smoke-filled taproom.

Once the door was closed, Mina pivoted on the bench and faced Catherine. Her sweet voice was filled with confusion. "Whyever did you say those dreadful things? That didn't seem in the least bit like you, Catherine. You did everything you could to aggravate your brother. How could you?"

Defiance still in her large, round eyes, Catherine pouted, "Oh, Mina, he just makes me so angry. Ever since I returned from Miss Hedgecombe's he's watched me like a hawk. Even before Liam. I have to do something, else I'll go insane, and he's so easy to rile that I can't help myself."

"That's no excuse. You ought to do your utmost to behave when you're around him. I'd like to help you and Liam. It would give me immense joy to see you united in matrimony. But I won't help if you're forever baiting your brother. There's no point in it, and it only hurts. Don't you see that he can't help but think of you as a flighty schoolgirl if you're forever behaving like one?"

Catherine pondered this and then, shamefaced, she admitted, "Yes, I suppose you're right. I promise to stop baiting Compton, although it won't be easy, I assure you."

"Well, as long as you try. I'll do my best to help you and Liam. I'll deliver letters for you, and I'll arrange for meetings once we're settled. Does Liam say when he plans to come to Town in his letter?"

"Yes, in seven days."

"Fine. We'll see him then. In the meantime, don't do anything foolhardy. If you can prove yourself to your brother, he may realize you haven't made an error in judgment in loving Liam. For that's what he thinks. Don't you see? He doesn't think you're capable of making so important a decision on your own, and you've got to prove him wrong."

"How wise you are," Catherine marveled.

Mina stifled a giggle. "I'm not wise at all. That's simply what Clorinda Penshurst did in *When Love Triumphs*. Only she had to prove it to her uncle, not her brother. But it's all the same thing."

"How long did it take Clorinda?"

"Barely a Season."

The answer satisfied Catherine, and she promised, "In turn, I shall help you find a beau."

This earnest pledge warmed Mina, and she smiled at Catherine. Her friend was truly loyal and kind, but Mina was not certain she needed anyone to find a beau for her. If she was destined for love, it would simply happen. Of that Miss Mina O'Kieffe was certain.

Before the carriage crossed the Thames it pulled to the side of the road, and the earl hitched his horse to the rear of the barouche and climbed inside. "Far too crowded on Westminster Bridge," he remarked as he settled opposite Mina.

The barouche lurched forward. Nanny and Catherine were napping and Mina, anxious for her first view of London, edged to the window and peered outside. "Oh, my," she said, unable to disguise her disappointment. This was not the grand London she had read about in Samuel Pepys's diary, nor the city poets honored in immortal works. Billows of smoke hung low and gray over the rooftops; traffic slowed to a snail's pace, the street being clogged with all manner of transport; the river was a sluggish brown hue; and a host of noxious odors rose from the gutters.

"Not precisely what you expected?" the earl inquired.

Slightly embarrassed at being so transparent, Mina shrugged a silent response, crossed and uncrossed her ankles.

"Hardly a storybook London, eh?" he persisted.

At this remark, Mina's face lit up. It was as if the earl had read her mind. "I was thinking of Wordsworth, my lord, and I pictured a skyline of spires and domes glittering magnificently against a bright sky."

Arms folded across his chest, the earl was staring hard at Mina, considering this latest revelation. So the girl was acquainted with Wordsworth, he mused. Unfortunately, the direction of his thoughts was plain, and Mina sat up a little straighter, offended by the fact that he obviously considered her too simple for anything other than a shilling romance. Defensively, she exclaimed, "Well, I can read something other than Minervas, and I do!"

His curiosity was piqued. "Such as?"

"I've read all of Miss Austen's novels as well as those by Mrs. Radcliffe. But I believe my favorites are histories. The library at Thornhill Park was filled with them, old and new." The dim light of the enclosed carriage did not mute her enthusiasm. Her eyes blazed with interest and she leaned forward to inquire, "Have you read Scott's ballads, my lord?"

"Yes, admirable works to be sure, but romances as well."

She could not repress a laugh at the truth of his statement. It delighted her. "But don't you see the romance in history, my lord?"

"Hadn't thought of it." It was impossible to miss the crease that marred his high brow.

"Never thought of it!" she cried in disbelief. "Why, consider Bonnie Prince Charlie and the brave Highlanders at Culloden, or Owen Glendower's stand in Wales, or Henry Tudor's quest for an heir. 'Tis romance in its purest form."

"Perhaps." He rubbed his chin, giving serious consideration to Mina's idea. Innocent she might be, but not ignorant, and he readily commended, "I give your idea credit, Miss O'Kieffe."

"Thank you, my lord. Perhaps there is hope, then?" she parried.

"Hope?" He cleared his throat. His voice was not altogether steady.

"Why, yes. If I can convince you of the romance in history, then perhaps I can make a believer of you." Her elfin smile was contagious and with a single, terse nod, he returned her grin. Their eyes met at that moment, and the warmth she had experienced when he kissed her by the stream returned. It was an intense sensation and inexplicable, as if something was pulsing in the carriage between them. It confused her and, oddly enough, intoxicated her. She felt bold, and with a gay confidence she inquired, "Will we reach Berkeley Square soon?"

"Only a few more blocks."

Again, Mina poked her head out the window, knocking her bonnet off in her eagerness. The earl chuckled, but it was an indulgent laugh. It pleased him to watch Mina. She noticed so many things, so many details that he had overlooked for years. A grin tickled the corners of his mouth, and so they passed the remainder of the ride in companionable silence.

At Number 5, Berkeley Square, an elegant Palladian-style town house, the carriage stopped. Nanny and Catherine stirred from their naps at the noise raised by servants who scurried about the wagons to unload the mountains of luggage.

The earl stepped down and held the door open for the ladies. Mina, anxious to actually place her foot on London ground, was the first to exit from the depths of the carriage, and in her enthusiasm she stumbled on the curbstone. The earl caught her in his strong arms. There was a slight buzzing in her head, and Mina felt a strange inward tremor—perhaps it was the heat of the day; the city was warmer than she had anticipated.

As swiftly as he had assisted her, the earl set Mina away from him, placing her safely on the sidewalk; and when she looked up to thank him, she found his attention was directed elsewhere.

A cabriolet was passing by, and seated beneath the partially folded leather hood was the most beautiful woman Mina had ever beheld. Her complexion was like alabaster, her lustrous hair black as midnight fell in long curls about her bare shoulders, and she was wearing a daring dress which fully advertised her womanly charms.

The earl tipped his hat and the woman nodded, the barest hint of a smile on her full ruby lips.

"Who's that?" Mina wondered aloud, and Catherine, who had stepped down behind her, responded, "Alexandra Audley. One of the famed demi-reps and, if last Season's rumors are to be believed, under the protection of my brother."

Unaccountably, this information caused a sinking sensation in the pit of Mina's stomach. "Is he very much in love with her?" she ventured to ask.

"Love? Hardly. I don't believe Compton would allow himself to love a woman like Alexandra Audley—or any woman, for that matter. She's merely a habit and a convenience and if Compton marries, his wife, unfortunate creature, will merely be, as he has often stated, a comfortable match. In truth, I don't believe a man who would say that is capable of love.''

This news merely served to reinforce Mina's already sad opinion of the earl. He was, as she had earlier discovered, a coldhearted man who did not believe in romance. Tragically, this blindness closeted him in a world that lacked true joy or pleasure. His was a life in which propriety and its perfection were all that he could claim. And as they entered the Palladian-fronted town house, Mina had yet to figure out why this fact distressed her so.

Chapter Four

It was eight o'clock in the morning, and across Mayfair no lady of Quality had yet stirred beneath the canopy of her bed. Young and old alike, they needed their beauty sleep and dared not venture forth at so unholy an hour, fearing an unhealthy pallor might beset the complexion or mauve half-moons sprout beneath the eyes. There was, however, one notable exception to be seen at Number 5, Berkeley Square. As the sun crested the rooftops, Mina padded across the Turkoman carpet of her bedchamber, threw open the shutters, and eagerly peered outside.

Cavendish House, being situated on the upper slope of Berkeley Square, afforded Mina a broad and unobstructed view of the morning goings-on. The neighborhood was a veritable beehive of activity. Across the square—which was really not a square at all, Berkeley being set out in an elliptical form—carts were unloading goods at a commercial establishment. No sign identified the proprietor or his trade, and as white lace curtains were drawn across the front bow window, Mina was left to wonder what business was conducted with the smaller but no less elegant building beneath the sign of a pineapple.

A sound directly below drew Mina's attention to the street. Two young chimney sweeps, breeches tattered and feet bare, trudged down the sidewalk. In their wake, a smaller lad walked double time to keep pace, lugging an array of ash pots which bumped and clanged in ear-splitting discord.

An open wagon was parked by the gutter, and an ill-kempt woman, her skin dark as old leather, was perched atop its seat. She called out, "Over 'ere, you shavers, and 'urry it up, oi says! We 'aven't got all day, and it'll be no porridge for the loikes of you, if we don't finish 'em jobs for these gentry-coves and get back to Old Bigby roight quick. 'E'll be expecting us."

"Aw roight, aw roight," the boys groaned. "Keep yer bloomers on, Nell."

Fascinated by this scene, Mina leaned farther out of the window. It was easy to imagine Mayfair in the old days before it became so fashionable a residential district. A mere hundred years before it had been the site of one of London's last medieval fairs. After King James granted a patent for a cattle sale to be held on the Great Brookfield during the first week of May, the event came to be called the May Fair. Mina had read about the May Fair in one of her favorite histories, and she knew that it had been a cause for general jollification to celebrate the coming of spring. Each May the neighborhood had come alive with the shrieks of riders on the roundabouts and swings, and the beckoning call of sly hucksters and honest merchants; the air was thick with the spicy aroma of fresh sausage roasting over open fires at the food stalls. The fields surrounding Curzon Street had been cluttered with tents and booths as city dwellers flocked to enjoy the entertainment. Mina closed her eyes and imagined herself strolling through the May Fair, passing gamblers and gypsies on her right, Indian rope dancers on her left, and straight ahead a mountebank extolling the virtues of a decoction of mistletoe and black walnut guaranteed to cure baldness, insomnia, and all manner of cramps.

It was in the midst of this daydream that the earl chose to exit Cavendish House. He paused on the top step to adjust his beaver hat and flick a speck of lint off his jacket when out of the corner of his eye he noticed a peculiar shadow rippling across the cobbled sidewalk. He looked up, and the sight he beheld was shocking indeed.

Mina, her golden brown hair unbound and dangling below the window, was garbed in nothing more than a nightdress of pure white linen. Palms placed on the sill, she rested her weight on her hands, this particular position making her otherwise chaste gown appear highly provocative. The lace trim at the bodice was pulled lower than the seamstress had ever intended, ruched tight against her figure, and a wholly unladylike expanse of creamy shoulder was revealed to any and all passersby.

The earl was reminded of the Miss O'Kieffe he had observed in the rowboat at Thornhill Park, and the sight was altogether unsettling. Worse, he now knew the color of her enticing green eyes. Too, he had tasted the delights of her lips, and he experienced a stab of longing for their sweet softness. It was unthinkable to have such intimate thoughts about a girl in one's own charge, an innocent girl who was, after all, little more than a romantic and slightly hoydenish twit.

He cleared his throat, and Mina, hearing the gravelly sound, glanced below to see his face, a prominent scowl marring the fine line of his aristocratic brow.

"Oh," she squeaked, her meanderings about a Mayfair's past fading while she felt the color rising in her face. She had violated the very rule she had lectured Catherine to heed; she had been caught behaving in such a fashion that the earl could only opine she was naught but a flighty schoolgirl. Looking down at her nightdress, she uttered another dismayed "Oh" and ducked behind the curtain.

"Precisely what I might have said, Miss O'Kieffe," he drawled in that faintly disapproving manner with which she was becoming familiar.

After a brief hesitation, she peered around the curtain. "I

suppose you're going to tell me this is hardly an auspicious start for my stay under your roof?''

''Precisely.''

''Well, I hadn't forgotten your words in the coaching inn, if that's what you thought,'' she ventured to explain. ''Nor did I intentionally set out to disobey your wishes, my lord. Not really. But 'tis my very first morning in Town, and I didn't want to miss a thing. Not even the activity belowstairs. Though some people might consider merchants and chimney sweeps beneath their notice, 'tis all fascinating to me. It puts me in mind of the old fairs. 'Tis all so elegant now, and the landscape has much changed. Even the Tyburn is gone; 'tis near impossible to credit, the notion of a river vanishing beneath the earth. But if I close my eyes I can picture Queen Anne aboard the royal barge, floating up the Tyburn and disembarking at Brook Street. I've heard said the brook flows beneath this square, perhaps below this very spot, and that if one were to be quiet as a mouse, a body might hear the ring of the water passing beneath the stones. Can you imagine?'' She concluded this lengthy discourse on a sigh and added wistfully, ''Those must have been glorious times indeed. Don't you agree?''

''Precisely, Miss O'Kieffe,'' he drawled again in a voice that bordered on the impatient and prompted Mina to hide her head behind the curtain.

''Ah, Miss O'Kieffe.''

It was startling to hear him calling her back to the window in a rather conspiratorial fashion. Popping her head back out, she inquired, ''Yes?''

''If I might offer some advice, I suggest curbing your curiosity—admirable and well-founded though it may be— until the rest of the household has decided to rise and face the day.'' The smile twitching at the corners of his mouth was at odds with his cool words.

''Certainly. And when might that be, my lord?''

''Close to noon at the earliest, I'm certain.''

''Oh!'' She regarded him in dismay.

''Precisely, Miss O'Kieffe. Precisely.'' He shook his head in amusement. There was the flash of a twinkle in his eyes.

Her heart was suddenly racing in response to the crooked grin he cast her way. "Good day, my lord." She could think of nothing else to say, though she longed to know where he was bound and why anyone would be so silly as to stay abed on so glorious a day.

"Until later, Miss O'Kieffe." He tipped his beaver hat.

"Yes, until later, my lord," she whispered and remained at the open window until he had disappeared up the slight hill that wound onto Charles Street. To think the earl had actually understood why she wanted to watch the goings-on in the square, and he had not scolded. Fancy that. One minute he was stiff-backed as a schoolmaster and the next he was near teasing her like a brother. *Quite impossible*, she thought. *He could not be both, could he?* Well, she would not question why he had been so pleasant. It was ever so much nicer when he smiled, for then she did not have to worry what she had done to deserve his critical regard. Then she did not have to feel as if he held her in bitter contempt. Hopefully, she would see more of this pleasant man during her stay in Town.

When the countess and Catherine finally stirred, it was, as the earl had predicted, close to noon. In the interim Mina made good use of her time. After an enormous breakfast of ham, kippers, and eggs smothered in a creamy herb sauce that could only be French, she explored the library and gardens.

A Cavendish residence had occupied this prime parcel of land since 1690. The current house had been built some seventy years before in the then-popular Georgian style by the earl's great-grandfather. More recently, the dowager countess—when she reigned at Number 5—had embellished the design with some Palladian touches. Roman-styled marble columns supported the front portico of the stately mansion, and balconies had been added along the western wall so that the ballroom opened onto a terrace descending to the gardens. The two styles did not create a bad combination, and like many other homes clustered about Berkeley Square, it stood flush with the sidewalk. A passerby might not conceive of the grove of elms that stretched out behind the house, hidden behind the privacy of a high stucco wall.

Upon inspection, the library and gardens met with Mina's approval. She was well pleased that some former earl had been so fond of books. The collection was astounding, and Mina located several volumes of interest. The garden was an equal source of pleasure, for one of the earl's ancestors had clearly shared Mina's love for nature. Bordering the grove of elms were beds of rosebushes, their crimson and high-pink blooms splattering the idyllic scene with vibrant color. It was almost like being in the countryside, and Mina was pleased with her discoveries. Her stay at Cavendish House would be doubly delightful. The quiet hours she intended to spend curled up on a garden bench with one of those beautiful old volumes promised to be special ones.

She was in the garden when the earl's butler, Hughes, informed her that the ladies had descended from the second floor. Mina quickly found her way to the dining room, where the countess, Catherine, and Nanny Saltmarsh were nibbling at a repast far scanter than the hardy one Mina had earlier enjoyed.

"Good morning, my dear," Nanny greeted and nodded her approval of Mina's rounded morning dress, a white muslin striped with yellow, and matching canary shoes. "Doesn't she look lovely, my lady?" Nanny addressed the countess in a manner that was unique to Amanda Saltmarsh, who could at once sound outright chummy while maintaining a socially acceptable distance from her superiors. It was that quality, coupled with her venerable years, that had secured for her a place at Thornhill Park which was more family than servant and that would continue to serve her well at Cavendish House. Nanny was not housed beneath the eaves in one of the rooms usually reserved for servants; she had been given a chamber down the hall from Mina. "I do believe Miss Mina would have been a match for Lady Elaine. You remember Lady Elaine, don't you?" she asked the countess, preparing to launch into a monologue about Mina's exceptional mother and her stunning come-out in '87.

"*Mais oui*, I recall the Lady Elaine. A lovely girl." The countess handed Nanny a cup of frothy Swiss chocolate. It was one of Nanny's two vices—the second being a penchant for a sip of sherry now and again—and the countess smiled with success as the faithful nurse quieted, her attention occupied with savoring each sip of the rich liquid.

"Catherine, *regardez*. Have you ever seen so many invitations?" The countess gestured towards the silver salver on the table before her. Tongues had been busy the past twenty-four hours. Word was out that the Dowager Countess of Brierly was staying this Season at Cavendish House with two eligible young ladies, and the cards had been delivered by an army of footmen from every corner of fashionable London.

"Ah, look. Lord and Lady Russell are hosting a musicale Friday next, and we've been asked to dine with Viscount Egremont before the opera," she remarked while sorting through the stack of envelopes, eyeing the return seal before opening each. "I understand Lady Jersey shall be in town by week's end. We must make a special effort to visit with her as she is at once a dear friend and a most important connection, if we wish to see Mina properly launched," the countess explained.

"You'll be seeing Lady Jersey for vouchers?" queried Nanny.

"Quite so, Miss Saltmarsh. We shall depend on her good graces to secure one for Mina. The girl simply must be seen at Almack's." Nanny did not respond. She yawned and began to stir her chocolate, so the countess returned to the invitations. "Ah, *fantastique*! Here's the one I was searching for. 'Tis from Lord and Lady Derby-Clement for a ball three nights hence."

"Derby-Clement. Derby-Clement." The name diverted Nanny from her cocoa. "Seem to remember that name. Believe Lady Elaine had two offers that night. Have a greenhouse, don't they? Behind the dahlias, she told me later on. 'Twas first Abington and then that stripling Bowdler. Both gentlemen presented their suits to the marquess the next morning, and both were turned down flat,'' Nanny said on a cavernous yawn.

Across the table Mina wished that the dear woman would not babble on about her mama. Heaven only knew how much Society would recall of Lady Elaine, but Mina knew well the rest of the tale. Within weeks her grandfather had agreed to a betrothal between her mama and her da, and although Mina loved her da dearly, she suspected that Society had not held him in equal regard. It was one of Mina's sincerest wishes to be admitted to Almack's as her mama had been, and she fervently prayed that nothing would prevent that happening.

''Quite so, Nanny, quite so.'' The countess offered an offhand remark—any would have done, for already the elderly nurse was dozing where she sat—then turned to the girls. ''Well, my dears, where shall we go today?''

Catherine shrugged indifferently, her thoughts on Liam.

Mina's response was immediate. ''I had hoped, my lady, to see some of London.''

''Excellent notion. *Eh bein*, I suggest a carriage ride in the Park at the fashionable hour. How does that sound?'' The two girls nodded their assent, and the countess rose. ''Excuse me, my dears, I've correspondence to attend to. Until five.''

At the precise hour of five, the ladies set out from Cavendish House in the earl's open town carriage. There was a veritable crush of curricles at the entrance to Hyde Park, and once their carriage had swung into the parade line, Mina gaped at the sight. Hyde Park was teeming with Society. The broad paths and walkways were jammed with carriages, riders, and pedestrians, and Mina wondered how anyone managed to pause and chat without being run down by the traffic.

It seemed the countess enjoyed a nodding acquaintance with more than half the *beau monde*. She acknowledged those friends with a dip of her head which was, depending upon the individual, often accompanied by a smile. The girls sat in the seat across from her. Mina was torn between keeping her eyes averted from so many strangers and staring at them like a thoroughly ill-bred shop girl. After several attempts, she perfected a tilt of her head that allowed her to peek from beneath the brim of her bonnet without being seen. Catherine, on the other hand, experienced no such compunctions. She was twisted about in the seat, ankles and crinolines revealed, craning her neck every which way.

"Stop looking for the lad, my dear," the countess said in a kind but firm voice.

"You could tell?" Catherine's expression collapsed.

The countess nodded. "So could half the *beau monde*. No point in giving the tabbies anything to chatter about—they'll only wonder who you're searching for, if they don't already know." She paused to nod at the occupants of a passing carriage. "He ain't here, and you'll only give yourself the megrims if you go on like this—and don't look so pudding-faced. Be patient. I'm certain 'twill work out."

"Do you really think so, Grandmère?" came the hopeful query.

With an enigmatic look at Mina, the countess responded, "In the end, *certainement*. And in the meantime, if you two young ladies should decide to visit Mina's relatives when they're in Town, I would certainly be obliged to permit that."

"Oh, Grandmère! You would let me see him!" Catherine bounced a little on the seat. A jubilant smile lit her eyes. "Thank you, Grandmère. Thank you so much."

"*Mais non, ma jeune fille.* There is nothing to thank me for." Grandmère winked at both of the girls as she stressed, "Remember that, *s'il vous plaît*. There is *nothing* to thank *me* for."

A carriage pulled alongside and a distinguished male voice boomed out an effusive greeting. "My Lady Cavendish, how delightful to see you and your charming granddaughter."

A positively flirtatious glimmer lit the older woman's countenance at the sight of the robust, white-haired gentleman in a gleaming barouche. He was accompanied by two girls and a young gentleman. "Sir Thomas, the delight is mine," the countess trilled, lowering her lashes as if she were barely out of the schoolroom.

Sir Thomas Barcroft, a widower with twenty thousand a year and estates in Hampshire and on the Borders, was out for an airing with his grandchildren. His daughter's girls, Sarah and Elizabeth, had not yet made their come-outs, being fifteen and fourteen respectively, but Sir Thomas saw nothing wrong in treating the girls to an occasional spin about the Park when he was able to wrench them loose from their over-protective papa. The young man seated beside Sir Thomas was their cousin, Percival Barcroft, the last male in the Barcroft line.

"My dear Countess," Sir Thomas returned, "you look positively ravishing. Why, I was just saying to Percival that I wondered who the two young ladies were with the Lady Catherine. Wasn't I, Percival?" he inquired of his grandson.

"Quite so, sir," Percival Barcroft responded. He was a pleasant-looking gentleman of two and twenty years with gentle eyes and a quiet demeanor to match. He smiled in greeting as his grandfather and the countess made the necessary introductions, and Mina was touched by the impression that he was genuinely shy.

Soon it was time for the carriages to proceed. Farewells were exchanged. The countess extracted a promise from Sir Thomas to bring his granddaughters to Cavendish House for tea, and Percival gravely intoned that he hoped to see Miss O'Kieffe in the future.

On their third circuit of the Park, Mina recognized Captain Ramsey atop a magnificent midnight-black mount. He was riding in their direction and was as splendid as she recalled.

"There's that charming Captain Ramsey," the countess said. "Knew his grandparents well. Grandmother was a Braughton. Fine family regardless of what my grandson may tell you."

The captain was not wearing his uniform today. He cut a nonetheless dashing figure in a bottle-green coat of superfine, ecru trousers, and gleaming riding boots. His stallion was a lively beast, prancing alongside the Cavendish carriage.

"My lady, this is indeed a surprise and an honor," he addressed the dowager countess in most proper form. Then with a merry grin, he turned to Mina. "How fortunate. I had not thought to see you for some time, Miss O'Kieffe. How has your stay in London been thus far?"

"Overwhelming!" came Mina's candid reply. "Why there's ever so much to see, and I'm certain I shan't get to visit everything in a single Season."

The captain laughed, revealing beautiful white teeth which stood in stark contrast to his ink-black hair and bronzed complexion. The chit was thoroughly delightful and quite a dasher. A real golden girl with sunlight-burnished curls framing her elfin face; she put him in mind of the country, something fresh and vibrant. He could not help but wonder what her true position was in Brierly's household, for the earl would have to be a nodcock not to fall under the enchantment of this lassie. "And the Park, does it meet with your approval?"

"Oh, yes! Although I never expected so many people and animals. They stir up ever so much dust, don't they?"

"Indeed they do," he concurred and then returned his attention to the countess. "My lady, I was planning on repairing to Gunter's for a refreshing ice. Would you and your lovely charges care to join me?"

"How considerate, Captain. We would enjoy that immensely." The countess instructed her coachman to head back towards Berkeley Square, where Gunter's, the finest confectioner's in England, was housed under the sign of the pineapple.

An olive-skinned man greeted the captain at the entrance. "Ah, Capitáno Ramsey. Welcome," he said.

"Thank you, Signor Vitelli."

"Please to come this way, Capitáno. I save the best seat for you and your beautiful friends." Signor Vitelli ushered them to the alcove at the front window, and they were seated in a circle around an elaborate wrought-iron table.

The room was a kaleidoscope of color. Large baskets of geraniums hung from the walls and were perched atop stands throughout the room, making Mina feel as if she were in a garden. Starched lace curtains were looped back from the bay window with red and green tassels, and the walls and ceiling had been plastered as white as the lace. The room was divided into several small areas by a series of low railings which were candy-striped in red and green. Waiters, balancing brass trays and rushing between tables, were dressed in white shirts and trousers, and their cravats were also green and red.

"Oh, this is truly lovely," Mina enthused. She glanced about her, making certain she had not missed a single detail. "What a splendid place!"

"I'm pleased you like it," Captain Ramsey said in a low voice that was meant only for Mina's ears. "Pleasure becomes you, Miss O'Kieffe. I do believe the green in your Highland eyes has deepened considerably."

Mina turned slowly towards him, and on her lips there was a knowing grin—the same one she bestowed upon her brothers when their teasing crossed the boundary between reality and make-believe. The captain was behaving no better than one of the twins when they were wont to badger her. "Could that be *blarney* green, Captain Ramsey?" she inquired, accentuating her Irish lilt.

Instead of taking offense at Mina's remark, he threw back his head and laughed, realizing the girl was not as naive as she appeared. What a minx she was! Innocent, but not muffin-headed.

" 'Twas perhaps overstated," he conceded, "but 'tis no shallow compliment, for your eyes do remind me of the Highlands. They are that green."

Mina accepted his compliment with a polite "Thank you," but her voice told the captain she would not be easily gulled.

"May I be so bold as to say that I hope we shall be friends?" he asked, having made a spur-of-the-moment decision that it might not be all dull to cultivate a friendship with so charming a young lady. It might very well improve his reputation, if mamas could see he did not have evil designs on every girl in Town.

"I would like that very much," replied Mina, quite

exhilarated with her success. She had been in Town less than a full day and already she was making friends.

Captain Ramsey ordered strawberry ices for the ladies, while he enjoyed a cup of dark espresso coffee. The ladies were having a gay time listening to the captain describe the pandemonium on the streets of Brussels after Waterloo when Mina's gaze was arrested by a figure looming outside the bow window. It was the earl. He turned to enter Gunter's, and she choked indelicately on a spoonful of ice.

Beneath the table she gave Catherine a warning kick, but dared not glance at her. The earl was only a few steps away.

"Grandmère. Ladies. Captain." He executed a quick bow, his face dark with displeasure. Gone was any vestige of the pleasant gentleman with whom Mina had conversed that morning. "I saw my carriage and came in with the hope of finding you, Grandmère. You quite forgot your appointment with Monsieur Camenbert, the new chef. He's waiting at the town house this very moment. Shall I escort you, ladies?" He gestured with his hand, long, expressive fingers pointing towards the door.

The countess turned a thoroughly displeased gaze on her grandson and stated, "Your concern is most ill-placed. I am quite capable of remembering appointments. *Mon Dieu, vous êtes incroyable!* Monsieur Camenbert, indeed. Despite your opinion, I am not in my dotage, Compton."

If Mina did not know better, she would have thought that was a blush fanning his high-sculpted cheeks. But such a thing was impossible. Very little ruffled the Earl of Brierly, and if anyone could maintain an impeccably proper façade, it certainly was he.

"Never meant to imply such a thing, ma'am," he protested.

"Didn't you?" the countess persisted with mounting asperity. "Well, you managed a fair imitation."

Catherine crushed a linen napkin to her mouth, repressing a titter, and again Mina issued a warning to her friend. She delivered a pinch to the girl's thigh, hissing beneath her breath, "Clorinda Penshurst wouldn't do that."

None of this went unnoticed by the captain, who winked at the both of them. His twinkling eyes darted among the glowering earl, the beautiful, irked countess, and the wide eyed girls.

It was an impossible situation, for there was a laughing devil in his eyes, and if Captain Ramsey did not stop looking at her in that fashion, Mina was certain to go into whoops at any moment. If he had been one of her brothers she might very well have given him a swift kick to the shins—anything to wipe that mischievous look from his face. Suddenly, Mina realized she had a soft spot for the captain, who was more prankish schoolboy than rake. He was truly incorrigible, and the earl had been right to warn her away from the likes of him. A man like Captain Ramsey could break a girl's heart, and she was very glad that they were only going to be friends.

The night of the Derby-Clement ball arrived, and Mina was standing in her dressing room amidst a scene of utter chaos. Gowns and petticoats, shawls and crinolines littered the room. Although she and Catherine had already discussed what to wear in minute detail, she was unable to make up her mind. The maid had set out seven different gowns and with each one a pair of shoes, gloves, a reticule, and lightweight shawl. The array of clothing boggled Mina, and she began to wonder if a single ball deserved all this fuss. Verily, she was beginning to question if town life merited such ritual. This was the fourth change of clothes required this day, she having first gone from a morning dress to a walking suit for a ride in the Park, and then having changed again for dinner.

"All of this dressing and undressing is quite tiresome," she complained to Catherine.

"I suppose that's why I never placed much stock in fashion. Waste of time. I'd rather get there and enjoy myself than tarry over my toilette. But 'tis really not all that dreadful, and besides," Catherine reminded, "if you keep up this pace, soon you'll have worn every one of those lovely outfits your gamekeeper's wife so expertly stitched."

"You're right. How about this one?" Mina picked up a simple gown of powder-blue velveteen."

"No, won't do at all. Even though 'twill be chilly this evening, you must wear something cool and certainly not new. There's always a horrid crush at the Derby-Clement affair. The air's bound to be stuffy and with such a crowd, you might even get punch spilled on you. They invite everyone, and they all come! This rout is always the first of the Season. 'Tis almost as important as a ride in the Park or vouchers to Almack's."

"Did you attend last year?" asked Mina.

"Of course. Grandmère would never miss it. It was at the Derby-Clement ball that Liam and I first waltzed. 'Twas really not the thing, of course"—she paused—"but I couldn't resist the chance to be held in his arms." Catherine sighed at the memory of Liam's embrace. "He always holds me as if I were about to break."

Oh, how romantic, thought Mina, and she asked, "Had it been long since you'd seen him last?"

"Six weeks. Do you recall his trip to Bath late last winter? In truth, 'twas not business that occupied his time in that city. He had come to see me."

"You were meeting secretly?" There was a touch of awe in this question.

"It was secret, yes, but not a lover's tryst. I'm not a total scapegrace, you know. A school friend from Miss Hedgecombe's invited me to visit. She and her husband were diligent chaperones." She paused, a faraway look in her eyes. "Those weeks were wondrous. Sometimes it seemed as if naught but Liam and myself existed in the world."

"What did you do?" Mina asked, spellbound, for the idea of lovers cocooned form the world was highly romantic.

"We took long walks and talked endlessly. In truth, we did nothing special. But that was the wonder of it, for until then we hadn't had the chance to know one another. We didn't even know if we wanted the same things in life."

"How could it be otherwise?" Mina asked with a tinge of outrage. "Why, it would be impossible to fall in love but have nothing else to share with a man. 'Twould be, I venture, more gruesome than marriage without love. It goes against the nature of love and 'tis quite impossible!"

Catherine cast a rather superior look at Mina as if to say *You can be hopelessly idealistic at times*. She endeavored to explain. "My dearest friend, 'tis not always so. Take Liam and myself. He rescued me during the peace celebrations—which was prodigious romantic—after which we fancied ourselves in love. Through autumn and the new year we stole moments together in the orchard at Brierly or in Sutton Valence. But until that time in Bath we'd never really talked or shared our ideas and dreams. Why, we might have discovered we hardly suited at all."

"Cupid wouldn't be so cruel," Mina insisted.

"In our case, he wasn't. Liam and I share a wealth of interests. We both enjoy singing and walking in the country, and we both want our home filled with children and pets. To be precise: three sons, two daughters, a family of spaniels, a hutch of rabbits, and several songbirds. Those three weeks in Bath were glorious. We were so close, and I came to see that my life would never be complete without him. Then we had to part. Liam returned to Thornhill Park, and I traveled to London with Grandmère. He was going to be at the Derby-Clement ball, and I do believe it was the most nervous night of my life when I entered that town house, terrified that he might have had a change of heart."

"Not Liam!" Mina exclaimed.

"Of course, I know that, but when you're in love, Mina, you'll understand how the silliest little fears can loom larger than life."

Mina pondered that for an instant. Then, urging Catherine to finish the tale, she said, "He was there, of course."

"Yes." Catherine smiled. "Later he told me he'd waited on the curb until the appointed hour. 'Be damned with being fashionably late,' he said, for he'd suspicioned my fears and was determined to be waiting for me the second I entered."

"But what about the earl? Wasn't he with you?"

"No. Grandmère and I attended with one of my great-uncles. Compton was off at his club."

"Then how did he discover you'd seen Liam?"

" 'Twas the waltz."

"Oh."

"I know it was reckless, but I couldn't resist. The music was so compelling, and I foolishly thought we might not be recognized in the crowd. Of course we were spotted, and word reached Compton before dawn. We even had our names in the books at White's. That was the beginning of all our troubles."

"Your brother was outraged?" Mina guessed, already knowing the answer.

"To say the least." Catherine shivered, remembering. "I've never seen him in such a taking."

There was a thoughtful pause. Speculatively, Mina asked, "What was it that made him maddest, do you suppose? The waltz or the gossip or Liam?"

"I don't know," Catherine replied. "He insisted I'd committed a triple crime. First, I deceived him; he had discovered my encounters with Liam in Sutton Valence after his edict that I not meet with any gentlemen unless a chaperone was present. Then there was the waltz. Waltzing was bad enough, he raged, but with an O'Kieffe it was *unforgivable*! He firmly believes that I must marry a man of equal or better rank, and your brother hardly meets those requirements." With a sad sigh, she finished, "I think there's very little hope of ever convincing him otherwise."

"Farradiddle!" Mina scoffed. "There's always hope, and no one can be as stodgy an old graybeard as your brother would like us to believe he is. Besides, he's got an O'Kieffe living under his roof and hasn't yet grown horns or been cast down into eternal perdition."

Catherine's eyes widened. "What's this? Do I hear you championing my warden and tormenter?"

Though she was not certain of the reason why, this question made Mina blush. "Championing your brother? No, not exactly." She paused to gather her wits and then switched subjects completely. "Come, we've not much time. Which gown shall you wear? How about my red organza? You're welcome to borrow it." Mina gestured towards an exquisite creation.

"I'd rather save it, if you please."

"Ah, yes, you must save it for Liam," Mina agreed,

feeling a bit wiser than she had been only forty-eight hours earlier. "It won't be long, Catherine dearest."

"Even a day is too long." Catherine ran her fingers over the glossy scarlet fabric and on a long sigh, she concluded, "I'm not certain I can be as patient as Clorinda Penshurst."

Chapter Five

In the end, Mina selected a dancing frock of pink gauze over satin. It fell from the shoulders in a froth of bows; its sleeves were daring short puffs. Her light brown tresses were pulled to one side by a pink riband, the lustrous curls cascading about her shoulders. In the privacy of her bedchamber, Mina thought her appearance quite acceptable. But once she left that haven, she was not certain she had made the best choice. She was, in truth, uncertain of many things, and as she slowly descended the circular staircase to the marble rotunda, she concentrated on composing her nerves.

Her first ball. Tonight she would become a part of her darling mama's world. This was what Mina had yearned for during the lonely years. Yet now that the time was at hand, she was gripped by a terrible fear of rejection. One inner voice tormented her with all manner of dire snubs and embarrassments, while a second scolded her for such ridiculousness. *Didn't everyone accept you at the Park?* that second voice queried. *And hasn't the dowager countess made it clear that Mina O'Kieffe is an old family friend?* The answers were, of course, yes. She was being a niddicock about nothing. Making a mountain out of a molehill. After all, this was only a ball, not an inquisition.

Only *a ball*, she groaned inwardly. This thought gave birth to an entire universe of new worries. What if no one danced with her? What if she trod on the feet of every gentleman who partnered her? What if she spilled punch on the earl? Or very simply became tongue-tied throughout the entire soiree?

At the bottom of the stairs she forced a small smile and hummed one of the tunes Catherine had played on the pianoforte during their dancing lessons. Eyes closed, she curtsied to an imaginary partner, extended a slender, gloved arm, and stepped forward, She feigned a waltz, one arm raised as if resting on a gentleman's shoulder, and around the hall she twirled. Her fears slipped away, her mood lifted, and a light giggle escaped her lips. Spinning about the far side of the rotunda, her eyes opened, and she caught sight of the earl lounging against a marble pilaster. Garbed all in black save for the crisp waterfall of white linen at his throat, he was an arresting sight, and she froze, arms poised in midair. The expression in his arctic blue eyes was predictably cool, and Mina had no way of knowing how long he had been watching her.

"Is that a waltz, Miss O'Kieffe?" he inquired gravely. She sucked in a gulp of fortifying air and offered him a shy nod, for she was not certain how to react to this changeable man.

His deep-set eyes roamed over her, taking in every detail of her exertion: the gentle rise and fall of her chest, the high color in her cheeks. Her emerald eyes glistened like a forest moist with early morning dew; decked out in pink, she resembled a sweetbriar rose on a willowy stem. The earl was certain he had never seen a lovelier young lady. "You look lovely, Miss O'Kieffe," he told her. "Quite breathtaking, indeed. It will be an honor to escort you as a member of the Cavendish party this evening."

The compliment was delivered in tones all too somber for Mina's taste, but from a man as persnickety as the earl, she decided it was high praise. "Thank you," she whispered, endeavoring to catch her breath. She shivered, and he saw the delicate quiver of her shoulders.

"'Tis chilly in this hall. Shall we wait in the drawing room?" He offered his arm, and she slipped a gloved hand in the crook of his elbow as they strolled into the room, where a fire had been lit.

Silence stretched awkwardly between them.

Candlelight played across Mina's hair. She was even lovelier bathed in the warm gold of the fire, and the earl was endeavoring to notice anything except the way her dress hugged her slender waist. He walked as far away from her as he might without being rude.

Mina hated the silence. It grated on her nerves, and impetuously she said the first thing that came into her head. "I'm very excited about tonight."

"Ah, 'yes, I'd quite forgotten. 'Twill be your first ball." This was safe ground, the earl decided, recalling how his three sisters reacted to their first balls. He began to relax, lips curving into the semblance of a smile. The tone of voice he achieved was distinctly brotherly. "Shall I give you a few pointers? Don't dance with any gentleman more than twice. Don't wander into the gaming rooms. Don't accept any invitations to see the greenhouse, and most important of all, don't step on your partner's toes while dancing."

She giggled. "That's precisely what I was thinking when I came downstairs."

"You looked as if you'd the hang of it." There was a lull in the conversation. Then the earl began to speak slowly, as if searching for the right words. "I shan't scold you for this afternoon."

"You're referring to our encounter with Captain Ramsey?"

"Indeed. 'Tis clear enough my sister and grandmother are in sad need of being kept on leading strings. The captain is of a fine family, I grant you, but I had wanted you and my sister to maintain a respectable distance from him. You see, young girls find the captain handsome and charming, and they're often swept off their feet by men of his ilk." He paused to determine Mina's reaction to this statement and was somewhat perplexed by the smile tugging at her mouth. "This is quite a serious matter, Miss O'Kieffe," he reproved. "What I am trying to say is that the captain's reputation is not spotless. I shouldn't like to see you hurt, nor do I believe your brother would appreciate my allowing that to occur.''

"I understand, my lord, and I appreciate your concern. But please put your mind at rest. In Gunter's I recognized the type of man the captain is. As you say, he's charming and handsome and quite gay company, but he's far too glib with his compliments, and even I know a Banbury tale when I hear it. Verily, he puts me in mind of my brothers. Not one of them—save Liam—has a serious bone in his body, and woe to the woman who might think otherwise.''

"Your good sense is quite admirable.''

"Oh, 'tis nothing,'' she mumbled, her smile dipping downward to a frown, for his remark sounded decidedly backhanded. Mina could almost imagine the earl saying, *Your good sense is quite admirable for a birdwitted girl who believes in love.*

"Then we understand each other, and you'll stay clear of the captain?''

"How can you ask that? He's not a bad man, my lord, and as I stand little chance of being swept off my feet by Captain Ramsey, I would like him for a friend.''

"Miss O'Kieffe, young ladies do not make friends with men like Captain Ramsey.'' The earl's remark was only partially true. Friendship was possible between ladies and gentlemen, but it was rare, and the earl experienced a prick of some alien emotion knowing that Miss O'Kieffe fancied such a special relationship with Captain Ramsey. Too, he recalled her confession in the coaching inn. It was a shame that any young girl should be so lonely, he decided. This particular thought had a distinctly unsettling effect on him, though he had no inkling why.

"How strange. I thought we were already friends, for the captain asked and I agreed.'' This remark from Mina served merely to deepen the scowl about the earl's darkening eyes, and she augmented, "Let me assure you the captain possesses few of the qualities I had hoped for in the man with whom I shall fall in love. Please agree to let me be his friend, for I don't wish to go against you, but I am fond of his company and wouldn't like to fabricate excuses to avoid conversation with him.''

The earl threaded both hands through his thick blond hair. He did not like having to make this choice, but he saw little alternative, especially if he hoped to maintain a modicum of sanity in his household. And he certainly did not want Miss O'Kieffe to go about behind his back. He had had quite enough deception with Catherine. ''Very well, Miss O'Kieffe. I see no harm in what you propose as long as you remain on your guard and that your relationship progresses no farther than friendship. For at the first hint of your so-called friendship becoming subject for speculation, I'll deny you all contact with Ramsey. Is that understood?''

''Yes.'' She looked so much like a chastised toddler that he added in a conciliatory tone, ''You *do* understand that rumors about yourself and the captain would scotch any chance of making a suitable match, and as that's the reason behind your visit to London, it would be foolhardy to jeopardize those chances.''

Unaccountably, Mina's throat closed up. She had never thought the sole purpose of her visit was to find a husband. Romance would be splendid, but being a part of Society was reward enough. Mina would not consider her trip a failure if she returned to Thornhill Park unbetrothed. Obviously, the earl thought quite the opposite. It made her feel as if he considered her a chattel to be disposed of as neatly and efficaciously as was possible.

The fire crackled and on the mantel a clock ticked. The earl became uncomfortably aware of the silence in the room.

''Your perceptions of men are quite unique. Would that my sister displayed as much common sense. Tell me,'' he remarked, ''have your conclusions about my character altered since our first encounter? Am I still the insensitive villain you accused me of being? I believe your precise words were 'poor creature.' '' Immediately, the earl regretted this curiosity. Zounds! What had possessed him to ask such a thing?

For her part, Mina was mortified. A flurry of thoughts filled her head, and she wondered, *Is he truly a poor creature*? True, he did not believe in love, but he was capable of kindness. The advice he had offered just this night had not been tendered merely to keep her on propriety's straight and narrow path. It had been genuinely given to set her at ease. A man such as that was no poor creature. But was he a man she could consider a friend as she did the captain? Of a sudden it occurred to her that while she understood Captain Ramsey, she was confounded by the earl in a way that made her shy and giddy. It was a disconcerting realization, and as she was not certain of its meaning, she did not wish to be candid with him.

Fortunately, there was no chance for any response. The countess and Catherine entered the room in a swirl of taffeta and silk. In the next instant, the earl was squiring the three ladies through the rotunda and into an awaiting carriage.

The Derby-Clement town house was situated on Brook Street off Grosvenor Square, and though it took only a few minutes to reach their destination, it was another twenty before they could disembark from the carriage, for the line of vehicles waiting to discharge passengers was long. As Mina stepped up to the entry portico, strains of a lively gavotte reached her ears, and she experienced a tremor of renewed trepidation.

"Come now, chin up," whispered Catherine by way of encouragement. "You look splendid, and we'll be with you the whole time."

At this, Mina squared her shoulders, raised her chin, and focused straight ahead, well prepared to face whatever the night might bring.

Each room in the Derby-Clement mansion led into another. The house extended an eternity, terminating in a ballroom that was ablaze with light from hundreds of candles in a center chandelier and in crystal sconces mounted between mirrors. The effect was dazzling. The lights reflected dozens of times within the mirrors; the crystal sparkled, casting rainbows on white walls; and those tiny prisms of color were complimented by flower garlands draped over the archways and above the windows.

Dancing was already in progress when the Cavendish

party entered the ballroom. Sir Thomas spotted the countess and hurried in her direction, his grandson in tow. The orchestra broke into a rousing Polish dance, and Mina and Catherine were immediately seized upon to make a set, Mina being partnered with Percival Barcroft.

Mr. Barcroft was as shy as he had been in the Park, his gaze being directed at the air above Mina's head. She experienced a surge of empathy, and as they joined the other couples on the dance floor, she whispered behind her gloved hand, "This is my very first dance."

"Ever?" he asked with an astonished glance in her direction. She nodded, this confidence making Mr. Barcroft feel more experienced than he usually did in the presence of young ladies. A hint of color came to his complexion, and he hastened to assuage her fears. He promised to whisper the steps to her, should she forget.

It was an energetic set, and afterwards Mina was in desperate wont of refreshment. Mr. Barcroft, having escorted her back to the spot where the countess and Sir Thomas were conversing, went in search of something cool to drink. He returned shortly with two cups of orgeat and sat down in a spindly chair beside her.

They sipped their punch in silence until Mina spoke. "Do you live in London, Mr. Barcroft?"

"No, in Oxford. I'm reading to be a don," came the halting response.

"How marvelous."

Her remark surprised him, for it lacked the censure to which he had become accustomed. Most young ladies either stared at him nonplussed when he spoke of his academic interests or quickly excused themselves for livelier company. Only one lady of his acquaintance had ever expressed an interest in his aspirations, and Miss O'Kieffe reminded him of Margaret Hamilton, the girl in Oxford with whom he had shared his dreams, but whose parents forbade any alliance with a man whose sole interest was academic. Miss O'Kieffe did not look like Margaret Hamilton, who was, in truth, quite plain by comparison, but the light in their eyes was the same. Genuine. Curious. Kind. Mr. Barcroft could not resist confiding, "I wish my parents thought it was marvelous."

"Well, we can't live our lives pleasing others. We must follow our hearts," asserted Mina.

Finding it very comfortable to talk with Miss O'Kieffe, he continued, "I agree, but my father believes in family obligation. He argues that guaranteeing the line should come before academic pursuits. We're not an old family, but he's determined to keep the Barcroft lands in the family. He feels my ambitions conflict with his, and there's no middle road in his view."

There was a frown on Mina's face. " 'Tis a shame. Many people share your father's view, which must, in my opinion, make for a great deal of unhappiness," Mina remarked. Of course, she was thinking about Catherine and Liam and how the earl's beliefs about propriety and family would condemn them to misery.

Miss O'Kieffe was a most exceptional young lady, decided Mr. Barcroft, a young lady with whom it would be pleasant to spend more time. Thus, for the first time since he had come to Town, he inquired, "If you would be willing, Miss O'Kieffe, I would be honored to call on you at Cavendish House."

"That would be splendid." Mina was pleased to have found another friend.

"Perhaps I might take you on a tour of London. Have you seen the Tower?"

"No, not yet, and I would enjoy that immensely."

Once that was settled Mr. Barcroft took leave of Mina, Sir Thomas having commanded, by way of suggestion, that he dance with his third cousin, a rather spotty young lady who had not yet stood up that evening.

After that Mina danced with Captain Ramsey and several other gentlemen, two lords, and a tall German count, Heinrich von Ruttiger. She was quite tired by the time her last partner led her off the dance floor. Next to her the countess and Sir Thomas continued their conversation, and Mina glanced about the ballroom in search of Catherine.

She caught sight of her standing with several other young ladies and, intending to join them, she stood.

"Miss O'Kieffe?" The low drawl sent shivers through Mina.

"You startled me, my lord."

" 'Tis a bad habit of mine." This was the earl who had offered kindly advice and had laughed on the stoop of Cavendish House.

"I've kept your advice in mind," she spoke, saying the first thing that popped into her head.

"No crushed toes?" His voice was smooth as velvet.

She swallowed hard and answered shyly, "No. No crushed toes."

The orchestra struck up a minuet. "Then 'tis safe for me, I suppose. May I have the honor of this dance?"

A dance with the earl! Her heart thumped hard against her chest, and miraculously her feet were no longer tired. With a sweet smile, she nodded her acceptance and allowed the earl to lead her onto the floor.

Gracefully, he executed a bow, and Mina, on shaky legs, gave a low curtsy in return. His eyes captured her gaze, and he took her hand, a spark of light jumping to life within the cool blue depths as their fingers touched. A smile tickled at the corner of his mouth, but he controlled it, his staid expression matching the precision of the stately rhythm. It was as if he commanded the music to his step and, in turn, Mina to his every movement. They moved in elegant counterpoint, Mina mirroring each fluid step taken by the earl.

His gaze remained intent, disconcertingly so, and Mina glanced away lest she embarrass herself with a scarlet blush. Then, drawn by his presence, she could not resist the impulse to peek at him, and from beneath lowered lashes she studied the earl. There was nothing about this man, from his lean jaw and startling blue eyes to his excessively broad shoulders and narrow waist, that would cause any woman to find fault with his appearance. There was nothing foppish or contrived about him, and Mina was struck by the masculinity he projected. If she had her way she would have preferred this sometimes-stern earl over all of the other gentlemen who had stood up with her this night. She was blissfully content holding his hand and gliding through the minuet.

They walked forward three steps and bowed deeply. Then he raised his hand aloft, and she pirouetted beneath their raised arms. Again, their eyes locked, cobalt blue never wavering from lush green, and she felt as if, in some mysterious way, he had entered her. She was his to command in this dance, and he led her masterfully through the languid moves. They approached and retreated, turning slowly and gliding past each other, ending in a stately, sweeping pose.

While the other couples moved towards the refreshment room, Mina remained rooted to the spot where she had been when the music stopped. A free hand flew to her face. She was unaccountably flushed. Her cheeks were blazing hot and, despite the slow rhythm of the minuet, her breathing was shallow. Not understanding what had happened to her, she looked to the earl for an explanation and watched as his lips thinned, destroying any vestige of a smile. It was as if the sight of her angered him, and a cool look descended upon his countenance.

Without a word, he escorted her to Catherine, leaving Mina feeling queerly deflated that their dance was over. She ached with unaccountable emptiness as she watched his retreating back, knowing that she would not see him again until it was time to depart.

The next afternoon saw a prodigious number of gentlemen callers at Cavendish House. Sir Thomas and Percival Barcroft called, as did Captain Ramsey and Count von Ruttiger. There were also several gentlemen desirous of renewing their acquaintance with the Lady Catherine. Mina joined the countess and Catherine in the salon with their guests, and although none of the gentlemen stayed longer than thirty minutes, she was exhausted when the last one had departed.

The countess hurried upstairs to change for a ride in the Park, and Catherine followed, ever in the hopes of spotting Liam. Pleading a megrim, Mina begged off this excursion.

In need of quiet and privacy, she slipped down the hallway and into the library.

This shelf-lined room was heavy with the scent of lemon wax and leather, which reminded Mina of Thornhill Park. Libraries were perfect harbors, and this particular room with its vaulted ceiling was no exception. There were, Mina estimated, at least two thousand books in the collection. Surrounded by so many friends, she was content. Mina slipped out of her shoes and curled up in a chair with one of the musty volumes.

It was a wonderful tale—an old romance about a young beggar girl in merry olde London who is rescued during the Great Fire by a notorious rake. Naturally, the beggar girl and the rake are instantly besotted with one another, and he reforms, offering the girl the honor of his name and the love of his heart.

In the end, the rake holds his beloved and whispers, "The sweet laughter in your eyes doth pierce the armor of my heart." Mina could not resist repeating the words aloud. They were utterly romantic and, to Mina's mind, beautiful beyond belief.

"Who's there?" called a deep voice.

Mina peered around the back of the chair, noticing for the first time that the earl was seated behind a heavy desk at the far end of the room. His booted feet were propped atop the massive piece of furniture, and an open book rested face-down on his chest.

"I didn't startle you again, did I?"

"Not this time." A smile curled her rosebud mouth.

"You're back already from the Park?"

"No. I didn't go."

He grinned sympathetically. "Pace of Town life got you down, has it?"

"Yes, I begin to comprehend why so many ladies lie abed 'til midday. This constant round of visiting is most enervating, and I confess that I miss the country. 'Twould be wonderful to gallop across the fields. Why, even a nice long stroll would be sufficient, but it appears everyone in London believes exercise is as deadly as the cholera."

"So London's not standing up to those romantic ideals," he remarked in a low, almost teasing tone. Gone was the frigid quality that often clung to his words. This was the man she remembered from the other morning, the earl she preferred.

"Oh, no, there's nothing amiss with London, my lord. What I've seen of the city is truly wonderful. What's disappointing is how everyone spends their time. Even Catherine is prodigious different. I have met someone, another friend, with whom I share similar interests. Mr. Percival Barcroft, Sir Thomas's grandson, has promised to take me to the Tower."

The earl mumbled something that sounded suspiciously like "the pale one," but Mina was certain she must have been mistaken.

When she asked him to repeat himself, he merely remarked, "The Tower, you say? Didn't know you were interested in the Tower."

"Of course, I am," Mina declared. "I most earnestly hope to see all the sights in the metropolis, particularly those historical."

"Ah, yes," he began dryly. "The romance in history is what you called it. Does Barcroft see this . . . this"—he was having a most difficult time spitting the word out—"*romance* as well?"

Turning around and sitting a bit straighter, Mina said, "Oh, yes, we're in perfect understanding. Mr. Barcroft shares my feelings. He's currently pursuing a course of study devoted entirely to history."

A furrow formed between his eyes. "That's nice." After a pause, the earl continued, "Understand he called today. That's good news. Do you think he's the one for you?"

Her immediate instinct was to respond Heavens no! but she did not say that. Instead she answered in a snappish voice, "You sound overly eager to have me off your hands, my lord."

"I have my duty, Miss O'Kieffe." His voice was cool once more. "And I never shirk my duty." He stood hastily, the book that he had been reading left open on the desk.

After he departed, Mina walked across the room and picked up the book. She recognized the volume at a glance. The earl had been reading one of her favorite poems, Scott's romantic ballad entitled *The Lay of the Last Minstrel*.

Mina knew the story by heart. 'Twas a bit like *Romeo and Juliet* set in the Highlands. Young Margaret Branksome is prevented from marrying Lord Cranstoun, her family's hereditary enemy. But unlike Shakespeare's ill-fated lovers, Margaret and her lord are wed at last, Lord Cranstoun having rescued Margaret's young brother from the English.

The book was opened to the scene in which Lord Cranstoun, garbed in knightly regalia, returns the Branksome heir to his family. "For pride is quell'd, and love is free," says Lady Branksome as she yields her daughter to Cranstoun.

Mina considered those words—*Pride is quell'd and love is free*—wondering for the first time how love might be bondaged to pride, if somehow the earl believed he could not love save at the expense of his pride. Perhaps he was not so coldhearted? Perhaps he was a victim of pride, and that, not an empty heart, would keep the earl from ever experiencing love.

Chapter Six

The next week raced past. Mina adjusted to the never-ceasing social events, and life at Cavendish House took on a certain pattern. Each morning, there were visits to the modiste or visits from the countess's hairdresser; in the afternoon, there were rides in the Park; on alternate days, the countess received callers at Cavendish House, during which time Mina visited with Count von Ruttiger, Percival Barcroft, and Captain Ramsey; and in the evenings, there were routs or the opera or balls and dancing with a long list of eligible suitors. There was also a trip to the Tower with Percival Barcroft, after which he took Mina to Gunter's for raspberry ice.

Mina seldom saw the earl, and so it came as a surprise when she received an invitation for a walking tour of Mayfair. She was delighted. On the other hand, Catherine, who was present when Mina received the terse note from her brother was horrified. It was incredible that her brother suggest anyone devote time to walking through the neighborhood and equally insane that Mina proposed to accept his offer. In vain she tried to convince Mina of the boredom such an outing would bring, but Mina would have none of it. She accepted the invitation, for there was nothing she would have enjoyed better than a tour of Mayfair, and the following morning at the unfashionable hour of nine they set out from Cavendish House.

Knowing how devilish starched-up the earl could be, Mina prepared for their outing with special care, choosing a modest walking dress in subdued green tones. The earl dressed with the utmost propriety, shunning the fashions so aspired to by dandies, and Mina was, she believed, simply acting out of a desire to prevent his raising an eyebrow at her appearance. She did not want the morning to be spoiled by anything. She merely wanted to guarantee that the pleasant earl she had seen on several occasions would be the earl who greeted her in the rotunda. It did not cross her mind that the extra moments she spent before the pier glass were in any way akin to a desire for his approval of her as a woman.

She had chosen well. The sensible dress was also exceedingly flattering, showing off her tiny waist and the gentle swell of her figure to perfection. Not only did the earl take note, so did the first footman as he closed the front door behind his employer and Miss O'Kieffe. She was a stunner, the footman thought with an admiring glance, and it was plum peculiar what a striking couple she and the earl presented. Two golden beauties they were. One tiny and delicate, the other tall and solid.

Deep in thought, the footman scratched his balding pate. The oddest thing was the earl, whose very countenance was altered. The strain had vanished from about his eyes, replaced by an expression of simple pleasure. The footman considered it a miracle.

The earl and Mina began their outing at the northernmost boundary of Mayfair, where Tyburn Road crossed Oxford Street on the way to the gallows. It was early. Traffic in the roadways was light, and they shared the sidewalk with London's common folk. Coal blacks and chimney sweeps scurried down sidewalks, bakers trundled their carts of hot buns to the Exchange, and farmers drove wagons laden with cabbages, spring potatoes, and chickens towards the markets.

"I like the city at this hour," said Mina. "Look! The houses are waking up." She pointed to one of the mansions, and the earl watched as two white-capped parlor maids pulled back the draperies and opened the windows on either side of the front door. "It's opening its eyes."

The earl barked a short laugh at this image and agreed. "I'd never thought of it like that. You've a clever imagination, Miss O'Kieffe."

" 'Tis all the books," she retorted with a playful grin, wishing that she might skip alongside the earl, but refraining from doing so for fear of the scowl it would certainly provoke. She did not wish this pleasant man to disappear. His company was far preferable to that of the dour earl, and quite enjoyable, in fact.

"You ride frequently at Thornhill Park, do you?" he asked.

"Almost daily. 'Tis surprising we never crossed paths before that day." She made oblique reference to her fateful plunge into the orchard stream.

"Not so very surprising. I usually take a more southern route, going by the Pluckley road to check on my tenants and the dikes along the Stour. It makes good sense to combine those pleasurable rides with estate business. No sense in wasting valuable time. Don't you agree?"

"Yes," she responded automatically, but she was thinking that she did not agree at all. Didn't he ever do anything that had nothing to do with responsibility? After a few minutes' silence she asked, "How do you tolerate Town life? What do you do without the open fields of Brierly and estate affairs to occupy your time?"

"There are quite a lot of details to which I attend while in Town. Hardly a day passes that I don't visit the City and confer with my man of business. And as to maintaining my sanity," he said with a near-boyish grin quivering at one corner of his mouth, as if he were confiding a great secret, "there are occasional morning rides in the Park, my weekly round at Gentleman Jackson's Salon in Bond Street, and visits to Manton's Shooting Gallery. But this is more precisely to my taste: walking through the city in the early hours, as much and as far as possible."

" 'Twas what you were doing the morning after our arrival?" He nodded a positive reply, and she said, "Thank you for including me today."

Ahead was a half-timbered building. The sign swinging above the door was painted with a picture of three ducks taunting a dog. There were not many such hand-painted signs remaining in London, the office of the high mayor having requested their removal over the past three-score years for the safety of pedestrians passing beneath them. That such a sign remained on this building was a sure clue that it must be one of the original inns remaining from when Mayfair was a village situated about the brook field and marketplace.

"The Dog and Ducks." Mina deciphered the pictorial meaning of the painting. "Wasn't that sign painted by Mr. Hogarth?" Her face was rosy from the brisk walk, and her green eyes sparkled with delight.

The earl nearly missed a step, which would have sent him stumbling on the cobblestones. Egad! The chit was putting him to shame, for he did not know a Hogarth from a Rembrandt, but he would be damned before he let her know that. She already had him reading Scott's ballads. Would he soon find himself touring the galleries of the British Museum?

"Hogarth?" he blithely remarked and squinted to feign intent perusal of the sign. "I believe you're right," he said, hoping that Miss O'Kieffe had not suspected his ignorance. What an unusual girl. He had come to think all females were like his sisters or his grandmother, but Miss O'Kieffe was continually showing him otherwise. Regarding her upturned face studying the sign in such wonderment, he was seized by a wholly unaccustomed desire to please her and could not resist asking, "Would you like to step inside and take a look?"

"'Tis a public tavern, my lord." She was clearly surprised by his suggestion. It was not the sort of thing she had come to expect from him.

"But 'tis early enough an hour that I feel certain we'll find little activity save that of the landlord tidying from last night." He eyed her intently, a moment of anxiousness laid bare at the possibility that she might refuse to accompany him into the Dog and Ducks. He need not have worried. Mina eagerly accepted, and arm in arm they walked up the wooden steps, the earl bending in the doorway to enter the low-ceilinged taproom.

A portly gentleman was sponging off a trestle table. "Welcome, milord," he said, wiping his hands on the apron tied about his middle. A trifle awkwardly, he added, "As you can see, we're not ready for customers."

"'Tis of no import, good sir. My young friend was desirous of seeing your renowned establishment."

"Oh, 'tis exactly as Hogarth's biographer described," enthused Mina, capturing the attention of the landlord.

"You've read about the Dog and Ducks, have you?" he remarked, puffing up with pride. "Don't often get folks who appreciate the history of this place. Me name's Foster, and the Dog and Ducks's been in me family for nigh on one hundred and fifty years. It would be an honor to serve up a light repast for your enjoyment. Please, milord, milady," he said, pulling back a chair for Mina.

Master Foster brought them cider and brown bread with potted cheese. The bread was steaming fresh from the ovens, and the cider was cinnamon-spiced. Master Foster was pleased that his guests were enjoying the fare, and as they relaxed, he answered Mina's questions about the old building.

"See that etching over there?" The landlord motioned to the near wall. "*Execution of a Fencing Master* it be called, and Master Hogarth painted it, he did. Right here in the Dog and Ducks."

"Whatever did the man do?" asked Mina as she studied the detailed drawing of a slender young man standing on the gallows, the streets around the wooden structure crowded with a motley audience of jeering Londoners.

"Killed a constable," Foster answered. "Cook was his name—the fencing master, that is. Constable was John Cooper. Died in a fracas at the May Fair. 1702. Now Hogarth, he was a mere stripling then, but his father what owned the coffeehouse remembered it well and told his son about it. Hanged him up on Tyburn hill, they did."

The expressions of the throng of spectators presented twisted caricatures of pleasure and pain, poverty and jaded comfort, while the fencing master wore a look of ethereal resignation, a look that placed him above both the highborn and the meek.

"How noble Master Cook appears. Don't you agree, my lord?" Mina asked the earl.

"Noble?" the earl repeated in disbelief. "To my mind, 'tis rather horrendous." He ran an expressive finger along his jaw and shook his head. "Perhaps Master Cook was innocent, but surely you don't find this romantic? Surely you don't deny the brutality depicted here?"

There was truth in what the earl said, and some of the glimmer fled Mina's eyes. She frowned a little as she studied the picture again. Slowly, she said, " 'Tis not all ugly. There is some beauty in every man."

"And I venture you find that romantic?"

"Perhaps that isn't exactly the word I would choose, for you would be right"—she smiled—"to say I was frivolous. But just as hope exists in romance, so, too, I look at this and feel hopeful. The fencing master is proof that despite ugliness there can be still be something pure and good above it all."

They were silent a moment, each turning over what the other had said. It was quite stimulating to discuss ideas without squabbling, they each thought, wondering if this was a part of what friendship was all about.

On leaving the Dog and Ducks they headed southward up the slope of South Audley Street to Copley's bookstore, where Mina discovered a copy of *Emma*, the new Jane Austen novel, and a display of the latest Minervas, from which—despite the earl's reproving frown—she selected two.

Next they entered Shepherd's Market, only half a mile from St. James's Palace at the far end of Piccadilly. It marked the site where the original May Fair had been held at the gates of London in 1686. A maze of small houses and shops, one on top of the other, clustered about the tiny marketplace, where two flower girls in soiled print frocks and old black chip bonnets were pushing a cart.

One of the girls called out in a singsong voice, "Primroses. Violets. Wallflowers. Penny a bunch. Flowers fer yer lady, m'lord."

On impulse the earl purchased a nosegay of wild violets. His look was serious as he presented them to Mina. She in turn smiled brightly and lifted the bunch of purple and white blooms to her nose. Their scent was faint. The dark leaves were soft, and she stroked her cheek with them. The deep green matched her eyes to perfection, and the earl could not tear his gaze from the sight of Mina as her lips brushed against the leaves.

An inward tension seized him for which he needed no explanation. He could remind himself until Doomsday that this girl was in his charge and that she was an innocent. But it would be to no avail. He wanted her as acutely as he had that day in the orchard stream. He was all too aware of her luscious eyes and pert mouth, and when she walked beside him, the rosewater scent of her honey brown hair drifted about him. Frustration tore at him. His jaw tightened and his breath hissed between his teeth as she looked him straight in the eye. A quiver of emotion darted along his nerves in response to what he saw, for within her eyes was reflected a longing so intense it was frightening. He nearly expected her to say, *Kiss me, my lord*, but her words when they came were not those he had expected to hear.

"I find it sad the old days are vanished forever. 'Tis not that progress is to be frowned upon, but wouldn't it be lovely if we could capture those other times, if only for a moment?" came Mina's soft words.

"'Tis the ever romantic Miss O'Kieffe speaking," he teased in an effort to control his reactions to their physical proximity.

"Yes, you're right," she said. Responding to his light tone, she added, "At least you're no longer mocking me about it."

They rounded the next corner, and the earl surprised Mina with his question. "If you could recapture a moment, what would it be?"

"A May Fair," was the instant response. "I would adore to attend a fair with the mimes and rope dancers and tumblers. Naturally, I could do without the cattle and pickpockets. But all the rest, the crowds and noise and bustle, would be fine fun. It's long been a daydream of mine." Slowing her pace, Mina asked, "And you, my lord, have you ever daydreamed?"

"Daydreamed?" That unwanted tension was returning, and the earl walked faster. "Not since I was a lad. Then I used to wonder what it would be like to joust with the Conqueror's knights." He was concentrating so hard on putting a distance between himself and the temptation of her alluring femininity that he scarce realized he had let that confession of a boyhood fantasy slip.

"A knight. What a splendid daydream for a boy to have. But what about now? Don't you daydream anymore?"

"No. Why should I? Daydreams are for children or incurable romantics." His tone was curt, for she was keeping pace with him. He could not escape the fragrance of rose water.

"That's wrong! They're for everyone. For lonely times when you can't have everything you want. It's much more pleasant to daydream than to mope. Don't you agree?"

When he did not answer she went on, "Do you have everything you've always wanted?"

"Can't say," he muttered indifferently, but he knew the answer. No, dear Lord, he thought, he did not have everything he wanted, and to daydream about it would be torture.

If Mina had suspected what the earl was thinking, she would have been stunned. Thank goodness she heard only what he had said.

The sun was midway in the sky as they headed back towards Cavendish House. At the corner of Curzon Street a sight caught Mina's eye.

"What's this?" she inquired curiously, pausing to inspect a small doorway in a wall which seemed to lead beneath the ground.

"Lansdowne Passage." He stepped one pace away from her.

"This is where you can hear the river?" She moved forward.

"So 'tis said."

She flashed a beguiling smile. "Let's go in, shall we?"

"No!" the earl nearly jumped.

"Whyever not?"

"Wouldn't be proper at all, Miss O'Kieffe," he said stiffly.

"How ridiculous. You took me into the Dog and Ducks. How can you refuse this now?"

"Very simply. 'Tis a wholly different set of circumstances. At the Dog and Ducks the landlord served as a chaperone of sorts, but in the passage there would be no one save ourselves. 'Tis out of the question."

"Nonsense. You're my guardian. Who else would I be safe with, if not you?" She offered a moue of persuasion, but the icy glint in his eyes made him appear thoroughly impervious to her efforts at charming him.

"There are some things that even a guardian is prohibited from doing, Miss O'Kieffe, and descending into an unlighted passage is one of them."

"Pooh!" she said with a stamp of her foot, and then, to the earl's horror, she proceeded to grab hold of his arm.

Tugging with all her might, she tried to drag him through the door.

"Stop that instantly!" He yanked his arm free and watched as she scampered down the quarried steps. The echo of her tinkling laughter was all that remained where she had stood an instant before.

"You unprincipled hoyden. Come back this instant," he ordered between gritted teeth.

"Will not," she called out, her lilting brogue echoing off the stone walls of the passage.

The earl glanced over his shoulder to see if anyone had heard the reverberation of her voice. Assured that no one of his acquaintance was in the vicinity and vastly relieved that the hour was still too early for most gossips to be up and about, he reluctantly followed Miss O'Kieffe into the passage. It was his duty as a gentleman and her guardian to retrieve her before she did something even more foolhardy. Or, he thought with a wry sense of foreboding, before *he* did something foolhardy.

In the passageway it was cool and musty and heavy with moisture. The earl quickly moved to Mina's side. He gripped her elbow to steer her towards the exit. "Come now, out of here."

"Sssh," she urged, shaking free of his grip. "Just a few moments, please." He reached towards her again, and she stepped back. "Please. Now that we're here, can't we listen?"

"Two minutes and then you'll come straight out when I say?" he hissed in impatience, grabbing hold of her shoulder.

"Yes. I promise."

He felt the tension in her body, heard the yearning in her voice, and he could not resist giving her this wish. He solemnly granted, "Two minutes."

They were still then. All about them sound was magnified. Mina heard her own breathing and his, and then a faint gurgle.

"The Tyburn!" she exclaimed in delight. She leaned towards him and whispered in excitement, the warmth of her words fanning his neck, " 'Tis a miracle."

"Yes," he drawled huskily, gulping deeply at the wave of sensation that washed over him. His voice was hoarse. "Yes, a miracle."

They stood together in the passageway for a long time, each achingly aware of the other.

She waited, hardly daring to breathe, not knowing what it was she expected to happen next, nor what it was that she wanted, and through it all she could not help wondering what it would be like if he kissed her again.

Finally, he wrapped an arm about her shoulder in a careless fashion and led her from the passage.

In the blinding light of the street, whatever spell there might have been was dashed, and if he had been able to see, the earl would have witnessed the brightness fade in Mina's face.

Chapter Seven

Snuggled beneath an embroidered satin counterpane, Mina was dreaming a pleasant dream in which she was being kissed by a tall, fair-haired man. They were standing in a narrow corridor. It was dark and cool, and Mina was chilled through and through, until his lips touched hers. Slender fingers caressed the nape of her neck. Then she was warm, so very warm, like a melting candle.

A glare of light streaked across the image, his lips lifted off hers, the glorious kiss ended, and she lost sight of the fair-haired man.

"Mina!" an impatient voice called.

Who had opened the bed curtains? she wondered in disgust, for she didn't want to wake up. She wanted to go back to sleep, to dream again, and to see the man's face.

"Mina, you slug-a-bed! What's gotten into you? Is our early bird finally becoming a sophisticated lady of the *beau monde*?" asked Catherine as she bounced around the other side of the rosewood canopied bed and pulled the flowered bed curtain wide open.

Rubbing her eyes, Mina struggled to sit up against a pile of lace-edged pillows. She was bewildered. "What time is it? And *what* is that muck all over your face?" she exclaimed, her eyes popping wide in astonishment.

Catherine's face was covered with a thick yellowish paste. Only her mouth and eyes remained in view, and they presented a bizarre sight within the grotesque mask. The noxious paste was drying at a rapid rate, and as it did Catherine's expressions were becoming more and more restricted. The goo was cracking and random bits were crumbling off.

"Saccharine alum," was the response, as if no other explanation were necessary.

"And what pray tell is saccharine alum?" Mina asked, casting her friend a wry smile.

"Surely Nanny has made a paste for you?"

"Never."

She heaved an exasperated sigh. Two yellow chunks skittered down the front of her dressing gown. " 'Tis for the complexion. One boils the whites of eggs and alum in rose water. The paste has much to recommend it, for its restorative qualities make the skin firm and clear." Explanations aside, she went on, her ebullient voice rising, "Hurry now, Mina, we must be dressed within thirty minutes. Why, 'tis nearly eleven and high time for us to be on our way."

"On our way? Where are we going?" came the perplexed response as Mina searched her memory, endeavoring to recall any social engagement to which she and Catherine were committed.

"The Burlington Arcade, that's where. So out of bed and into a walking dress. We've no time to spare." Catherine could barely contain her excitement. "No time for breakfast, either."

"Miss Mina isn't going anywhere without a full meal,"

put in Nanny, who was shuffling between a towering armoire
and a dressing table flounced with a charming ruffle of
heather floral damask. Now fully awake, Mina glanced
toward Nanny, who was performing the same ritual she had
done for the past six years. With meticulous care the dear
woman set a pair of gloves and a matching bonnet on the
dressing table. "Ain't going nowhere without something in
her stomach," she repeated twice and then directed Jenny,
the maid, to fetch a tray of chocolate and brioche.

"The Arcade at this hour?" queried Mina. "Whatever
for?"

"Trouble again, I tell you," Nanny grumbled, and Mina
wondered if the sun was too bright or if the temperature had
taken an upward turn for the worse.

" 'Tis not trouble. 'Tis a wonder. A delight. A marvel,"
Catherine sang and handed a letter to Mina. " 'Tis from
Liam. He arrived last evening. Three days later than he
promised, but he's here at last and is staying in Knightsbridge.
We're to meet him at Dawson's, the tobacconist, and
Grandmère has said we may go, taking Jenny with us, of
course."

"Trouble. Trouble. Didn't I warn the lad? A hornet's
nest, I said. And now you girls! Oh, the earl was right. A
scandal broth, he said, and we'll all be set afloat in it."
Nanny muttered to no one in particular as she took a seat on
a damask chair.

"I believe I may burst. Oh, do hurry." Catherine fluttered
her hands in a birdlike motion as she sped through the
connecting door to her bedchamber.

A few moments later Jenny returned with a tray, and as
Mina gobbled down two rolls with strawberry preserves, the
maid laid out a daffodil-colored walking outfit. Realizing
the import of this outing, Mina was swept up in Catherine's
excitement. It would be lovely to see her favorite sibling,
but above all else, the star-crossed lovers would be reunited.

Oh, what a glorious day it would be! True love united and
all would be well in Mayfair, Mina declared inwardly.

Well, almost, she conceded, knowing full well that the
greatest hurdle between eternal heartbreak and true love was

the Earl of Brierly. He was not, however, an insurmountable obstacle. Hadn't he proven that on their outing? And she vowed that soon the earl would be of such a frame of mind that he could no longer deny true love. Mina would see to that.

While she dressed, she placated Nanny. " 'Twill be all right. I promise to wear my bonnet and gloves, and Liam and Catherine will not be alone.'' Nanny, still perched on the damask chair, was not assured. Her nose and mouth puckered into obstinate lines, and she cast Mina a vastly prim and very disapproving gaze. Mina lowered her voice and said persuasively, "Nanny dearest, you must admit 'tis unreasonably cruel to keep them apart. And we have a plan. A marvelously wise plan. Catherine is endeavoring to convince her brother that she isn't a birdwitted schoolgirl, and once the time is right, I'll speak to the earl in Liam's behalf.''

The lines on Nanny's face were erased by a swell of sympathy. "Oh, Mina. You can't be having storybook endings in all of life,'' was her woebegone statement.

"Fustian. Of course I can. If one wants it, then anything is possible, especially when there's love,'' Mina attested. "You wait and see.''

When the two girls, accompanied by Jenny, departed Cavendish House, Mina remarked on Catherine's smart outfit and spirited appearance. "The nasty alum paste must have done its job, Catherine dearest. You look positively radiant.''

Lady Catherine was stunning in a sage-green dress with lace-trimmed lapels. Her jet black hair, wide-spaced eyes, and full mouth were the usual set of features for a gypsy, not a lady of Quality. An Oldenburg bonnet sat atop onyx curls, its wide brim heightening her naturally exotic appearance.

"Liam is going to be well pleased by the sight of you. You are, indeed, an angel,'' assured Mina. This reference to Liam's pet name for Catherine elicited a girlish blush from the angel, whose eyes, Liam asserted, were blue as the heavens.

Burlington Arcade was a bustle of activity. Fashionable shoppers strolled along the concourse beneath the vaulted glass roof as footmen scurried behind, their arms piled high with purchases, and shop girls in modest dresses, enjoying midday breaks, gawked at the swells entering the men's haberdashery. Mina curiously peered into each window. She would have liked to have lingered at the milliners, for a canary-yellow bonnet with gold ribands caught her fancy, but Catherine would have none of that. There was no time to spare, and she hurried them along towards Dawson's.

"Oh, there he is!" she cried and, in a most unladylike fashion, waved at Liam, who strode through the crowd. But he was not fast enough, and Catherine could not wait; she dashed the last few yards to his side and slipped her arm through his. They did not embrace, for that would have been certain to start tongues clacking, but their faces were close together, and Mina watched as they whispered private greetings to one another, the color in Catherine's cheeks rising noticeably.

It tugged at Mina's heart to see her brother so happy. The grin plastered across Liam's handsome face was near comical.

"Mina, my own darlin' sister, and how might you be this fine morning?" He gave her a crushing hug.

"Splendid. And you?"

"Fit as a fiddle." He smiled at Catherine and then looked back at Mina. "Don't need to ask how your stay has been, puss. You look fine as a ninepence."

"And as Da would have said, you look handsome as the devil himself, Liam O'Kieffe."

He laughed. " 'Tis good to see that Town life agrees with you."

"I've Catherine to thank," she reminded him and watched as her brother returned his attention to the angel. An indulgent smile lit Mina's elfin face. It was a satisfying sight to see her friend and brother goggling moon-eyed at each other. "Go on, you two," she urged. "Jenny and I don't want to intrude on your reunion. We'll stay a few feet behind and keep an eye out for the earl."

The lovers strolled on ahead, and Mina was fascinated by

the sight of them. Memories of her outing with the earl
returned with a rush. She vividly recalled how her pulse had
raced in Lansdowne Passage. And she remembered their
parting in the rotunda at Cavendish House. Yes, her words
had been the truth: their outing was the best time she had
enjoyed in Town. That was, however, only partially true.
What she had not told the earl was that he was the reason
why the day had been so special. She could have seen
Mayfair with Captain Ramsey or Percival Barcroft, who
would have lectured Mina as he had on their tour of the
Tower. No, without the earl Mayfair would not have been
the same. Mina did not doubt that one iota. He had made
the morning special because he had shared it with her.

Shared. It was a peculiar word to ascribe to anything
between herself and the earl. But indeed that is what they
had done. He had shared her delight at their visit to the Dog
and Ducks. It was as if they had discovered something
together. Something that belonged to them alone. And there
was no denying that he had fallen under the same spell that
had spun its magic about her in the passageway. Perhaps
there was a romantic soul waiting to be liberated from
beneath those layers of propriety. Mina smiled at the image
of the earl dressed in a suit of armor, participating in one of
the Conqueror's royal jousting tourneys. His boyhood fantasy was prodigious romantic, but Mina was certain the earl
would deny it should she tell him so. Ah well, one could
not tame a dragon overnight.

Daydreaming found Mina three shop-lengths behind the
lovers, and she was startled when someone addressed her by
name. It was Eugenia Grevey, overdressed as always in an
elaborate outfit and a top-heavy bonnet from which apricot-
tinted plumes extended every which way.

"What a pleasant surprise," Mina said and embraced the
red-headed actress with genuine pleasure. It was wonderful
to spot a familiar face among strangers, and Mina happily
regarded Genie, who on second glance, appeared to be
trimmer than when she had last seen her. Mina was about to
say how charming she looked when she noticed the bluish
smudges beneath Genie's hazel eyes. The actress was not

well, Mina deduced, longing to know what was wrong but reticent to pry.

Arms akimbo and without preface, Genie demanded, "What are you doing here by yourself, Miss O'Kieffe?" She sounded for all the world like a scolding mother hen.

"Oh, I'm not alone. Catherine and Liam are up ahead and Jenny, a maid from Cavendish House, is also with us," Mina hastened to reply. Then, realizing she had not been a vigilant watchdog, she checked the area for any sight of the unwanted earl.

Jenny, dawdling before a window display of beaded reticules, heard her name mentioned and hurried forward to bob a curtsy. Catherine and Liam spotted Genie, and as they strolled over to greet her, Mina hurriedly explained that this was the first time the couple had seen one another since their ill-fated elopement.

"I have a marvelous notion," Genie announced. "Why don't all of you come to my flat for a visit? 'Tisn't a fancy Mayfair mansion, but it would allow Catherine and Liam to visit without worrying about the earl."

"That's perfect, Genie." "How kind you are!" Mina and Catherine spoke at once.

"Come along, then," she encouraged, and the little entourage followed her out of the Arcade and in the general direction of the Thames. Genie leased two rooms on the top floor of a house at Adelphi Terrace, a row of buildings lifted on arches over the water. It was a good walk from Mayfair, but Mina enjoyed the chance to see more of London. She and Genie chatted as they went.

"How's Sean? And everyone else at Thornhill Park?" asked Mina.

"Fine, I suppose."

It was such a short answer that Mina ascertained something at Thornhill Park, her brother Sean most likely, was probably the source of Genie's malaise. "What is it, Genie?" she asked. She was excessively fond of Genie and was aware that something was amiss.

"Oh, nothing's wrong at your home, I assure you. Didn't mean to scare you, lambie."

"It's Sean, then. He sent you back to London?"

Genie sniffled. "I never thought it would happen. One of my friends at Drury Lane warned me. Told me I wouldn't be the first actress to get stars in her eyes and go off with a gent. Also said I wouldn't be the only actress to be turned out cold when the fellow got bored. I listened to Sheila, that's my friend at Drury Lane, but I went anyway. Thought your brother was different. Not a snob like them other coves what hangs around the stage door. I know I'm not a lady, but he treated me right nice those first weeks and"—she hesitated before going on—"I developed an attachment for him." She sniffled some more and withdrew a handkerchief from her reticule, with which she dabbled at her watery eyes. "Two nights ago Sean told me to pack my bags and head back to London."

"Did you argue?"

"If we'd fought I might accept it, but we didn't. It was worse." Her expression doubled with pain. "The twins were teasing at him. Saying how Liam was about to get leg-shackled, and if he didn't watch out, I was going to clip his wings. Sean didn't like that and when they wouldn't stop gabbing on about it, he simply said it was time for me to go back to London."

What devastating news. Genie deserved a happier ending than this, and Mina hastened to offer her assistance. "Well, perhaps if I said something to him. Or perhaps when I return home you might visit me. Yes, that would work, for when he sees you again, he'll certainly realize—"

Genie cut her off. "That's very kind of you, but no."

"Aren't we friends?" she asked in bewilderment. "I'd like to help you, Genie, and I'd enjoy your company at Thornhill Park. There's nothing wrong with that, is there?"

"There's nothing wrong with that, lambie. But I know where I'm not wanted, and I've too much pride to be throwing myself at a man who doesn't want me. Ah, it's sort of amusing in a sad way. There I was, full of experience, warning you about the pitfalls of London, and I was the one to get the gravy boat dumped on me." After a pause, she revived and went on, "How about you, lambie? Have you met any particular gentleman yet?"

"Several. A German, the Count von Ruttiger—who seems nice, but I can scarcely comprehend a word he says—and there's Percival Barcroft. He's from Oxford and has taken me to the Tower. We compiled an extensive list of the sites in London, and he's promised to take me to each. Next week we visit the Royal Museum to see the recently acquired Elgin marbles."

"Museums? Old buildings? Sounds as boring as those books of yours. Mr. Barcroft must be dull as ditchwater, if you ask me. Far too dull for the likes of you, lambie. Anyone else?"

"There's Captain Ramsey, a dashing Highland laird and a war hero wounded at Waterloo. You'd like him, I wager. He's ever so flirtatious and insists my eyes are as green as highland pines."

"A gent with a honey tongue, eh? Sounds a ramshackle sort."

"That's precisely what the earl said."

"Watching you like a hawk, is he?"

"Yes," she answered slowly. "He's been full of advice, and not altogether as loathsome as I thought him to be. The other day he took me on a walking tour of Mayfair. We even went inside the Dog and Ducks, and down into Lansdowne Passage to listen to the Tyburn. It was ever so romantic," she concluded.

"It was, was it?" A spark of lively curiosity ignited Genie's eyes.

"Listening to the Tyburn!" corrected Mina quickly.

"That's all?"

"Of course that's all!" she retorted hotly, her thoughts in a whirl of confusion, alternately recalling the brotherly manner in which he had escorted her out of the passage and the delicate purple and white violets which sat in a vase atop her dressing table at Cavendish House.

"Well, has he kissed you yet?" she whispered.

"Who? What? The earl? No!" Mina sputtered. A flaming blush spread up her neck and across her face. "Gracious, what kind of question is that, Genie? Whyever would you think that might have happened?"

The redhead restrained a smile at Mina's emotional denial. "Can't say, lambie. Thought there was something in your eyes, but I must have been mistaken."

They proceeded the remainder of the way in silence. Mina was trying hard not to think about kissing the earl and she glanced at Genie. Sadness once more clouded the actress's eyes, and Mina wished that Catherine and Liam were not laughing so gayly, nor looking quite so pleased with themselves. It was grossly unfair that they should be happy while Genie was miserable.

Genie's flat at Adelphi Terrace was, like its occupant, alive with dramatic touches. There were several elegant pieces of furniture, one of them being an over-sized French mirror suspended above a tiny fireplace. In a stroke of decorative inspiration, Genie had squandered her savings to purchase the mirror, for she envisioned the enlarging effect it would have on the small parlor. It made the room seem more spacious and magnified the light from the single window, which offered an unobstructed view of the Thames dotted with boats, their white canvas sails billowing in the breeze. Reflected in the mirror Mina saw an urn of peacock feathers sitting on a table constructed solely of stag horns polished to a gleaming and most unnatural state. An array of fringed shawls were draped over chairs, and the floor was covered with odd-sized Oriental carpets. The focal point of the cluttered room was an elaborate painting of a man and woman in period costumes. The brass plate on the frame was inscribed "The Greveys as Lord and Lady Macbeth."

"I was born to the theatre," Genie explained to Mina, who was gazing raptly at the portrait. "My parents and grandparents were members of London's finest companies." She lovingly stared at the painting and drew herself up with pride. "I know what most people say about actresses, but it's an honest profession. Unfortunately, I'm not as good as my mother and grandmother were. But I don't know any other way of life, so"—she shrugged her shoulders in a gesture of resignation—"here I am."

"You say that as though there's no other choice for you," remarked Mina as she untied the ribands of her bonnet.

"Well, is there?" Genie challenged.

"Of course—there always is." Mina and Genie sat on a worn velveteen settee while Catherine and Liam occupied the seat in the window embrasure. Mina thoughtfully regarded Genie, who was endeavoring to look cheerful. "Is that what you'd want, if you could have anything? To be the finest actress in London?"

After several moments' consideration, Genie replied with uncharacteristic reservation, "No, I don't think so."

"Well, what would you want, then?" encouraged Mina.

"I think"—Genie struggled to find the right words—"I think that I would most cherish a home and family of my own. That's something I sorely missed as a child, my parents being on theatre tours much of the time. Always wondered what it would be like to live in one place and to call it home."

Listening to Genie, Mina was seized with an overwhelming urge to throttle her eldest brother. Sean deserved to be horsewhipped for being such an insensitive bumpkin. Her dismay was evident, and Genie hastened to continue.

"Don't look so serious, Mina. I don't have any regrets. I've made a nice go of it. The theatre folk remember my parents, and Mr. Tarleton, the manager at Drury, always has a role for me."

Mina scarcely heard this. Her mind was wandering, already tackling the problem of Genie's love life. There had to be some way to help Sean and Genie. This Cupid business was fine work. A bit hard at times, but as she was already halfway to achieving perfect love for Catherine and Liam, Mina did not doubt that she could make miracles for Sean and Genie, too. There simply had to be a way, for Mina believed in dreams, and she would see that Genie's came true.

Perhaps a rescue would do the trick. That had worked splendidly in *Miss Minton's Marquess*. If Mina could locate a copy of that book, then she might recreate a similar incident with Genie cast as Miss Minton—who was pitched into the lake in Green Park—and Sean as the Marquess who saved Miss Minton from certain death when he plunged into the water and swam to her rescue. Then Mina remembered that Sean did not swim, and her thoughts wandered to *The Path to Heart's Haven*. Genie's happiness depended on other people, and in *The Path* Allison Braithwaite could not marry before her elder sister. In Genie's case, Mina decided, it would be necessary to marry off the twins, for once they surrendered to love they could no longer mock Sean. A house party—as in *The Path*—would enable Mina to match the twins with their own lady loves. She would invite her new friends to Thornhill Park, and Genie would come, as well as two beautiful debutantes who would fall in love with the twins. Yes, a house party with debutantes was the perfect scheme to guarantee that Genie's dreams became reality.

The afternoon passed quickly. They all quite forgot to watch the clock until the bells of Westminster chimed six times. Jenny, who had been dozing in a corner chair, sprang to her feet. "Lady Catherine, Miss Mina! Oh, we must hurry!" she cried. "Hughes will be wonderin' where I be, my lady. Oh, dear. Oh, dear."

This outburst astounded Mina and Catherine, for neither girl had ever heard Jenny utter more than two words at a time, and they hastened to calm her.

" 'Tis no disaster," Catherine said. "Grandmère knows you've gone with us. If anyone's in hot water 'tis Mina and myself." She then clarified, "My brother's schedule is as predictable as the winter solstice. 'Tis Compton's invariable custom to return to Berkeley Square exactly at half past six."

"If that's true, my dearest angel," Liam put in, "then you'd best hurry. It would be most unfortunate should you and Mina arrive home on foot at the same time as he. That would certainly raise questions, would it not?"

The girls agreed and hastened to gather up their bonnets and reticules. Genie walked with them as far as Piccadilly. They presented a gay sight, all four walking abreast and laughing at Liam, who was a nonstop source of tall tales. At the corner of Regent Street they stopped while two sweepers cleared the crossing. A carriage also waited as the barefoot boys completed their task.

A third lad hardly above four years approached Liam. "Eh, mister, penny fer a cartwheel?" he called and then performed a series of quick turns across the cobbled walkway. Liam tossed a coin, and the boy scrambled after it. "Oi can do 'andstands, too," he vowed earnestly, capturing Mina and Catherine's attention. The boy stood on his hands, prompting each girl to fish a coin from her reticule and hand it to him.

Then it happened.

"Land o' Goshen!" shrieked Genie.

Everyone followed the direction of her horrified glance.

"Fudge!" Catherine gasped and groaned alternately.

Liam let go a curse.

And Mina exclaimed, "Drat the man!"

There was the earl sitting in the waiting carriage with none other than Alexandra Audley. For the moment he was watching the boys in the street. Quickly, Liam grabbed Catherine's arm and propelled her behind him. Mina and Genie moved on either side of him, as close as they could possibly get, forming a wall of sorts behind which Catherine huddled in hiding.

"Eh, m'lord," the smallest boy called out to the earl, "penny fer a cartwheel?"

When the earl turned his head towards the lad's voice, he caught sight of the exceedingly nervous trio. Mina rolled her eyes heavenward and whispered a prayer that he would not suspect a thing, for her heart had risen into her throat at the fear that her plans would go up in a puff of smoke. She smiled weakly as he inclined his head in acknowledgment, his deep-set eyes crackling with suspicion as they took in the sight of Mina and her two companions.

Beside him Alexandra Audley raised a bare hand and touched his cheek. She was a woman who thrived on being the center of attention, and she could not tolerate anything which might divert the earl even for a second. She was also a woman skilled in the ways of beguiling a man. With a knowing smile, she trailed her fingers along his cheek in a teasing motion. Mina stared in fascination as the exquisite Beauty turned in the seat just enough to brush the front of her snug jacket against the earl's arm as she whispered into his ear.

The street sweepers completed their task; Liam threw out a coin. The carriage jolted to a start and moved past. Mina, who had been holding her breath, exhaled and gave a moue of disappointment, for she wished that she might have seen the earl's reaction to his mistress. Would he return her look with equal ardor? she wondered.

"What a hussy!" Genie declared. "Don't let that tart get your earl," she added in an aside for Mina alone.

"He's not my earl," was Mina's quick response. "I assure you that I don't care a fig who he spends his time with."

But this was not entirely true, and a very odd thing happened. Again, Mina found herself wishing that Catherine and Liam did not look quite so merry. And this time she reluctantly admitted that she was rather jealous at the sight of them. Indeed, she was quite eaten up with envy.

Two blocks ahead the earl chastised, "Alexandra, for God's sake, can't you keep your hands to yourself?"

"Oh, Compton," she sulked, ruby lips in an adorable pout as she withdrew her hands. The Beauty was wise enough to know when she had near overplayed her cards. "Please forgive me, my love. I could not help myself." This was spoken in a low purr. "I don't know what came over me. You must forgive me. 'Tis not my fault. I have so little control around a man like yourself." She peeked up at him from beneath her lashes, endeavoring to force a blush to her cheeks. Men were such simple souls, she thought as she smiled falsely. They could be easily gulled. All it required was a dose of flattery.

The earl, however, had not heard a word she said. He was thinking about Mina. What was she doing with her brother and that actress? He could not deny her the right to visit with her brother. But the actress was another matter entirely.

Nothing but trouble was sure to come of that association. Where Mina was, Catherine was likely not far behind, and no telling what ill-conceived behavior that actress might encourage. Good Lord, they might go so far as to assist his sister in meeting with O'Kieffe.

The minx was up to something. This was the girl who had flaunted his orders and every bound of propriety when she dashed into Lansdowne Passage. There could be no doubting that she was going to cause trouble for him.

Thus the Earl of Brierly determined it was necessary to keep a closer eye on Miss Mina O'Kieffe.

Chapter Eight

The next afternoon Captain Ramsey called on Mina at Cavendish House. He had agreed to escort her and Lady Catherine to Lane's Lending Library, where Catherine intended to rendezvous with Liam. It was another fine day for walking, and as they strolled down the street the captain, flanked by the two young ladies, was relating a story about a gypsy spy who had served the British on the Peninsula. It was such an engaging tale that not a one of them saw the earl as he exited Boodle's.

Beaver hat in hand, he stood on the top step outside his men's club and watched his sister and Miss O'Kieffe with the captain. There was nothing overtly improper about them. They could have been any group of acquaintances strolling through St. James's, but the earl was not so certain of their innocent intent. Where were they bound? Were they going to meet Liam? Or the actress? He recalled the sight of Miss O'Kieffe on Regent Street, unquestionably shocked by the sight of him and terribly nervous. She had indeed been guilty of some caprice and was likely embarking on another. Yesterday's decision was well made. Miss O'Kieffe was in need of vigilant watching. He gave it not a second thought as he proceeded to hotfoot it down the street in pursuit.

When they disappeared inside Lane's, he followed, only to be crushed amidst a horde of spinsters and dowagers. One of the day's popular authors was in attendance and had attracted dozens of loyal fans to the lending library. Poke bonnets and ostrich plumes bobbed before the earl's eyes. They blocked his view, and he lost sight of his quarry. He was surrounded, cheek to jowl, by women waving scented hankies at a rather effeminate poet who stood beside a marble likeness of himself, hair pomaded à la Brutus.

"La! My lord Brierly," one of the dowagers effused. "Come to see Beaully?"

He inclined his head. It was Lady Chester, a rather coarse woman, wife of a Welsh Border lord.

"Over this way, if you wish for a signatured volume." The woman had the audacity to grip the earl's waistcoat and pull him towards the foppish Beaully.

"Lady Chester, have you seen my sister?" he asked, unable to focus on the ghastly woman as she coyly fluttered her eyelashes.

"La! Yes. Saw the darling girl with the O'Kieffe chit and the dashing Captain Ramsey," she trilled, continuing to bat her eyelashes in that most ridiculous fashion.

"Must catch up with them," the earl explained and broke free of the lady's grip.

He managed to inch his way through the near-swooning females to the rear of the room, where several doors led to the various literary collections. At random he chose a doorway, ducked his head, and walked beneath the arch. On the left-hand side of the room neat lettering on the shelves stated Antiquities, referring to a series of books that appeared seldom touched when compared with those along the right-hand wall, there the label read Gothick Tales. There was no one else in the room, and he proceeded into the next one. As the earl passed through one archway after another, it became quieter and quieter.

A few steps inside the final room he abruptly halted. It was occupied, and he recognized at once Miss O'Kieffe's lilting brogue and the broad Highland burr in the captain's voice. They were standing on the other side of a shelf that divided the room into two sections. The earl backed up two steps and paused on the doorsill, his mouth dropping open at the words he heard spoken by Captain Ramsey.

"My dear Miss O'Kieffe, it would be the greatest, nay the most profound, honor if you would consent to be my wife," he proposed in an utterly sincere tone.

The earl had not intended to eavesdrop, but it would at this stage have been *de trop* to waltz into the room. There was no other course save to remain where he was and keep silent. He held his breath and waited for Mina's response.

She did not answer right away, and the earl longed to know what she was doing. Had the chit developed a *tendre* for Ramsey when he had forbidden her to do so? What sort of expression had crossed her countenance at this proposal? Were her green eyes alight with joy at the prospect of matrimony with the captain?

It was the captain who spoke next, words spilling out of him in eagerness to impart the news. "This is, I concede, a most sudden announcement. But a number of events have occurred which force my hand." He stuttered and started again. "Excuse me, I have little practice at this and did not mean to sound so graceless. The fact is my Great-uncle Angus has died, and his lands and title have passed to me. I am now Laird of Etive and Loch Awe, the Earl of Croick."

"Why, that's marvelous. What I mean"—Mina likewise stammered—"what I mean to say is that it's quite unfortunate about your uncle, but how wonderful for you. Imagine, the Earl of Croick. Now I must call you my lord Ramsey."

Her voice lowered to a whisper. There was a pause, and not a sound filtered from around the shelf. What were they doing? The suspense was unbearable. This was not, the earl imagined, Miss O'Kieffe's notion of romance. Was it?

He was standing on tiptoe, endeavoring to peer over the top of the shelf, when a nasal voice queried, "Looking for something in particular, my lord?"

"No," he hissed, piercing the unsuspecting clerk with a glacial stare.

" 'Scuse me," she huffed. "Only trying to help." And as she went towards the front room, she muttered to a young couple, "Got windmills in his upper regions, that one do."

Curious, the two young people glanced into the room.

"Good grief, 'tis Compton!" Catherine whispered frantically to Liam.

"Is he looking for us, do you think?" Instinctively, he pulled her behind a shelf.

Peeking around, she watched her brother for a few moments and then said, "No, I don't believe he is."

"Well, what's he up to, then?"

"Don't know." She leaned as far forward from behind the shelf as she could without toppling over, held her breath, and listened. There was dead silence save for two low whispers from the farthest room. "I believe that's Mina's voice," she whispered. "Good grief, he's spying on Mina!"

"Impossible! What a rapper, my dear, look again."

"He is, indeed," she attested, tugging Liam around the shelf so he might better hear the whispers.

"Don't make a bit of sense," Liam commented, shaking his head in confusion.

"It seldom does with my brother, but you can safely wager 'tis something to do with form. He's likely keeping tabs on her, making certain she treads the straight and narrow."

"Do you think she's safe?"

She repressed a titter, a hand flying to cover her mouth. "He's not liable to go berserk, if that's what you're asking."

"Well." Liam sounded uncertain. "It did cross my mind."

"Sssh," an annoyed patron hushed, and Catherine, having assured Liam of his sister's safety, led him from the room.

Back on the doorsill, the earl still did not know whether Miss O'Kieffe was going to marry Captain Ramsey. Minutes ticked by. Absently, he pushed long fingers through his hair, considering the nature of this proposal. It was shockingly precipitous. Good Lord, what did Miss O'Kieffe know about the captain? She had said that he reminded her of her brothers—charming but glib and irresponsible, and woe to any woman who thought otherwise. That was not the sort of man Miss O'Kieffe should marry.

More important, what did the captain know about Miss O'Kieffe? Did he understand her notions about romance? Did he enjoy walks in the early morning and history and books and riding as much as Miss O'Kieffe? These thoughts ran through the earl's mind so quickly that he gave no consideration to how utterly strange it was that he would even ponder such matters.

At last, their voices raised slightly. The earl could hear the conversation again.

"No, you won't have to address me so formally," the captain was saying in a curiously unsteady voice. "You must call me Duncan."

"Duncan." Mina tried his name and then said in her forthright fashion, "I had not anticipated such an offer, Duncan. We've known each other for scarcely a fortnight."

There was a touch of challenge in her words, and the earl let go a sigh of relief. Thank goodness the girl was showing a fair amount of sense. Surely Miss O'Kieffe would not seriously entertain the notion of marrying a man like her brothers. How could she expect loyalty from a man like that? She needed a man who would be steadfast, and the earl doubted that Ramsey was that fellow. Miss O'Kieffe would be mortally wounded by his rakehell ways.

"I'm going home to the Highlands, and it may be months before I return to England." He struggled to find the adequate words. "As earl I must have a wife, and it seemed a sensible notion to return to the stronghold with one on my arm. I could think of no other lady in all of the British Isles who would be a more perfect bride or better wife than yourself, Miss O'Kieffe. You're no simpering miss, which I greatly respect, and more important, you know me for the man I am. And I don't doubt that my clansmen would fall in love with your Highland eyes as instantly as I did," he augmented less seriously.

Another great silence followed this revealing speech. It

was the last thing the earl had ever expected to hear from Ramsey. There was good sense in his proposition, but, the earl knew, none of that would matter to Miss O'Kieffe. She was likely cringing, for the proposal lacked romance. The earl craned his neck but could not see over the shelf.

The sound of rustling skirts reached his ears, and it occurred to him that the captain might be kissing Miss O'Kieffe—which was something that, as her guardian, he could not allow. Even if they were to be betrothed, a gentleman did not kiss a lady in public. The earl would permit them until the count of three before he would charge in and demand to know why they were in so isolated a spot without a proper chaperone.

From between clenched teeth, lips barely moving, he quietly ticked off the numbers. "One. Two. Three."

It was another long moment before Mina broke the silence. "Oh, Duncan, I'm deeply touched. Would that I could say yes, for I well enjoy your company and believe you would treat me with honor and respect. But my answer must be no. The affection I feel for you isn't the love a woman must feel for a man, and I simply can't marry you or any other man unless that love exists."

"We could grow to love one another," the captain suggested, his tone disappointed but still clearly hopeful.

The earl knew Miss O'Kieffe's answer before she spoke, for although he did not accept her romantic notions, he was coming to understand them. Verily, he was startled to realize that he was coming to know Miss O'Kieffe very well in a number of ways. Indeed, he understood her better than Captain Ramsey ever would, the earl thought smugly.

"Isn't that what everyone says?" Mina returned, precisely as the earl had expected her to do. "Yet often it never happens. I'm sure we'd get along exceptionally well and we might have a lifetime of contentment—except for one dreadful possibility. What if one day you happen across a bonny lassie and fall madly and irrevocably in love with her? Think how truly miserable you would be, how hurt the girl would be, and how very unhappy I would feel."

The earl heard the captain's harsh sigh.

"Some truth to that. Suppose you're right. Well, I tried. Had hoped that you might say yes." There was another silence, and then in a revived voice Captain Ramsey, now the Earl of Croick, finished, "You'll make some lucky gentleman a fine wife, Miss Mina O'Kieffe. You're lovely and refreshing. You've got a good heart, and your love, when it comes, will be strong and true. What a lucky man he'll be."

She giggled. "There isn't any *he*."

"Oh, no? What about Brierly?"

"Poppycock!" exploded Mina. "The Earl of Brierly, indeed. You're the second person in as many days to tender that subject and, as before, I find it the outside of ridiculous."

"How so? The earl's handsome and eligible and most mamas would believe their daughters blessed to—"

She cut him off. "I could never love a man who denies love as the earl has done between my brother and Lady Catherine. Nor could I love a man who considers marriage merely a business arrangement or the pursuit of a wife little different from . . . from buying a horse at Tattersall's! Indeed, he would choose his cattle with more care, I venture. And I would not, nay *could* not, have any feelings for a man who would hold my family in contempt!"

The earl clenched and unclenched his fists. She might as well have called him a poor creature before a full assembly of the *haut ton* in Hyde Park. He was furious that she would so intimately discuss him with Ramsey.

He assuaged his wounded pride with the dubious consolation that she did not want to marry him. At least the chit wasn't harboring any silly notions. She was right. He did not believe in love, and he did hold her brothers in contempt. So why was he in a lather about a female who didn't give a tinker's damn about him? It was merely his pride, he argued silently. That was the full extent of it. His damned pride.

"That's strong condemnation," the captain noted. "It seems you're overlooking one possibility. Perhaps you'll have no control over whom you love." In a teasing fashion he proposed, "What if, despite your vows, one morning you wake up and discover yourself in love with the earl? What would you do?''

'' 'Tis impossible,'' she stated absolutely. ''Why on earth would I fall in love with a man such as that? What could *possibly* exist between us out of which some deeper sentiment might grow?''

This stung the earl. Although he was prepared to admit his faults, he was not prepared for Miss O'Kieffe's rejection. Damn it! Who did she think she was? What did she really know about him? He had never given the matter of wife selection any thought, but he was certain that he would not pick a wife as he purchased horseflesh!

Lost in thought, the earl made his way out of Lane's, his anger increasing with each step taken towards Berkeley Square. His memory clicked back to the night of the Derby-Clement ball, when he had asked Mina if her initial impression of him had changed. Well, now he knew the answer, and he did not like it one jot. Most of all he did not like the fact that, deep inside, a voice spoke a more profound truth, and he did not like what he heard.

It mattered very much what Miss Mina O'Kieffe thought, that voice said.

And still another voice called out unanswered questions. Questions the earl did not want to answer. Why did it matter what Miss O'Kieffe thought of him? And what was he going to do about it?

When Mina entered the dining room two mornings hence, she was pleased to see the earl at the end of the table. She did not like to eat alone. They exchanged brief greetings as Mina skipped up to the buffet to serve herself an enormous platter of food. Then, choosing a corner place next to the earl, she allowed her eyes to skim over her breakfast partner. His blue jacket matched the color of his eyes, and she could not help comparing him to the other gentlemen of her acquaintance. He was quite the most attractive man she had ever known—not unlike the romantic hero of whom she had often daydreamed. Her smile widened at the notion of the earl being the subject of a romantic fantasy. It was truly farfetched. Wasn't it?

"Is that a new cravat, my lord?" she asked with a gay smile while waiting for the footman to pull her chair away from the table. "'Tis quite becoming."

"Thank you." The earl was astonished to note the warmth that swept through him as he accepted the lightly delivered compliment. It made him feel like a schoolboy. Taking her cheery lead, he drawled, "I thought young ladies were supposed to eat like birds." He grinned at the sight of a mound of scrambled eggs, two croissants, and several slices of pork on her plate.

Unfolding her napkin and placing it across her lap, she replied, "That's the rule when dining out. But a lady is hardly expected to starve the rest of the time, is she? Besides, my lord, you're quite like a brother to me, aren't you? 'Tis not as if you're one of the gentlemen-about-town whom I have to impress—bring up to scratch, I believe they say—so I'll receive a decent proposal before the end of the Season."

He heard the teasing note in her demure voice and nearly gagged on a mouthful of kippers. "Don't be impertinent. I happen to know that you've already received a proposal."

"Yes, from Captain Ramsey." She shot him a questioning glance. "I suppose Catherine told you about it. Did she explain it wasn't a proposal of love? You would be most commending of his motives. 'Twas a very thoughtful but thoroughly emotionless proposal. We might have suited, for he would never have lifted an eyebrow should I gorge myself on all manner of delicacies, but there's no love between us."

She slathered a generous dollop of strawberry preserves on a croissant. Then, in a most indelicate fashion, she proceeded to raise a pinky finger to her mouth and lick off a dot of preserves which had fallen from the croissant. Through all this she kept her eyes on the earl, watching for his response. She was satisfied when he blanched visibly.

"Miss O'Kieffe," he began to lecture, only to be cut off in midsentence by whoops of girlish laughter.

''The captain would never have noticed such a thing. We're friends, you see.'' But the laughter died on her lips. She had expected the earl to be annoyed, but his reaction was unanticipated. There was something highly unsettling about his countenance. Why was he staring at her in that thunderstruck fashion? She looked into a pair of distant blue eyes and then swiftly transferred her attention to her plate.

The earl sat back in his chair. Stunned, he threaded one hand through his hair, eyes focused on nothing in particular and thinking very intently. Friends. With stunning revelation he realized that he had not enjoyed a particular friendship since his days at Eton, since he had come home that term break for Lady Day and inherited the title. His life had not been a solitary one. There had been numerous mistresses, and he had passing acquaintances with his former schoolchums. But he had not had a particular friend. Grandmère's lecture in the library at Brierly echoed in his mind. By God, she was right. He had allowed propriety and duty to rule his life, to override his own happiness. No wonder Miss O'Kieffe thought him a poor creature.

The course of his thoughts altered, and he recalled the words Miss O'Kieffe had spoken after their outing; she had said it was her best time since arriving in London. An incredible reality struck him with the impact of a thunderbolt. It had been the best time *he* had enjoyed in many years. A mere slip of a girl with an elfin smile and hopelessly romantic outlook had breached ten years of bleak adherence to some larger-than-life notion of duty. She had managed to make him forget his responsibilities, to help him laugh at himself, to overcome his jaded outlook, and to have him see commonplace things from a most refreshing perspective.

Yesterday outside Lane's Lending Library he had wondered why it rankled that Miss O'Kieffe thought poorly of him. Now he knew. He envied the easygoing friendship she shared with Ramsey. He wanted that friendship for himself. It mattered what Miss O'Kieffe thought, and he desired her good regard, but yesterday he had not known what he might do about that. Today he had the answer. He wanted her friendship. He would interest himself in her concerns—it would not be hard. He would put a horse at her disposal and see that she had at least two morning rides in the Park each week, and he would arrange another outing for her—perhaps a picnic at Hampton Court would be romantic enough to suit her fancy. Soon she would see that he could be the sort of man she wanted for a friend, and he hoped that she would change her mind about him.

"My lord," Mina broke into his reverie, "are you feeling all right?" She was alarmed by his sudden silence.

"I'm fine, Miss O'Kieffe," the earl stated with an uncommonly bright grin. "Splendid, in fact. Go ahead and enjoy your meal. How about another croissant?" With that he proceeded to dump three of the buttery French rolls onto his platter and two more on hers.

Their eyes met across the table, deep blue joining with soft green in an unexpected harmony of humor. Irrepressibly, she started to giggle, and within moments he was laughing with equal abandon.

On a balcony overlooking the Duchess of Darien's columned ballroom, an orchestra began the introductory chords of a waltz. It was a captivating tune, and Mina experienced a pang of regret. The countess had forewarned the girls that they must not waltz this evening. The Duchess of Darien was an outrageous trendsetter, and the *ton* tolerated her excesses. It was fine if she chose to have a waltz played at her rout. It would not, however, be fine for the girls to dance when it was played.

"But, Grandmère," Catherine had pouted, "how can you naysay us? Didn't you say it was the most wondrous dance created?"

"*Mais oui*, I said that and *c'est vrai*, it is wondrous. But I did not mean for *mes jeune filles* to spin about the floor in public like trollops. *Comprenez*?"

"Why did Master Peterkin teach us, if you're never going to let us dance it?" Catherine had made a petulant moue.

"When the time is right to waltz, you will know. You'll not have to ask," her grandmother had advised in a stern voice. "Sneaking a waltz in a crowded ballroom is not wise. One invariably is caught. *N'est-ce pas?*" And with that setdown Catherine had ceased to protest.

Mina decided to remove herself from temptation's path by slipping out of the ballroom onto a deserted terrace.

It was a cool night for late June. A breeze blew through the treetops, and an iridescent full moon was suspended against the indigo sky. Silver light fell about her, casting elongated shadows on the flagstone terrace. She turned towards the french doors and rested against the railing to gaze inside the ballroom. Couples were moving into each other's arms. What a glorious sight it made, elegantly gowned ladies with jewels shining at their throats and gentlemen in swallowtail coats and striped silk stockings. Mina sighed a little sound of disappointment. What a shame that she had to be on the outside looking in instead of dancing in the arms of a handsome gentleman.

From the far end of the ballroom the earl had observed her departure. He ascertained something was bothering the girl, and motivated by his newfound interest in her welfare he strode across the room, intent on righting whatever wrong had brought such a frown to Mina's pretty face.

Outside he moved towards her, taking in the sadness of her expression. She was utterly downcast. Hesitating only a moment, he asked with friendly concern, "What's wrong?"

"The waltz." Mina barely got out those two little words.

"How strange. I thought the waltz was the delight of every young lady in the realm. How can it be the cause of such a despairing look?"

Mina pouted in frustration. "If I could waltz, then I *too* might be smiling as gayly as the ladies in the duchess's ballroom. Your grandmother, however, forbade us the pleasure, and I can't help but be gloomy. Nay, cross as crabs!" She enunciated each of these words separately, adding three gentle stamps of a slippered foot for punctuation. "There really are too many rules, and I'm finding it most unpleasant to heed them."

Strains of music drifted onto the terrace, and Mina stepped towards the french doors for a better view. The earl was reminded of an urchin he had once seen gazing at Christmas candies in a shop window. As the earl had offered a treat to that child, he now acted in Mina's behalf.

"If your papa were here, he would dance with you, wouldn't he?"

Eyes still focused on the dancers, Mina replied, "Yes, I suppose so."

"And that would be within the boundaries of the rules, would it not?" the earl pressed onward.

Mina nodded, not understanding the point of his questioning.

"Would it not also be acceptable for one of your brothers to ask you to waltz?"

"Yes," she said on a wistful breath.

Throwing caution to the wind, the earl asked, "Well, how about me? As your guardian, might I do for a partner?"

Mina whirled to face him with amazement and hope. "Do you really mean it?" she wondered aloud, the breath catching in her throat.

He grinned. "I wouldn't have suggested it otherwise. I may be stodgy, but I'm not cruel. Miss O'Kieffe"—he made her an elegant leg—"might I have the honor of this dance?"

Wordlessly, she nodded her acceptance. They moved closer to each other in small, tentative steps. Having never really waltzed before, Mina was stricken by hesitance. The earl was equally unnerved by the situation, being rather confused by his bold offer. Less than a pace separated them when he put an arm on her shoulder and drew her closer. His hand found the curve of her waist and quite tenderly circled her. Shyly Mina set her left hand on his shoulder, her right hand in his left one, not daring to actually hold him, rather letting her hands simply rest against him. The music drifted on the night breeze, and they moved, slowly at first, to the enchanting rhythm. He was a graceful dancer and executed the circular steps with ease. Mina relaxed, surrendering herself to his expert skills. Soon they were waltzing the length and breadth of the terrace as though it were a ballroom expressly created for their enjoyment.

Together, they did not dance as mere mortals. They were moving on air, Mina thought, as the song played faster and they spun incessantly around the terrace. Turning, turning, turning in endless circles of rapture. It was as exhilarating as she had imagined. Better! None of the books had done it justice. Her heart beat wildly, her breath came shorter, and she could not control the smile that came to her lips.

The sensual music became a part of Mina, enhancing her awareness of the earl, the pressure of his hand where it grasped her waist, the strength of his thigh against hers as they swirled across the flagstones. His grip about her waist tightened, and of a sudden she was acutely aware of the full length of him. A sweet ache ran through her. So this was what a man felt like, she thought with a giddy ripple of laughter, tilting her head back to gaze into his face.

There was nothing hard or cold about the man who returned her heated regard. His countenance was as open as her own. On and on they swirled, their eyes fused together, his blue ones speaking of forbidden desire, her green ones echoing that yearning mixed with wonder at the newness of her feelings. The arm that encircled her waist pulled her closer, his hand moved to the nape of her neck, and he bent to rest his jaw against her forehead. In this intimate pose, his lips faintly brushed against her brow, his breath fanned her skin.

When the music stopped, they remained as they were for infinite seconds. Time stood still, and Mina, eyes closed, listened to her heart. She realized with shock that his was beating as fast as her own, and the waves of warmth that pulsed through her body were coming from his.

"Oh, my lord," she breathed on an airy whisper. "Thank you so very much. This meant the world to me. Truly."

The earl remained silent, struggling against the fierce longings that threatened to ravage his self-control. He was so taut that he might snap at any moment and sweep her off her feet. He could have her then, he was certain of it, in the garden beyond the terrace. She would not resist. And he would be done with the passion that had gnawed at him for weeks, the passion he had fought to suppress. It was an awful, unleashed thought. The hand that had held hers moved slowly upward to her lips.

A strange tremor rippled slowly through her, all the way to her toes, as the earl outlined the shape of her mouth with a slender finger. This was forbidden, and yet she could neither move away nor utter a single word of denial as long as his heart beat against hers. His nearness was the only reality of which she was aware.

Then he took her arm, pulling the white satin glove back to reveal satin-smooth skin. He lowered his head and slowly he kissed her bare skin.

Mina's eyes widened. The breath caught in her throat. Her heart skipped a beat. She dared not move. She dared not breathe. His lips scorched her flesh where they rested, making her tremble. Seized by an irrepressible urge, she reached out and allowed her fingers to touch his bent head. The fair hair was gloriously thick. It beckoned her to run her fingers through it. And she did.

"Miss O'Kieffe!" Jolted out of his passion-laden fantasies by her ingenuous response to his improper kiss, the earl jerked away from Mina's touch. Reality returned to him, as did a modicum of self-control. But the wrong words rose to his lips, not proper words of apology but angry words that he should have directed at himself, not at Mina. "What are you doing? You should never let a gentleman take such a liberty!" he thundered to cover his own weakness and painful frustration. Was he mad? Dear God! He had wanted to be her friend, but he was damned near ravishing her. He had been treating her like some lightskirt, not like a lady in his care, a lady who trusted him to behave like a gentleman at all times.

Mina looked up at him in confusion. Her eyes reflected the profound hurt that was spreading outward from the core of her soul. Then suddenly her expression altered. Furiously, without thinking, she slapped him smartly across the face.

The earl winced and drew back, his misdirected anger turning to astonishment.

"I do beg your pardon for forgetting the rules," came her overly calm statement. Mina's voice was a study in controlled politeness. "Thank you for educating me so graphically." She watched as a deep flush suffused his face where her hand had met his cheek and then, shoulders squared, her head held high, she walked back towards the ballroom.

"Miss O'Kieffe! Come back!"

There was remorse in his plea, mixed with an undercurrent of something like pain. Mina heard and wondered about it, but she did not turn back.

That night before she extinguished the candle on the bedside table, Mina opened the copy of *Emma* which the earl had purchased for her. She savored a long, hard look at the nosegay of violets pressed between the pages. Resting her head against the pile of lace-edged pillows, she wondered at the tears that were gliding down her cheeks, and she feared the truth of what had happened that night. There was an ache in her heart, and it would not go away.

Nothing would ever be the same again.

Chapter Nine

"Of course, Elise, I agree with you completely," Lady Jersey, one of the high priestesses of Almack's, said to her bosom friend the Dowager Countess of Brierly. They sat on a rose damask settee beneath the slanted gaze of a Chinese emperor glowering from a tapestry on the wall in Lady Jersey's town house. "The gel can't help who her father was. Don't worry. She's charming and I remember her dear mama, Lady Elaine. A veritable exquisite." Displaying her infamous wont of tact, Lady Jersey added, "Though not a terribly bright chit. You'd think with the offers she received she might have had the wit to escape that Irish merchant."

"Quite so," the countess began and, not wanting to comment on Lady Elaine, went on quickly, "I'm so pleased you understand about Mina. *C'est bien.* You're most reasonable.''

"Enough of that flummery, Elise. Don't need to gull me. The gel shan't be denied a voucher. Good lord, blood tells all. Five hundred years of Thornburys must account to more import than a single and exceedingly unfortunate accident of matchmaking.'' She ended with an ill-bred chuckle.

The subject of this discussion was seated at the opposite end of Lady Jersey's drawing room, a chamber of considerable proportion decorated in the Chinese motif which the prince regent had popularized. Mina nibbled at a tea cake and cast an occasional glance at the two older women, but was unaware of what they were actually saying.

Catherine was perched beside Mina on the ornate chaise with carved dragon arms. Anxiously, the darker-haired girl whispered, "What is it, dear friend? You're prodigious absentminded this morning. Not coming down with the ague, are you?''

"Nothing like that,'' Mina assured. But, in truth, she was not certain. Ever since the rout at the Duchess of Darien's she had not felt quite the thing. She was unable to concentrate on anything for more than a few moments, her thoughts continually wandering to the earl. In her mind she saw him standing by the orchard stream, mud-splattered and angry as the devil; buying the nosegay of violets from the flower girl; and heaping a mountain of croissants on her breakfast platter. He made her want to laugh and cry, to jump for joy, to run and hide all at once—though she did not understand why. Mina's hand stole to her breast. There was a pain there, but, of course, it was not really a pain. Was it? The question only added to her mounting confusion.

" 'Tis good you're not getting ill because I believe Grandmère has obtained your voucher.'' Catherine popped a third watercress sandwich into her mouth.

Nibbling without much purpose on the same tea cake, Mina answered with an air of preoccupation, "That's nice.''

"Nice!'' Catherine dropped her fourth watercress sandwich on the table. "Is that all you're going to say? I thought that more than anything you wanted to go to Almack's, as your dearest mama had done. How can you say *nice*?" When Mina failed to respond to this prodding, Catherine loosed a sigh of frustration. "Mina! What's wrong with you? Why aren't you listening?"

"I'm sorry. What did you say?"

Mina barely heard the questions. Catherine received no answers. And the conversation continued in this halting vein until Catherine finally moved to stop it. They were seated in the earl's carriage when she blurted out, "Grandmère, look at Mina. There's something amiss, though she denies it."

The countess fixed a keen eye on Mina. She too was worried about the chit and suspected that her pallor had something to do with her grandson. She knew he had followed Mina onto the terrace last night, and she had observed them return to the ballroom wearing very different expressions from those they had worn when they left the room. They had both been in high dudgeon about something. But she did not know what had passed between them. She could only hope whatever it was would, in the long run, be deemed progress.

"Perhaps you're tired, my dear," the countess suggested sympathetically.

"Perhaps," was Mina's dull response.

"She does seem a tad hag-ridden, doesn't she?" Catherine infused gracelessly and received a quelling stare from her grandmother.

"Let me check your head," said the countess, and after determining that Mina did not have a fever, she gave her an encouraging pat on the hand. " 'Tis your first Season. Such reactions are not uncommon for a gel in Town her first time. 'Tis the excitement. The hectic schedule. *C'est tout*. Nothing more. I suggest a nice rest. Perhaps you'd rather not accompany us to the musicale? You needn't feel obligated to attend everything." This remark failed to elicit even the tiniest response. Mina merely stared at her reticule. This would not do at all. And determined to shatter Mina's malaise, the countess boldly suggested, "*Peut-être, c'est l'amour*."

Mina's gaze jumped instantly to meet that of the countess. "Love," she repeated, high color staining her cheeks.

"Oh really, Grandmère, don't be silly," Catherine said in typically havey-cavey style. "Whoever is there that Mina might have fallen in love with?"

The question hung in the air between the three women. Mina fumbled with the clasp on her reticule. No one spoke. The clip-clop of horses' hooves on the street became oddly magnified. And, in the heavy silence, the truth came to Mina. The unthinkable had happened to Miss Mina O'Kieffe. She was in love with the Earl of Brierly.

Oh, that it were not so! her thoughts cried. How could this have happened? He was toplofty, coldhearted, and a thoroughly disdainful aristocrat, yet her heart leapt into her throat at the mere thought of him. For he was handsome and when he smiled his eyes turned a warm, gentle blue; he could be kind and understanding; and he was the one gentleman who truly made her stay in Town special. He was a man, while the kindly Percival was merely a boy. And he was sincere, while the dashing captain had been a practiced flirt.

It was an impossible situation, and Mina could imagine no happy ending coming from it. She winced, imagining his reaction should he discover what lay within her heart. He would laugh as he had done in the stream. Oh, how he would laugh in mockery, for despite the measure of understanding he appeared to have gained for her sensibilities, he did not believe in romance.

Last night she had suspected the horrible truth, but she had managed to deny it, hoping that in the light of day she would discover that she had been merely overset by the earl's odious behavior on the terrace. It was not to be. The truth had nagged at her. There was no escaping it, and the countess had forced her to confront reality.

How had he become the center of her universe? When had she allowed this betraying emotion to creep into her heart? For this love, she condemned, was a betrayal. A betrayal of the very principles she believed resided at the core of the human condition. This love for a man who did not understand the meaning of the word was a travesty.

Oh, despair! Oh, misery! Oh, grave injustice! No Minerva herione had ever suffered so cruel a fate. Mina shut her eyes against the truth, but that did not make it go away, and large teardrops began to trail down her cheeks. She opened her eyes and stared hopelessly at the countess and Catherine.

"I know, my dear," consoled the countess. "Don't cry. 'Tis not the end of the world."

" 'Tis worse," Mina wailed. "How could I let something like this happen?"

"But I thought you knew," the countess commiserated, withdrawing an elegant lace handkerchief from her reticule and handing it to Mina. "None of us has any control over it when it happens."

"I thought I knew everything there was to know about love," Mina sobbed. Her faith and confidence ebbed downward with tears of self-pity. "It's supposed to be beautiful and perfect. Not painful."

Catherine glanced back and forth between Mina and her grandmother. Slowly, the bewilderment vanished from her expression, to be replaced by surprise. "Oh, Mina, you've fallen in love with my brother!" she exclaimed.

The result of this remark was a renewed torrent of tears down Mina's face, to which Catherine swiftly responded, "Please don't cry, Mina. This is wonderful! I never thought *anyone* would love my brother. How I've worried about him, but I shan't any longer. Dear, stodgy Compton shan't be condemned to a loveless eternity, thanks to you. Oh, he's so lucky."

"He doesn't know," was Mina's flat rejoinder.

"Whyever not?" Catherine's smile was fading.

"Whyever should I tell him?" Mina sniffled. "Your brother doesn't even like me, much less love me. What am I to do? Humiliate myself by confessing all to him? No." She raised her chin determinedly. Her straight little nose was slightly reddened by crying, her lips were tightly pursed together, and her green eyes glistened with unshed tears as she vowed, "He shall never know from my lips."

"You're mistaken, my dear," the countess said gently. "He likes you. *C'est vrai*. He likes you very much, but he's simply too afraid to admit it to anyone, least of all himself." She shook her head at the sadness of this. "*Pauvre garçon*. We can't allow him to live his life so miserably, can we?"

Mina paid little heed to this question. She was thinking about the countess's words. Did she really believe her grandson felt any warmth of affection for her? "It can't be true. The earl doesn't love me," she denied, her words laden with uncertainty.

To this Catherine rejoined, "What's happened to our romantic Miss O'Kieffe? If I'm correct, you ought not to be concerned whether or not Compton loves you. If your love is strong, then anything is possible, including Compton's love. Isn't that what you've always said?"

This attempt at optimism did not sway Mina.

Catherine tried again. "Grandmère's right. I know, for that explains why he was spying on you and Captain Ramsey at Lane's."

Even this revelation brought scant notice from Mina.

"This calls for intervention," the countess suggested.

"Intervention!" Mina and Catherine echoed in one voice.

"*Mais oui*, Mina, you must help my grandson to discover the true nature of his feelings. You shall simply have to force his hand. You shall make him jealous."

"Jealous?" Mina's mouth dropped open a smidge.

The countess nodded decisively. "You must make him believe he might lose you. As long as he believes you'll not marry, as long as he believes you'll return to the estate adjoining his in Kent, then he doesn't need to confront the future or his feelings. Only when faced with losing you to someone in Northumbria or Hampshire will he realize he's leagues in love with you already."

"Perhaps he'll never admit it," Mina countered dismally.

"Perhaps, but then many things about Compton have been different these days. He smiles more and he was even whistling the other morning." The countess leaned forward and gave a punctuating shake of her head. "Whistles! Imagine the Earl of Brierly whistling! I would have thought that impossible two months ago, but anything is possible when there's love. Anything.''

Mina recognized those very words. She had said them to Genie when her faith in love wavered, yet she had never understood how that could happen—how love could be less than a fortifying force. Now she understood only too well. But the countess seemed so determined, so very sure. Just as Mina had used to be.

"Oh, Mina, don't you see? 'Tis precisely like that book you bought on your outing with Compton," interjected Catherine.

"*Emma*?"

"No, peagoose! Not that prosey stuff. One of the other ones. Believe it was called *Clever Clarissa's Campaign*."

Mina nodded. "I remember." Clarissa had flirted outrageously with every tulip and dandy until Mr. Pemberton finally proposed. Perhaps . . .

"If it worked for Clarissa, 'twill certainly work for you, for my brother's not half the nodcock Mr. Pemberton was. And you'll be a far better flirt than Clarissa by far!"

On a tired but valiant sigh, Mina agreed. "Very well. I'll try."

"*Merveilleux*!" exclaimed the countess. "I knew you would not give up so easily."

On Wednesday evening the ladies of Cavendish House, having prepared Mina to do battle for the earl, were off to Almack's in King Street. Originally a gaming club, the assembly rooms under a governing committee of highborn ladies had become the exclusive temple of the fashionable world. The patronesses laid down stringent rules of conduct and executed rigid control over every entree to the establishment. No one entered without their approval; and no one, not even the regent himself, could enter after eleven o'clock. Mina knew the importance of her voucher; to be excluded from Almack's was tantamount to being banished from Society. Too, Mina knew the importance of this night. For within the walls of the famed marriage mart she would commence her campaign for the earl's heart.

Stepping down from the carriage, the three ladies presented a splendid trio. Mina, fortified by an afternoon of coaching from the countess on the myriad ways to enchant a man with a fan, a smile, and a giggle, wore a flattering pale blue frock; Catherine was decked out in a becoming shade of green; and the countess was particularly stunning, her statuesque form being clothed in shimmering gold lamé. A matching turban was intricately wound about her head, lending her a hint of gypsy beauty similar to Catherine's. The earl—as did all gentlemen who entered Almack's— wore the prescribed uniform: knee breeches, a white cravat, and a three-cornered hat.

Upon entering, Mina was deluged with requests to sign her dance card. Every young man she had thus far met in London was at Almack's, and they all wished to stand up with her. She was hard-pressed to determine whether under normal circumstances there would have been such a crush of beaux circling her, or whether it was the constant batting of her lashes and the flirtatious moves with a hand-painted fan that brought her popularity. Clarissa had not been half so successful, and Mina was feeling very lightheaded. She cast a quick glance about the room for the earl. He had better be watching, she thought, as she gave a thin smile to a gentleman from York; Mina was not certain how long she could continue the charade. From the corner of her eye she spotted Count von Ruttiger.

"Fraulein O'Kieffe. I believe the next dance is mine," said von Ruttiger. He clicked his heels together and offered Mina a sharp bow.

"Yes." She quickly glanced away from the angular Teuton who was peering at her through a delicate quizzing glass.

He offered his arm, and as they formed a set with three other couples, he said, " 'Tis gut this is not a waltz. Yah, Fraulein O'Kieffe, for I would not wish to sit out with you. You are such light dancer. Such pleasure to be your partner."

Mina smiled flirtatiously. "Do you like the waltz?"

"Pah. Peasant dance!" he retorted in sharp Germanic tones.

This violent response startled Mina. "Excuse me?"

"*Waltzen*." The count snapped the word out in two terse sounds. He and Mina turned respectively and danced for several bars with other partners. When they were side by side, he continued, "In my language *waltzen* means 'to turn.' *Waltzen*. It is a peasant dance from Landler in Austrian mountains."

Oh, how to diffuse this tirade? Mina wondered. Innocently, she queried, "An Austrian dance? I thought it was from France."

"Pah! The French are thieves always. Did you not know *waltzen* was imp of Germany, kidnapped and raised in France? The French lie and tell you it comes from Provence. But 'tis not true. And if it was, then would still be a peasant dance. Not fit for ladies!"

When the dance again took her away from the German, she felt distinct relief. Conversation with him was difficult, for his accent grew more guttural as he became incited from his vitriolic discourse on the waltz. She would never have asked the question if she had suspected it would bother the count.

The countess observed the proceedings from a seat on the edge of the dance floor. Mina was doing a superb job, she declared silently with a grin. Might accomplish more than turning her grandson's head. Might even get an offer. When the countess espied the earl, having just escorted the Rutledge chit back to her doting mama, she beckoned him her way.

"Done your duty dance by the gel, m'boy?" she inquired, nodding in Mina's direction.

The earl turned and observed Miss O'Kieffe, an especially dark scowl marring his features. The music stopped, and he watched as the German led her to the edge of the floor. She was not alone for more than a second as a cotillion was being formed, and her next partner, a lordling from Somerset, was swift to claim her.

"No. I haven't," the earl answered his grandmother in a voice that betrayed no emotion.

The countess, however, noticed a tightening of his lips. "*Mais non*? You have a good reason?"

"Take a gander for yourself, Grandmère." He motioned

towards Mina, who was charming in her celestial blue gown, and he winced visibly as she emitted a pretty titter at some comment from the Somerset lordling. "Can't get within twenty paces of the chit. She's a veritable diamond of the first stare. Every buck is orbiting about our own Miss O'Kieffe. Look at her out there," he declared with a touch of disgust. "The girl's smiling at every booby who glances her way."

" 'Tis the first time the gel has had admirers, Compton," the countess said with an air of reasonableness. "She's young and pretty and ought to enjoy herself. Is that so wrong?"

"The hoyden's doing more than enjoying herself. Why, she's an incorrigible flirt." He cast a blighting stare at his grandmother. "And even if I could get within earshot of her, I wouldn't be able to get a dance. I have it on good authority from numerous and disappointed gentlemen that her card was full almost instantly."

"Well, 'tis all for the best, then," concluded the countess. "*La guerre est finis*."

This remark elicited a perplexed expression from the earl. He had not the slightest notion what she was babbling on about now.

The countess explained, "All the attention Miss O'Kieffe is receiving. She is a success, and as this is the marriage mart and her marriage is one of the reasons behind her visit, we've almost accomplished our purpose. *C'est vrai*, the gel's a great success!" Her countenance brightened at the gathering sneer this elicited from her grandson. "*Mais oui*, can't have Mina rusticating in Kent. Needs a husband, and you were going to help her find one. You do recall that, don't you?"

The earl was heard to growl something about duty be damned. A new dance began, and his gaze fixed on Mina as she danced a country set with Percival Barcroft.

Following the direction of the earl's regard, the countess remarked, "Sir Thomas and I have entertained several notions of a match there. What do you think, Compton?"

"What? That milquetoast!" came the ill-conditioned retort.

The countess was not the least surprised. She had expected him to say as much and would have been vastly disappointed if he had said otherwise. Unruffled by the rude remark, she went on, "He's a harmless lad and would make a fine husband. Barcroft has six thousand a year. Not a fortune, to be sure, but they would get along."

"Six thousand. That's a pittance! And even if Barcroft had twice the sum, he's not right for Mina." Thoroughly oblivious to the fact that he had referred to Miss O'Kieffe by her given name and scowling the very devil, he added for good measure, "If the puppy dares to ask for her hand, I'll turn him down flat."

The countess's eyes were aglow with expectant victory. Oh, this was developing precisely as she had envisioned. Not quite as quickly perhaps, but as long as this affair continued a natural course, she could wait a while longer before helping her grandson do the right by Miss O'Kieffe. She would give him four more weeks; then she would step in and arrange matters. Didn't want the gel pining away too long.

"Turn Barcroft down, will you? How would you know who's right for the gel, by the by?" she challenged.

There was a decidedly stubborn set to his lean jaw as he replied, "I know."

"You're certainly not suggesting yourself, are you?" queried the countess, wondering if she had pushed him too far.

"Egads! Grandmère, there you go again. Off on one of your birdwitted fancies. Put that silly maggot out of your mind. We'd hardly suit at all, Miss O'Kieffe and I, hardly at all. Why, whatever would we find to talk about?"

"Whatever, indeed?" was the countess's pithy reply. "Speaking of marriage, have you given any thought to your duties? Must secure the succession, n'est-ce pas?"

The gaze he set on his grandmother was acid.

Undaunted, she demanded, "Alors, do you intend to secure the Cavendish line? You're hardly in your salad days, you know."

He gave a bark of laughter. "You're baiting me, Grandmère, though for the life of me I can't say why."

"We were talking about marriage," she persisted innocently.

"Whose? Miss O'Kieffe's or mine?"

"Why the two of you, of course," she said slowly, but her words did not have the slimmest effect on the earl.

He was watching Mina again. She unfurled a painted silk fan and peered over the top at the surrounding court of swains. Being the center of attention lent an added radiance to her piquant face. Four gentlemen stood about her, grinning foolishly and hanging on every word and pretty smile she offered from behind the fan.

"An incorrigible flirt," he condemned, then turned and strode away. He danced with the Rutledge chit again and stood up with a long line of blushing debutantes. But he could not forget Mina's upturned nose, her rosebud lips, or those lush emerald-colored eyes. He heard her lilting sweet accent and recalled the way her eyes sparkled when she laughed. Every detail was etched in his memory, and he shrugged elaborately, attempting to dismiss her image from his mind's eye.

The chit was playing havoc with his peace of mind, and he intended to put a stop to the mayhem once and for all. If they could not be friends, then that would be the end of it. It was near hell to act as her guardian when he wanted her in the most shockingly intimate way. He would give friendship one more try, then he would do the necessary and put as great a distance between them as was possible; he would offer her hand to the first willing gentleman. By God! Did it matter so much who the chit married? For marry she would! The only answer to his excruciating dilemma was separation. He would not have her dangling about his household for another Season or making neighborly calls at Brierly this autumn. That would be hell on him, and it simply would not be safe for her.

A few days later Catherine was getting dangerously impatient. She was beginning to resent anew the curtailment of her relationship with Liam and was not content merely to visit at Lane's. When was Mina going to plead her cause to the earl? It could not be soon enough. She wanted to announce their love to the world. To shout it from the top of London Bridge. They would run away if they had to, again and again and again, she declared rebelliously.

"I wish he might attend the opera with us," she said to Mina. "Verily, I may simply stay home with a megrim and meet him in the garden. 'Twould be more pleasant, by far."

"And if you were caught it would be a disaster," Mina admonished as she adjusted her bonnet ribands. The girls were headed for another rendezvous at the lending library. "Don't you see that if you're caught it would hurt both of us? In your case your brother would be convinced once and for all that you're not responsible enough to know your own mind. He might even marry you off like your elder sisters, without so much as a warning. And as for me, my prodigious flirting will have been for naught. Do you really imagine your brother would give me a second's notice if he refused to allow you to marry my brother? Please, Catherine, for both our sakes, don't be rash."

"I did warn you that I couldn't wait long," Catherine reminded her friend on a heavy breath and then, seeing Mina's fairly desperate look, she added, "I'll try. I'll wait a bit longer."

Mina had to be content with that.

This afternoon the lending library was not crowded, and while Catherine and Liam escaped to one of the back rooms, Mina perused a volume of poetry by Lord Byron. A shadow fell across the pages, and she glanced up to see the earl standing before her clutching his hat in one hand, a book in the other.

Her stomach fairly knotted in panic at the sight of him. They had not talked since that incident on the terrace at the Duchess of Darien's, nor since Mina had made her discovery and embarked on her campaign to make him jealous. She wondered if he had noticed her at all last night. She wondered if he had felt the slightest consternation at the way she had flirted with those gentlemen. Was there any hope of winning his love?

"Good afternoon, Miss O'Kieffe. How are you?" he asked, equally surprised to see Mina. Impulse had driven him to Lane's to obtain a copy of Byron's latest work for her. It had seemed a nice gesture of friendship, and he had hoped that she would accept the gift in the spirit in which it was intended. Glumly, he saw that she had already obtained one.

Unable to stop the fluttering of her heart, she could not quite get the hang of talking in complete sentences. He asked several questions of little consequence about the weather and the volume of poetry. She responded in polite monosyllables, her attention directed not at his face but at the thin book in his hand.

Puzzled by Mina's uncharacteristic restraint, the earl formulated a question to which she could not respond with a simple yes or no. "What was your impression of Almack's, Miss O'Kieffe?"

"Do you wish to hear the truth, milord, or a polite response?" She peered closely at the book he held. It was a copy of Lord Byron's poetry, and her heart skipped a beat at the thought of the earl reading Byron.

"The truth, of course."

She concentrated to keep her voice even. "In truth, I thought it stuffy and the cakes stale and the lemonade watered down abominably. 'Twas not at all the picture I had painted."

"Not losing that rosy view of the world, are you? If I didn't know better, I'd say you were beginning to sound like me," he finished with a gentle smile.

"Never!"

"Stale cakes aside, you did appear to be enjoying yourself."

He had noticed! Her heart somersaulted with excitement, but she schooled her expression and simply said, "I suppose." What was she to say? That she had presented such a gay picture only for his benefit? That he was supposed to be pea green with jealousy, not calm as a church deacon?

With a grimace he observed the pain about her eyes. The sight tore at him; he could not bear to see those beautiful eyes altered. She put him in mind of Catherine the night he fetched her home from the inn at the Border. Zounds! An unwelcomed thought occurred to the earl, and he forced himself to voice his fear. "If I didn't know better, I'd say you were behaving like a young lady in love."

"What would you know about that, my lord?" She felt the warmth of color that stole up her neck and riveted her gaze on his face, searching for mockery but finding naught but sympathy.

"I have read a few books in my day," he said and then recited Tristan's lines to Isolde with such feeling that Mina feared she would cry right then and there. "Ah, I struck a nerve, did I?" he said kindly, observing the stubborn tilt of her head, the betraying quiver of her lips. "Surely this is cause for celebration. Why the Cheltenham tragedy? Can it be the young man doesn't know of your *tendre*?"

Her gaze dropped to the floor. She wanted to laugh, perhaps as much from nerves as from the irony of the situation. Clearly she was not destined to succeed as Clever Clarissa had. There would be no storybook ending for Mina. It was only with the most supreme effort that she maintained her voice beneath an hysterical pitch. "I would rather not discuss this, my lord."

He stared at her bent head, twinges of guilt returning. He did not want to hurt her any more than he already had. Would that he might see her happy. He stepped forward and raised a hand as if to stroke her shoulder. He wanted to erase her unhappiness, but he withdrew his hand and simply said, "I respect your sensibilities, but 'tis my duty, you understand." In fact, he was quickly coming to loathe those responsibilities. He did not wish to fulfill them in any way. But as a man of honor, he had no choice. He was bound to do so and therefore continued, "I was given the responsibility to act in your eldest brother's stead. If there's a young man trifling with your affections, I must know his name."

Mina choked. Her gaze flew upward to his in panic. "What would you do?"

"Merely ask him what his intentions were." The earl did not like this business one bit.

"That isn't necessary," she countered swiftly, wishing

that she might disappear in a puff of smoke like a djinn from the tale of *The Arabian Nights.*

"Don't be timid, Miss O'Kieffe. Is it Barcroft?"

She averted her eyes, studying the floor once again. "No."

"That's good. The lad's too young for you. Is it von Ruttiger?" His kind smile disguised his own turmoil.

"No," came a second muted reply.

"Good. Couldn't have you moving off to Bavaria. My sister would never forgive me," he said most sincerely.

Unable to bear his kindness any longer, Mina cried out in a strangled voice, "Stop! Please, my lord. 'Tis not necessary for you to do anything."

His brotherly voice betrayed none of the ambivalent emotions stirring within his soul. "Very well, perhaps not now, but you just give me the nod, Miss O'Kieffe, and I'll do the necessary. Bring him up to snuff. Don't you worry," he ended, giving her a reassuring smile of great fondness.

Chapter Ten

"This calls for drastic measures!" Catherine declared roundly. Mina had just finished detailing her latest encounter with the earl, and Catherine was well into planning phase two of the assault on her brother's heart.

The two girls were strolling down the Embankment on their way to Genie's flat for tea. Naturally, Liam would be there. Intermittent thundershowers had been falling since early morning, and they hurried towards their destination before the rain began again. It was dank and chilly, more like autumn than midsummer, and Mina was as gloomy as the gray clouds that hung low over the city.

"I'd hoped you wouldn't say that," Mina said with a dreary sigh. The plan to make the earl jealous had backfired, and Mina was hard-pressed not to dissolve into a puddle of hysteria at the thought of another unmitigated disaster such as the one in Lane's. "I let you talk me into one rag-mannered scheme, but I shan't be haring off on another one, I assure you."

"Fiddlesticks," retorted Catherine. "You still love him, don't you?" Mina looked so utterly downcast—as though she had a case of the pox—that Catherine backed off a bit. "Perhaps we should take a break from our efforts. We must take your mind off Compton."

Mina glanced at her dubiously. "How do you propose to accomplish that?" A gust of wind blew off the Thames, and Mina grabbed hold of her bonnet. The sky was darkening, clouds were rolling over the chimney pots, and rag boys and street sweepers were scurrying for shelter.

"Vauxhall." The wind tossed Catherine's answer in the air, and her skirt billowed about her. It was going to rain. Cyclones of dust swirled in the street, and the girls bent against the wind.

"What did you say?" yelled Mina over a violent clap of thunder, and Catherine's response was again drowned.

They reached Genie's building precisely as a deluge of water let go from the skies. Jenny scurried to open the door, and once safe inside the vestibule, they leaned against the banister to catch their breath. Outside the rain beat a staccato tattoo against the building.

"Vauxhall Gardens," Catherine repeated. "Liam has agreed to escort us. He'll hire a box, and Genie will come, too!"

Instantly, Mina brightened. "'Tis a superlative idea, Catherine. I've always wanted to go to Vauxhall. Will there be fireworks?" she asked. For the first time in two days she was thinking about something other than the earl.

"Yes, fireworks and a concert and dinner and dancing. But I haven't told you the best. It will be masquerade night."

They were almost to the landing when Genie's door burst

open and the actress called down, "Spied you from the window. Aren't wet, are you?" Seeing that her young friends were all right, she hurried them inside. "I've got a surprise! You'll never guess, not in a million years."

The sight that greeted them was indeed unexpected. Every piece of furniture in the small parlor was buried beneath clothing. There were capes of satin, gowns of gossamer silk, velvet cloaks, and vibrant colored petticoats. Liam stood in the middle of this chaos, a green satin mask covering his face.

"Won't this look splendid on my sister? 'Tis sure to do the trick," he announced.

"Liam, what are you doing?" Mina and Catherine asked at once.

"Helping out. Had some costumes delivered from Drury Lane. Great idea of Genie's to hire these things for the masquerade. Paid a small fee and promised to return them as is."

Catherine began to sort through the exotic costumes while Mina gave Genie a hug of thanks before joining in the search. "What an ever so heavenly idea. Finding something to wear is like going on a treasure hunt."

"Well, lambie, I figured you'd be needing a little something to distract you about now," said Genie. With a knowing grin she observed the telltale blush that tinted Mina's cheeks.

Peals of laughter drew their attention to the center of the room. Catherine had discovered a court jester's outfit, and she was struggling to slip the collar over Liam's head. He was a most unwilling mannequin.

"Oh, no, you don't!" He tussled playfully with Catherine, who laughed as she forced the ruffles about his neck. The girls, including Jenny, could not help giggling. Liam's head of crisp black curls atop the enormous collar was suggestive of a nursery drawing of pretty-faced cockleshells in Mary-Quite-Contrary's garden. Tiny bells sewn to the collar tinkled as he moved to stand before Genie's French mirror. He joined in the laughter at the sight he presented.

"You may all chuckle now," he said, "for I assure you that I shall not wear this in public. Not even to a masquerade."

"I quite agree," tittered Catherine. "You'd be far better as a Cavalier." She placed a cockaded Cavalier's hat on his head.

While Genie and Mina searched for something to wear, Mina relayed the latest developments on her progress, or more appropriately her lack thereof, with the earl.

Genie commented, "From all you and Catherine have told me, it seems the earl has a soft spot in his heart for you. Like as not, the gent's too confused by his feelings to see it clear. Can't expect him to change overnight." She paused to examine a velvet robe, checking to make certain the seams were intact and the inevitable moth holes were too small to be noticed. Then she went on, "Sometimes love hits like a bolt of lightning and you don't doubt what's happened. Other times it comes in bits. It can be like a child's puzzle. Your earl is looking at the pieces, but he can't see the whole picture. Know why not?" Mina shook her head, and Genie answered her own question. "He can't see the picture because one of the pieces is missing."

"What's that?"

Genie gave a low laugh. "You're going to have to discover that for yourself, lambie. And when you do, the earl will know his heart as surely as you know yours."

"If I don't know what I'm looking for, how will I find it?" asked Mina, pulling a long face to show her frustration.

"You don't look for it, lambie. It happens. Like love. The trick is you've got to recognize it. That's when it fits in with the other pieces."

Mina breathed a vexatious sigh. "This love business is certainly not as simple as the books described."

"Never was, lambie. That's what we was all trying to tell you."

Masquerade night at Vauxhall Gardens arrived at last, and a hackney cab bearing Mina, Catherine, and Liam pulled up to the entrance. Wearing costumes heightened the thrill of the evening—which had begun when the girls climbed over the wall at Cavendish House; they had waited patiently until the earl and the countess departed to their respective social engagements before exiting into the garden. Mina and Catherine were exhilarated by their daring—their eyes sparkled, and their complexions were radiant.

Liam assisted his angel, who had been bouncing excitedly on her seat, and then turned to help his sister descend from the carriage. Mina's hands shook in anticipation as she placed the forest-green domino over her face and tied the satin ribands securely behind her head. Then she accepted her brother's hand, stepped from the carriage, and paused on the bottom step to gaze at the veritable fairyland before her. Trees glimmered with miniature lights from paper lanterns of blue and white and red and green. From within the gardens came the strains of musicians tuning their instruments.

Mina was exquisite in this setting. Her costume had been designed for Ariel, the sea sprite in *The Tempest*. It was of the sheerest sea-green muslin, dipping daringly low off the shoulders, with an Empire-styled bodice; its skirt cascaded in transparent layers about her shapely legs. She would never have worn anything so revealing were it not for the anonymity of the domino. There was something vastly romantic about going to a masked ball in a daring gown, one's face hidden behind a mask. She felt very bold, and she was going to have a glorious time. Tonight she was not Mina O'Kieffe. She could be anyone. A sprite. An actress. Or even a countess. She could forget the earl and all the rules she was required to obey while living in his household. She would dance and laugh and perhaps even taste champagne. No one would ever know the identity of the masked woman in sea green.

Vauxhall's pleasure gardens were crowded. The season being in full swing, daring members of the *beau monde* flocked there for entertainment of a more stimulating bent than that to be found at Almack's or a staid musicale. The Quality mingled with an assortment of lightskirts and overdressed cits. There were young bucks escorting gay Cyprians—their dresses a tad shorter than was accepted as being in good moral taste, displaying slender ankles and a fine view of calf. Titled ladies and gentlemen entered the gardens alongside merchants for whom the four-shilling entrance fee was a vast extravagance.

As Liam escorted the girls into the gardens, Catherine was dancing circles about them, excessively merry and beautiful in a Grecian-styled outfit.

"She looks like the angel Gabriel with eyes that shine like a bit of heaven," Liam commented to his sister.

Mina had to agree and realized that Liam was the only man who would ever make Catherine happy. Yes, they were in love, but there was something else between them. A balance in their natures. They were both wild and gay and fun-loving, but where Catherine lacked common sense, Liam stepped in to keep her on an even keel. She was an exuberant girl and would run any other man ragged, as she had her brother—yet Liam knew how to please her and, in turn, Catherine heeded his advice. They were a perfect match. Mina wondered if this was the secret ingredient of which Genie had spoken. Somehow she did not think that it was the piece for which she was searching.

A row of boxes draped in scarlet velvet faced the orchestra, and a dance floor was positioned between the two. Liam led the girls past the waiting throng to one of the private boxes where Genie and her escort were waiting for them. Genie's friend, Clive Luttrell, was a nice young man who bore an uncanny resemblance to Sean. They were of the same build, chunky and square, and like Sean the young man's ruddy complexion was accentuated by highlights in his coppery hair.

Clive Luttrell was, Mina concluded, evidence that Genie had not recovered from Sean. She shivered. What a dreadful, lonely fate. Would she one day be seeking the company of gentlemen who resembled the earl? Is that where love would lead her?

"What's wrong?" Liam asked, having spotted Mina's momentary frown.

"Nothing." She essayed a smile.

"You're certain? I wouldn't call a forced smile nothing. Care to confide, puss?"

Her brother's concern warmed Mina, and the smile came easier. "I was thinking about Sean and Genie."

Following the direction of her gaze, he understood and nodded. "Darling puss, always concerned for others. Come on now, chin up. We're here to enjoy ourselves, and I'll have none of that gloom and doom. If Genie can, you can, too." Then he reached across the table, grabbed a slender-necked bottle, and poured its contents into five fluted glasses set around the table. "Have some champagne. Only a bit, mind you. Can't let my little sister get disguised, you know."

They toasted to love and summertime, and as Mina sipped her champagne she surveyed the merriment of Vauxhall. People were still taking seats, and the orchestra was completing a rousing military march. She had a splendid view of the stage and applauded when Madame Vestris walked on to sing the infamous "Cherry Ripe." Although Mina was not certain of the meaning of the words, there was no mistaking the invitation in the songbird's sultry voice, and she blushed furiously as several young bucks called out suggestively.

At the conclusion the crowd let out howls of appreciation. Madame's song marked the end of the first half of the night's entertainment. The musicians bowed to the crowd and filed off-stage as waiters materialized to serve a light dinner during the intermission: thin slices of ham with mustard, spring lamb, pears in wine sauce, and individual mocha gateaux.

When the dishes were cleared away it was time for the dancing to commence. Liam turned to Catherine, saying, "Angel, be a dear and let me have the first dance with my sister."

Catherine consented and flashed a beguiling smile at her beloved. "Only this one dance," she said flirtatiously, "else I shall perish."

"Silly gudgeon." He kissed her hand and then escorted Mina to the floor. It was very crowded, and Liam held Mina as Master Peterkin had. She smiled at her brother and then glanced over his shoulder at the other dancers. Most of them wore masks. Only a few were bold enough to do otherwise.

Then, out of the corner of her eye, an unexpected sight halted her wandering gaze. There, at the far end of the row of boxes, was the earl with Alexandra Audley. Instinctively, she averted her face. Why did he have to be here and ruin her night? He always popped up at the worst times! When Mina remembered the domino she wore, she relaxed, telling herself it did not make any difference who saw her. Thus reassured of her anonymity, she was able to focus her attention on the earl and his companion.

The lady was divine in black, her creamy breasts barely covered and dark hair cascading in wild curls down her back. And he was fair and lean, his masculine power evidenced in the way he lounged beside her as if he held all the world under his control. He was elegantly garbed in black evening attire, a style that accentuated his blond hair, making it appear almost as white as the triangle of pristine white shirtfront, and Mina thought that he had never looked so handsome. Neither Lord Cavendish nor his companion wore a mask.

Alexandra Audley leaned closer to the earl and fed him a morsel of gateau. He smiled at her, and Mina experienced a jolt of intense jealousy. How dare he cavort so publicly? she thought in an unexpected flash of anger. And how dare that hussy stare at him in that brazen fashion? The man was an out-and-out hypocrite, a bounder of the worst sort. Mina and Catherine must not incur the raised eyebrow of Society, but it was all right for him to openly carry on with his mistress. Mina was indignant and growing more resentful with each glimpse in their direction.

When the dance ended, Liam escorted her to their box. The others were laughing at one of Catherine's jokes. Liam ordered more champagne and then swept his angel onto the dance floor. Genie and Clive followed. No one noticed the depths into which Mina was swiftly descending. Her gaze narrowed intently on the scene in the far box as Mina sipped her third glass of champagne. Alexandra was whispering to the earl; then the Beauty stood up and left.

"Ah-hah!" said Mina quietly as a very wild and exceedingly daring thought seized her. She would show that toplofty, arrogant earl.

Without considering the consequences of what she was about to do, Mina made her way towards his box. The distance was not great, perhaps twenty yards at the most, but it seemed like a hundred miles to Mina. With each three steps she felt as if she had stepped back a fourth. His box appeared to be farther and farther away, and the laughter of the revelers echoed about her.

Then she was there before him. All other sights and sounds faded into the background as she looked straight into his eyes and tempted him with a bewitching smile.

At first sight of the slender girl the earl had realized she was coming to see him. This amused him, and he had watched from beneath half-lowered eyelids as she threaded her way to his box. When she reached his table and stood before him, he could scarce believe his good fortune that so delightful a wench would seek him out—usually the bold ones were older, hardness and years of experience engraved in their expressions and every gesture. But this girl was different. She moved with the uncalculating grace of a child; yet the dress she wore marked her as a woman. Soft lantern light glowed behind her, revealing beautiful legs beneath the transparent folds of the skirt; the clinging fabric outlined perfect breasts, a tiny tucked waist, and shapely hips. But it was her eyes that captured his greatest fancy. Large green eyes stared at him from behind the satin domino, eyes that shimmered in the half-light with a warmth the earl longed to return. She beckoned to be loved, and he felt his own body respond with an answering chord.

"Hello." Her voice was a sultry whisper.

"Hello," he returned, thinking that she was a nymph of a fairy tale breathed into life.

The music started again, and he noticed the wishing gaze she cast towards the dancers. "Would you like to waltz?" he asked.

Fearing to reveal herself if she spoke again, Mina answered with a flirtatious curtsy. The earl stared at her for a long moment, and she tried to still the trembling deep within her.

Then he pushed away from the table and stood. With a sensual smile, he bowed to her and moved closer—so close that she had to tilt her head to look up at him.

His eyes sparkled dangerously with wayward thoughts. She was a delectable tidbit, this beautiful forest nymph, and he would be a fool to pass up a chance to hold her in his arms even at the risk of Alexandra's fury. Perhaps, he thought with an intrigued grin, he had stumbled on a replacement for the cloying Alexandra. That Beauty had become very boring, a sure sign that it was time to disencumber himself from a tiresome liaison. She was too voluptuous, too bold, and too demanding. Indeed, he found his tastes definitely running towards a woman more slender, perhaps a bit shy—a woman with a trifle more mystery about her. A woman, in fact, like this honey-haired, green-eyed forest nymph. With that thought in mind, the earl reached out for her.

There was no tentative coming together of this man and woman. Mina, emboldened by the champagne, stepped into the circle of his arms. One muscled arm embraced her about the waist. The other one, which should have rested at her shoulder, cradled the nape of her neck, pressing her to him. And then they began to waltz. Around and around they swirled, a thousand tiny lights shooting past. Swirling images of faces and dancers, trees, waiters, and musicians blurred into a kaleidoscope of dizzying color. She closed her eyes and welcomed the broad platform of his shoulder upon which to nestle her head.

Oh, but she was sweet! thought the earl as his hands tightened about the mysterious woman he held. She was so tiny he was reminded of a delicate spun-sugar fairy atop a cake, and he feared she might break beneath his hold. Yet with each tightening of his embrace she did not crumble. Indeed, she melted into him with unrestrained abandon. He might have been holding a feather, he mused, save for the aching need this reed of femininity was awakening within him. He knew desire had no place in a public setting, and normally he would have exercised iron restraint until a more private opportunity could be found. But this girl was shattering his control.

They swayed together as his passion spiraled. He was drowning in an ocean of arousal. The girl in his arms was not brazen, as were most lightskirts. Her surrender was imbued with an implicit trust of him as a man. He sensed it in her ingenuous sigh of contentment when she rested her head against his shoulder—which, of itself, was a powerful aphrodisiac. He was acutely aware of the heat radiating from her body through the folds of the whimsical gown. The fragrance of rose water clung to her hair and, unable to resist, he buried his face in the velvet tresses. Knowing he had to get them away before he did something very foolish, he moved towards the outer edge of the dance floor.

Before Mina knew what was happening they were walking down a secluded path. The earl pulled her under the sheltering branches of a massive oak tree. Only their hands were touching, but a quiver of sensation rippled through her, bursting hot and splendid from her feminine self. Her whole body quickened. There was an unnerving pang deep inside her. This was not like that brief taste of excitement on the Duchess of Darien's terrace. That attraction had been forbidden, and that knowledge had served as a natural curb. Tonight the attraction was unchecked, and Mina was frightened of her reactions to the man she loved so hopelessly. There might be little danger of passion getting out of hand between his ward and the Earl of Brierly, but garbed as an anonymous nymph, there was nothing to protect her from the flesh and blood man who held that title.

"My lord," she said in an urgent, husky voice, "I must return to my friends."

"Playing coy, my darling forest nymph?"

His warm breath was heavy with the scent of liquor, the words slightly slurred. Mina's anxiety rose when she realized the earl was a trifle foxed.

"Do not naysay me, my darling nymph," the amorous-minded earl continued. He nibbled at her ear as he coaxed, "This evening shall be well worth your while. Fear not. You shall become a lady of great wealth, for I'll bestow many riches and pleasures on you before the night is out. Let me see your face."

"No!" Cold panic spilled over her.

"Your eyes are truly beautiful. The loveliest I've seen. Let me see the rest of you." He chuckled indulgently at her display of shyness. "Very well, if it makes you happy, then wear your mask. For the time being, at least."

When his mouth sought hers, Mina trembled like a water lily before a summer storm. Their breath mingled for an instant, and then the pressure of his lips sent shock waves through her veins. There was an urgency in his kiss, and all thought of returning to the safety of the dinner box took flight. She clung to him, savoring the taste of him, the scent of sandalwood, and the positively intoxicating sensation of his virile strength pressed against her slender form.

He murmured something and held her closer, pulling his head back to feast on the sight of her beauty. Her skin enticed caressing, and he ran his fingers across the delicate expanse of flesh divinely revealed above the bodice of her gown. She was ivory white in the starlight, and he lowered his lips to her shoulder.

"I must have you," he murmured.

Mina's heart sang in response. She would do anything for him. It did not matter if he loved her or not. Oh, but it did! the voice of conscience cried. Suddenly, she was terrified. She had never thought to steal a moment of pleasure at the expense of love. What was happening to her? What had become of her girlish notions of love? All the love that she had read about or ever imagined was chaste. Mina, ever the romantic, had heretofore never encountered real passion. She had not realized there was a hidden aspect of love that might take her against her will.

The longer she stayed in the earl's arms, the more she wanted to remain there for eternity. There was only one thing to do. She must escape—and she had to do so before something dreadful happened. She could not deny the pleasure that sped through her when his lips brushed against her skin any more than she could deny that what they were doing was wrong. He did not love her; he did not even know the identity of the woman in his arms.

With a moan, Mina pushed against the earl's chest and, catching him off guard, she was free. Without a backward glance, she dashed down the path towards the sound of the orchestra. The earl called after her in surprise, but she did not stop.

Honey hair tousled about her face, lips reddened by the unrestrained kiss, and trembling like a blancmange, Mina flushed hot and cold with embarrassment as she scurried into the box. The ever-wise Genie observed this and ascertained what had transpired, for she had earlier seen the earl at the end of the row and had later spied a churlish Alexandra searching the crowd after Mina had disappeared. Genie offered a sympathetic smile and said, "Appears you've found the missing puzzle piece."

Scarlet patches dotted Mina's cheeks and forehead. With an uncertain look at Genie and an anxious glance over her shoulder, she scooted down in the chair until she was hidden from sight.

"Almost lost your head, did you?" Genie chuckled. When Mina looked as though she might wilt to the floor, the older woman added, "Come now, can't be all that bad."

Wide-eyed and still endeavoring to catch her breath, Mina whispered, "He didn't even know it was me!"

"'Course not, else he'd never have danced with you in the first place. Men harbor some mighty queer notions about making a lady happy, and one of them is that a lady of Quality ought not to be treated like a flesh and blood woman." She gave a harrumph of disgust before continuing. "That's part of the reason he can't believe in love. He ain't supposed to feel any emotion 'cept some toplofty respect for a lady. But he does, and you, Cinderella, you've got the key to unlock the mystery for him."

Mina saw the brilliance of this and she exclaimed, "So he couldn't believe in love, for it could never exist in one of his businesslike marriages of convenience, nor would he allow love to flourish, for a lady must not know real love."

"That's the ticket, lambie."

"What happens next?" she asked, a trifle awestruck at the possibilities.

"That green domino is your glass slipper, lambie. Save it for the right moment."

When the earl took Alexandra home that evening, he did not stay with her. After a snifter of brandy and more of her pouting airs than he cared to witness, he headed back to Berkeley Square. He did not desire what she offered so willingly, but he was not certain what he wanted in its stead.

There was a nagging yearning within him, and as he passed through St. James's on unsteady legs, he scanned the faces of the women beneath the gaslamps. They paraded before the bow windows of the private clubs. Garish, willing, and available. But they were not what he wanted either. He was searching for something.

Images of a green domino and flashing emerald eyes swam before him. Was it the girl in the green nymph costume? He stopped and squinted into the darkness. But there was no one there. It was only his imagination, and he grumbled beneath his breath. Not likely to find that sweet morsel strutting the streets. Not the strutting type. Come to think of it, she had not really been the lightskirt type at all. Too trusting by far. Unless it was her first time. That might explain it. Or perhaps she was the adventuresome daughter of some cit, escaped from mama and papa for a risqué night in the gardens, in which case she was already snug in bed in St. John's Wood.

Upon reaching Cavendish House, the earl ambled into the library, where he poured a healthy dose of brandy. Idly, he twirled the snifter by its long stem and in the light of the dying fire watched the liquid swirling in circles. Then he drained it in a single swallow. Taking the decanter, he sat before a french door and stared into the garden. Between the trees two shadows elongated and shrank. The dark forms came to life and drifted past the rear wall. The earl rubbed his eyes.

"Lord, I'm drunk as a wheelbarrow," he muttered as he tilted the decanter to his lips. A drop of brandy escaped his mouth and, inelegantly, he wiped his chin with the back of his hand. Long legs propped on the desk, he closed his eyes and leaned his head against the wall by the open door.

A breeze blew across the terrace. High up in an elm a branch creaked, the hush of a hundred thousand leaves whispered like tissue paper, and giggles drifted on the wind. Giggles? The earl opened his eyes and slurred, "Impossible. Must be a trick of the night. Too much brandy." Peering into the garden, he again spotted those unusual shadows, and this time they looked like female figures.

He stepped onto the balcony and squinted. Who could it be? Housemaids sneaking off to meet with grooms? Mina and Catherine? It was not an unreasonable suspicion. But what could the girls be up to?

Nothing moved. There was not a sound in the garden. Must have been his imagination, the earl decided with a drunken shrug. A lot of things must have been his imagination—wonderful things, such as an innocent, green-eyed forest nymph—for how could a Cyprian have been so sweet? Sweet as Mina, came the unbidden thought, followed quickly by self-reproach. What an utterly debauched mind he possessed!

"Sweet Mina. Is that you, sweet Mina?" he whispered, thoroughly unaware of the devastating truth his sodden mind had uncovered. "Sweet forest nymph."

He staggered and turned back to the house. A movement on the second floor caught his eye. The old nurse, Nanny Saltmarsh, was standing at a window, a spectre in white, candle in one hand. What the devil was the old girl doing up so late? Walking in her sleep, no doubt.

Shrugging his shoulders, he reeled into the library, where he plopped down in a large leather chair. His eyelids dropped closed, and his head spun. There were those giggles again. He was sure of it. Female giggles. High and clear and delightfully familiar. But his eyelids were too heavy, and he could not open them to investigate the source of the girlish laughter.

Chapter Eleven

"I've lost the green domino!" Mina cried in alarm. At this dramatic discovery, she pawed through the folds of the gossamer green skirt. "Wherever can it be?"

"Sssh. Keep your voice down," Catherine admonished on a moan. The champagne she had imbibed the night before had given her a dreadful headache. She rubbed her forehead in a circular motion. "Where did you lose it?"

"If I knew where, then it would hardly be lost, would it?" Mina retorted. She crossed her arms and drummed her fingers impatiently on them while she gave the matter thoughtful consideration. She had been wearing it during the carriage ride home, but she could not recall when she had taken it off. Had she been wearing it when she and Catherine crept through the garden? Had she lost it at Vauxhall or somewhere nearer to home? If she had dropped it in Cavendish House, it could be found by heaven knows who. Gracious, what a coil that would be!

"Don't get in such a taking," Catherine told her. "Jenny can stitch up a new one. What difference can it make?"

On an exceedingly piercing and nervous laugh, Mina replied, "A great deal of difference. First, it's my glass slipper and second, it might very well be our mutual death decree." She received a look of extreme befuddlement from Catherine, who mouthed the words "glass slipper" and "death decree," a scowl deepening between her pretty eyes. Mina blanched noticeably but went on, "You're going to be prodigious angry when I tell you something about last night.

'Tis truly dreadful what I did. You see, your . . . your brother saw me in the domino last night."

"So?" Catherine drew the single word into a long and apprehensive question.

"In truth, we . . . um . . . talked."

"Talked?" Catherine covered her eyes. Her head was throbbing harder, and this unexpected confession was not helping.

"More than talked." Mina tweaked at the green dress.

Catherine peeped between her fingers. "Stop mincing words, Mina. What did you and my brother actually do, if it was more than talking?"

"I danced with him," she said and, blushing profusely, added, "Then he pulled me into an arbor and kissed me."

This was hardly the ominous news Catherine anticipated. Rather it was music to her ears, heralding the end of her troubles.

"Oh, this is famous!" she enthused, her headache miraculously abated. "He kissed a girl in a green domino. But 'twas really you! This is splendid. The domino is surely a glass slipper; he'll find it and come to you on bended knee like Prince Charming. You'll marry Compton, and I'll marry Liam!"

"I hardly think it's going to happen like that," snapped Mina, wondering with dismay if her own romantic ideals had sounded so totally implausible. "Can you imagine your brother behaving like Prince Charming? Like as not, he'll put two and two together and then we'll all be in trouble. Instead of a glass slipper, the domino shall give away our escapade and set us in line for a ferocious raking down."

"Egad!" Catherine gasped, her headache returning with tripled force. "You're right, and there's no telling what he'll do. Why, he might even challenge Liam." She paled at the prospect of her beloved and her only brother driven to a duel.

Mina picked up her skirts and in great haste left the bedchamber to enter Nanny's room at the end of the corridor. It was a comfortable chamber decorated in shades of blue, with a four-poster bed and a chaise upholstered in blue-and-white flocked chintz. Matching curtains were tightly closed, and Mina opened them to reveal a view of the rear gardens. She peered in the direction of the yew hedge.

"Oh look, there it is!" she said to Catherine, who had followed. Pointing excitedly towards a small green object on the pebbled path, Mina declared, "I must retrieve it immediately."

Out of the door she flew, along the hallway, past gilt-framed Rubenses and Gainsboroughs, and down the wide marble staircase.

"House on fire?" a disapproving voice cackled. Nanny was standing at the foot of the stairs, arms crossed, the wrinkles in her pale face were accentuated by displeasure as she stared down her nose at Mina. Nanny's gray brows went up. "Not so fast, Miss Mina. Mustn't run in the house. Ain't ladylike. Back up those stairs and come down in a manner befitting a lady. Up with you," she urged with a waggle of her aged finger.

"Yes, ma'am," Mina said, barely able to hide her frustration. She trudged back up the stairs, turned, and descended in an appropriately ladylike fashion.

"Much better, m'dear. Much better," the mobcapped woman approved. Then, seeing the direction in which Mina was headed, she added the inevitable, "Don't forget your bonnet, Miss Mina. Lady Elaine never went outside without her bonnet. Always took care of her skin, she did."

"Yes, ma'am. I won't forget," said Mina on a quick turn with a half curtsy.

The domino lay on the gravel where she had seen it, and once it was safely in Mina's hand, she sped back towards the house. Around the rose garden she skipped and, not watching where she was going, she charged up against something very firm and solid.

"Mercy!" she exclaimed.

"And good morning to you, too, Miss O'Kieffe," the earl drawled.

Mina stared up at him in horror. He was smiling, highly amused about something. Did he know she was the woman in green from Vauxhall? Mina searched his eyes for any sign of recognition or suspicion, but found nothing. Nothing at all. The deep-set blue eyes were inscrutable. She crumpled the domino in her hand, making it as small and invisible as was earthly possible. She had not thought their first encounter after Vauxhall would be like this. It was exceedingly disconcerting to be caught off guard, and she wanted to get away.

"Good morning, my lord." She automatically bobbed a curtsy and tried to inch past him, but he blocked her way. He was standing far too close to her, too close to prevent the unnerving palpitations of her heart.

"Been for a walk in the garden, Miss O'Kieffe?" he inquired with the tilt of one blond brow. "And in such a hurry, too." His eyes came alive, and he leveled a horrendously blighting stare at her. "Heed your nanny, Miss O'Kieffe. She's a wise woman. Knows much about what is and isn't acceptable for a young lady." The blighting stare softened, then twinkled into a smile. "I'm off to my club. Have a pleasant day, Miss O'Kieffe."

She watched him exit by the garden gate, beaver hat on his head, a charcoal short-tailed coat fitting his broad shoulders to perfection, and she heaved an immense sigh of wonder at his physical perfection, of relief at his departure, and of perplexity at his light mood. At the very least, she thought, he ought to be suffering with a splitting headache! He certainly was not behaving like a man who had been out until the wee hours.

From the other side of the wall, Mina heard someone, a very earl-like someone, whistling the refrain of "Cherry Ripe."

"Ooooh!" she exclaimed, stamping her foot and stuffing the domino in her pocket. Had he seen the domino? she wondered. Did he suspect her? And why on earth was he so deuced jolly?

The earl could not repress the grin that broke across his face in uncharacteristic abandon. His step was unusually light, and he tipped his hat with a chipper "Good morning" at every passerby.

Still wading through the events of last evening, he had managed to sort what had happened into two sets of facts. There were those facts that were undeniably true and those that were swathed in mystery. Mentally he compiled list number one, to which he assigned the following: True, he had danced with a lovely young woman in green. True, he had been and still was extremely attracted to that same woman. True, that girl bore an uncanny similarity to Mina. And true, he would like to know her name, find her, and make her his.

The second list was comprised exclusively of questions, and to each question he had ready but unsatisfactory answers.

Who was the woman in green? A novice lightskirt? Or a merchant's daughter come to the masquerade for excitement? And why did she so strongly remind him of Mina? Perhaps it was simply an obsession. Possessed as he was with the thought and image of Mina, had he transferred her image to the other girl? Who had been giggling in the garden? Housemaids? What was that slip of green fabric Mina had tried to conceal from him? Perhaps he had imagined it. Was it possible that Mina was the green forest nymph who had melted into his arms with such complete surrender?

It was preposterous, of course. Such a conclusion was unthinkable. It was merely a coincidence that the eyes of the girl with whom he had dallied were the same rich emerald green as Mina's. Impossible. It was only coincidence that the girl at Vauxhall had responded to him with the same sweet abandon Mina had shown on the Duchess of Darien's terrace. Outrageous. Mina masquerading as a seductive forest nymph in Vauxhall, indeed.

The notion made him laugh and quicken his jaunty pace. For as preposterous, impossible, and outrageous as it might be, he knew he would be immensely disappointed if Mina were not that woman. He had to find some way to discover if she was the green forest nymph. Here was a puzzle indeed, and Lord help him, he wanted the worst to be true.

Dining *en famille* developed into a miserable affair for Mina. Sitting at the same table with the earl was sheer torture. Try as she might, she could not follow what the countess said about the Italian soprano at the opera, nor what Catherine said about the new modiste on Half Moon Street. The memory of Vauxhall was still fresh, and the earl, seated at the far end of the table, was the focus of Mina's attention.

In the garden the previous morning, she had been too anxious to consider little else save the missing domino. Now she could concentrate on naught but the earl and what had happened in the secluded arbor. She squirmed in her seat. Between spoonfuls of green turtle in sherry she stole glimpses of the earl's chiseled face, his deep-set eyes, and sensual lips. She recalled the touch of those lips on her bare shoulder and trembled. She met his eyes, but saw nothing in the icy blue depths to make her think he was the man who had so passionately declared his desire for her.

The earl, for his part, was—to state it mildly—in a vile humor, the source of which was of primary concern to the girls. He stared daggers at the countess when she tried to engage him in conversation about the auction of Arabian stock at Tattersall's, he complained that his prosciutto was too salty, and he criticized one of the footmen for a poorly tied cravat. By the time dessert was served, everyone in the dining room was assiduously avoiding his gaze, and Mina squirmed in her seat some more.

"Do you think he knows about Vauxhall?" she whispered to Catherine.

"How could he?" was the silently mouthed return.

"The do-mi-no," Mina also mouthed, exercising due caution to make certain that the earl was not glancing in their direction.

"No, be-cause—" Catherine mouthed distinctly, then paused to pop a forkful of peach tart between her lips.

Mina waited with bated breath until Catherine was done chewing.

"Be-cause he would have ex-plo-ded with fu-ry," Catherine finished, her silent communication being augmented by facial contortions of the worst sort.

"O." Mina's lips rounded in confirmation.

At last the interminable meal was over. The ladies rose to take their coffee in the grand salon. Thinking her ordeal was at an end, it came as an entirely unpleasant surprise when Mina was summoned to meet with the earl in the library.

"Whatever can he want?" Catherine asked Mina, who paled considerably.

"He must have found out about Vauxhall. Perhaps one of the footmen saw us leave and told him," said Mina.

"If that were the case, then why would he be asking to speak with you alone? It makes no sense."

The answer was clear as a candle to Mina. If he knew they had been at Vauxhall, Catherine's indiscretion was far less heinous than her own. Catherine had merely gone to the pleasure gardens, while Mina had courted pleasure, disguised as and acting no better than a wanton. Her punishment would be dire, indeed, for Mina well knew the risks she had taken. Until that night the girls had enjoyed the countess's tacit consent to visit with Liam. Although they had acted against the earl's wishes, they had comported themselves like ladies. Vauxhall was another matter entirely. It was the sort of behavior that could ruin one's reputation. It was precisely the sort of behavior the earl considered beyond the pale. Oh, why hadn't she thought of that before traipsing off? How excessively childish of her—and not entirely unlike the flighty, thoughtless Catherine—not to have realized earlier what Lord Cavendish would think of her recklessness. It was precisely too late now, and she would have to face whatever consequences arose from her precipitous actions. Shoulders squared and head held high, Mina entered the library.

He was standing by the hearth, back to the door, arms spread wide to rest on the wood-carved mantel. His head was bent in an exhausted pose.

"You asked to see me, my lord?" she asked, then bit her lower lip between her teeth to prevent its trembling. She folded her hands to prevent their shaking.

"Close the door firmly behind you," he said in a voice that made her stomach churn. She did so, and he raised his head, turned away from the fireplace, and pushed his fingers through his hair. He watched her closely. She was more beautiful than ever tonight. Her hair was gathered at the top of her head with a green and yellow grosgrain ribbon; thick curls twirled about her shoulders, giving her the frothy appearance of a honey-sweet confection. His gaze traveled from her eyes to her mouth, sweet and pertly full, and he watched as her lower lips gave a betraying quaver. The girl was nervous as a catbird, he noticed. She had been edgy during dinner, too.

What was she hiding? Was it Vauxhall? *That would indeed be something worth hiding, my pretty nymph,* he thought with increasing satisfaction. *Are you my pretty forest nymph? Your eyes are surely as beautiful.* He recalled the tempting waltz he and Mina had shared at the Duchess of Darien's, which could have become as heated as the embrace he had shared with the girl in Vauxhall. But would Mina have masqueraded at Vauxhall? And if the answer was yes, why would she have sought him out for an interlude as the forest nymph had?

The bells in the mantel clock chimed nine and recalled him to the present. He coughed twice and then said, "Had a visit from von Ruttiger this afternoon. Made an offer for you."

Mina looked somewhat taken aback. Her eyes widened. All fear of having been caught at Vauxhall evaporated. "As in marriage?" The question almost lodged in her throat. "I had not guessed he harbored such feelings for me." She paused, and for a long moment it was very quiet. Far too quiet. Why wasn't the earl saying anything? What had he said to the count? Egad, he hadn't given his consent, had he? "Well?"

"Turned him down," he said shortly.

"You turned him down!" she nearly shouted. "How dare you do something like that without consulting me first! Whatever made you suppose you might know what I wanted?" She was glad not to marry the German, yet her relief rapidly turned to anger at the earl. If he had so easily turned him down, he might as easily accept another offer without her consent.

"Remembered what you said in Lane's. You told me von Ruttiger wasn't the fellow you wanted," he said reasonably. "Your brother *did* authorize me to act in his behalf. He must have thought my judgment was acceptable in some way."

"Well, I don't," she retorted indignantly. "Your judgment is of no account to me for we're as different as wine from water."

"Not so very different," he ventured gently, a devil dancing in his eyes. "What about the Dog and Ducks? Croissants and preserves? Walking and riding and history? I've developed quite a liking for Scott, you know, and I'm considerably more interested in history. And that's your doing." He added in a low, silky voice, "You've taught me quite a few lessons this Season, Miss O'Kieffe."

The amusement in his gaze further incensed Mina. Totally disregarding the substance of what he had said, she continued to rail, "What would you know of what lies in my heart?"

She was positively entrancing when angry. The natural color in her cheeks heightened; her eyes flared diamond chips against emerald. The earl fully expected that Miss O'Kieffe would stamp her foot at any moment, and at that prospect, he suddenly was laughing.

"You—you odious beast!" His laughter was the final straw, and she could not help the tears that clouded her eyes. "Stop that!" Of course, she stamped her dainty foot.

"Still as rag-mannered as you were that day in the stream." He shook his head, chuckling. Taking in the sight of her eyes shimmering with tears, the bewitching color in her cheeks, and her honey hair, which he knew was soft as silk, he added, "And still quite as pretty. No, prettier, I believe. There's a glint in your eyes, the glint of a hoyden, and I believe it's begging me to lean over and take you and . . ."

He stopped in midsentence; his words faded away. There was a long, heavy silence. Why did Mina torment him so? He stepped away from the hearth, took four paces, and towered over her. She filled him with such contradictory emotions. One moment he wanted to shake her senseless and in the next, he wanted to kiss her.

"Don't you dare," she said on a whisper. "Don't you dare mock me. You p-p-poor creat—"

She never finished. The last word was captured by his lips as he soundly kissed her until she gave a little sigh of surrender and relaxed in his arms. A salty taste mingled with the sweetness of her mouth. Mina was crying, and the earl reluctantly lifted his head and stepped back to regard her.

The sight of her was spellbinding. She raised one hand to touch her lips in a curiously vulnerable gesture, and tear-spiked lashes brushed against flawless cheeks. She took a deep breath, but no words would come. She could do naught but stare at him.

Certes! He blinked. It was as though a flash of lightning ripped through the room. There was an arrested look on his lean features. By God, he loved the chit. He had been in love with her since that night at the Duchess of Darien's. Or perhaps it was the morning she leaned out the window, or was it when she stamped her foot in the orchard stream?

Having never been in love, he felt a gauche fool. And knowing her feelings towards him, he could not very well say, "Excuse me, Miss O'Kieffe, I've suddenly discovered I'm head over heels in love with you and wonder if you might overlook the fact you've vowed never to love a man such as I." No, he could not say that. It would not do at all.

If she was the girl in the green domino, then he was certain she harbored some warmer feeling for him. But he could not risk his newfound emotions without knowing the truth. He must first find out if she was the forest nymph.

He looked down at her face and experienced a rush of emotion, part joy, part tenderness, and something that might have been fear. His cool composure slipped, and he struggled against a surge of feelings too intense to control.

In a shaking voice, he said the first thing that occurred to him. "Please accept my humblest apology, Miss O'Kieffe."

"There's no need to apologize," Mina said on a sharp

intake of breath. If he had stabbed her, the pain could not have been sharper. That he would apologize for kissing her was proof that it meant nothing. Nay, that *she* meant nothing to him. Mina lowered her gaze to the tips of her kid slippers and swallowed the tears burning her throat. If she had not been so discomposed, she would have read the naked look upon his face, the look that exposed his own awakened heart.

The door opened. Any distraction was a relief, and instantly they turned to observe the countess on the threshold. "Not interrupting anything, am I, my dears?" With a swish of taffeta skirts she blazed into the room, looking august, curious, and scheming. Taking note of the grayness that had settled about the earl's mouth, she trilled, ''Mina, Compton does not look himself. Assist him to a chair *tout de suite*! Give him a hand. *Ce n'est pas* correct. You must help him into the chair—don't merely point at it!''

The earl pushed Mina's hand aside. "Perfectly capable of standing on my own two legs," he grumbled and crossed the room to get as far away from Mina as he could.

"Thought I heard raised voices." The countess shot a narrow gaze at her grandson. "Weren't fighting, were you?"

Mina cast a sideways glance at the earl, who pushed a lock of hair off his forehead and shot a supplicating glance heavenward. His grandmother could not have chosen a more ill-timed moment to intrude. "We were discussing Mina's offer from von Ruttiger."

"Had an offer, did she? 'Tis cause for celebration, *oui*?"

"Oh, no!" Mina hastened to inject, not quite understanding the countess's jubilant tone. She sounded as if she were already planning the nuptials. Didn't she want the earl to marry her? The woman could be so peculiar at times. 'Twas no wonder Catherine was such a skittlebrain.

"Turned him down," the earl said with such a self-satisfied grin that the countess surmised why he was looking like a man who had just made a profound and unsettling discovery. Her glance alternated between him and Mina. Clearly her grandson had come face to face with love. Of a certainty, he knew his feelings. It was also clear that he had not shared them with the chit. What was wrong with the dolt now?

"Thought you were going to help Miss O'Kieffe," the countess went on. "Turning down an offer from von Ruttiger ain't help. *Alors*, she has been on the rounds, has a voucher for Almack's, and has mingled with the *crème de la crème*. Nothing left for it but one thing. You must host a gala ball for Miss O'Kieffe." Now the lad would be caught off guard, she thought smugly.

Only the flexing of his cheek muscle betrayed the earl's annoyance with this latest ploy. It passed quickly, superseded by a sort of giddy sensation, and he ladled a wry smile at his grandmother. She was not going to bamboozle him this time!

"Excellent notion," he said promptly, startling both women, who had expected him to lodge a mild protest at least. *Yes, indeed, a superior notion,* he thought, running a lanky forefinger up and down his chin. His quick intellect saw myriad opportunities in such a plan, and he took another moment to consider the proposition. "You must make all the plans Grandmère, but I insist on one thing. It must be a theme ball. A May Fair. And the guests will wear costumes."

Mina, scarce believing she had understood correctly, stared at him, and seeing that he was indeed serious, she beamed a smile of delight. "Oh, thank you, my lord!" she cried, and giving no weight to what had passed between them before the countess entered, she dashed across the library, threw her arms about his neck, and kissed his cheek. "What a romantic notion!" she declared, not realizing the import of her own words.

Their meaning was not, however, lost on the earl, who decided that in a matter of seconds he was getting quite good at this frivolous stuff. And it was not all that bad. All that remained was for him to discover if Mina was the forest nymph, and he believed that he had found a way to do exactly that.

Chapter
Twelve

Within a fortnight the morning parlor at Cavendish House, a sunny retreat papered in pale green silk and looking out onto the garden, was in a state of pandemonium. There were only nine days until Mina's May Fair, and a score of details remained to be settled. The exquisite room was buried in mounds of lists, bills and other slips of paper; the countess, having organized the event as if she were a general preparing for battle, set all items pertaining to the décor at one end of the room, notes on menus and food at the opposite side, and guest lists and invitations in the middle. No detail was unattended. There was a well-defined division of labor among herself, the girls, and the staff, and she demanded strict adherence to all deadlines. The plans were designed to function like clockwork, and no shirking would be tolerated.

In the northernmost corner of the room, occupying a gold-filigreed Louis XIV table, were four different menus; and there would likely be a fifth and sixth before the countess had made the final decision as to what would be served. There was going to be a full buffet for the guests, but whether they would dine on roasted goose or poached salmon had yet to be decided. The only certain thing was the destiny cake. Mina had once read about the elderberry pastry in a book of medieval nursery rhymes. She wanted it at her ball, and luck was with her. After several queries Cook had located a recipe from a second cousin who worked for Baron Swynford. The kitchen staff, to Mina's delight, was frying hundreds of fanciful destiny cakes.

On the opposite side of the room, running the full six-foot length of an inlaid cherrywood console, were various sketches for the décor. Overall, the countess intended to employ an abundance of flowers. From the moment guests alighted from their carriages and walked up the garland-draped staircase to the entrance of Cavendish House, there was to be a prevailing sense of springtime throughout the mansion. The interior of Number 5 would be bedecked with artfully arranged boughs of pink flowering clematis; blossoming orange trees from the greenhouse at Brierly would line the rotunda; and in the ballroom the countess would display the famous Brierly orchids, also transported from the castle greenhouse, greenish yellow in hue and renowned for their powerful sweet scent. In the dining room, there would be ice sculptures standing among banks of yellow and white roses. One sculpture would be in the likeness of a rope dancer, and the second was to depict the dog and ducks in Hogarth's sign.

Strewn about a circular marble table in the center of the morning parlor were the last of the gilt-edged invitations. Already, some three hundred of the engraved ivory cards had been sent. The countess was at present sorting the acceptances and preparing the final ones for delivery that afternoon.

Catherine and Mina were engaged in a mild disagreement about the decorations for the rear garden. The earl had agreed to hire concessionaires with swings and roundabout rides which would occupy the space beyond the elm grove. Mina wanted to erect small tents in the garden, one for a juggling show and the other for gypsy fortune tellers. Catherine disagreed.

"And while you're about it, my dear," the countess put in affectionately, "how about a few cows and ducks?"

She was teasing, of course, but Mina, who was taking this May Fair quite seriously, did not see the jest in this. "Live animals and a duck pond. What a famous idea!" she exclaimed.

Catherine groaned as if in exquisite pain. "Mina."

Then Mina blushed, realizing her error. She admitted,

"Of course that wouldn't work. The crowds would frighten the beasts."

"Ah-hem," a male person coughed, and all heads turned as the earl ambled into the morning parlor. He greeted his grandmother formally, first with a bow, followed by a kiss on the cheek, then turned to the girls, asking, "Everything going smoothly?"

He was in one of his exceptionally fine humors. Of late he had been like this a great deal. A day seldom dawned that the earl was not in high spirits, a phenomenon that was noted by each of the ladies in her own way. Catherine made a little frown. She did not understand her brother at all. Where was the stiff-rumped tyrant who had ruled her life with an iron hand these past years? Grandmère understood what had happened and grinned knowingly at the miracles wrought by an event so significant as a thawing of the heart.

Mina simply stared at him, wondering all the while what this mysteriously pleasant earl was about. Odd, she thought, but these past days he reminded her of her brothers, as Captain Ramsey had. But she scoffed at the notion. Any true similarity between such opposite personalities was not possible. Was it?

"Tell me," the earl inquired conversationally, "have you ladies decided on costumes yet?"

"No," Catherine said with a pout. " 'Tis a terribly hard decision, further complicated by Caroline Beaufort and the Ladies Anne Haworth and Pamela Sumerville."

"Pray, what have the good ladies done to complicate your life, sister dearest?"

"*On dit* they plan to attend as shepherdesses, and I had wanted to be one, but would never do so with so many others. I want to be original!"

The earl laughed. "And so you are and shall be. How about you, Miss O'Kieffe?"

"I've browsed through several books for inspiration but have had no luck either."

"Then I trust none of you will object that I took the

liberty of having several costumes made for your selection. A friend of mine recommended a designer. Madame Rabelais has extensive experience with fancy-dress balls, and I'm assured the selection she presents shall be excellent.''

"I know *la Madame*," the countess effused. "How brilliant of you, Compton, to have obtained her services. She was the most promising apprentice at the old king's court in Versailles. Many of the most magnificent costumes *en toute de la France* were made by Madame Rabelais when she was a mademoiselle before the Terror."

"Oh, Grandmère, will you be wearing a costume?" asked Catherine.

"*Mais oui!* I would not attend Mina's May Fair any other way. The May Fair is for the young, and I confess to feeling gay and young at the prospect of hostessing the Season's most original costume ball. 'Tis most exciting.''

"What will you wear, my lady?"

"Let us wait and see what Compton has ordered from *la Madame*," she suggested before thanking her grandson.

"I agree, my lord. 'Twas prodigious kind of you to go to such trouble. I'm sure I'll find something among Madame Rabelais's costumes that I like very much," said Mina, turning a radiant smile on the earl.

His eyes glinted roguishly. "I hope you will, Miss O'Kieffe," he said sincerely, then he inclined his head in farewell. "Ladies, until dinner."

The remainder of the morning passed most productively. The final invitations were addressed. The countess and Mina concurred that salmon would be better than goose, and Catherine, after dispatching the final invitations into Hughes's care, wrote a note to Liam.

At half past eleven the butler reappeared on the threshold. "A Mr. Sean O'Kieffe has arrived to see Miss O'Kieffe, my lady."

Startled, Mina looked up from the menu.

"Show him in, Hughes," the countess commanded, then shuffled her papers together and rose. "Come, Catherine, you and I shall check with Cook about the pastries while

Mina visits with her brother." They departed the morning parlor while Mina awaited her visitor.

Sean was in Town and had come to call. This struck Mina as very strange. Although she had never been away from home before, it did not seem likely that Sean would take time to pay a brotherly visit. He had never written while he was gone—as Liam regularly did—nor had he ever brought her a souvenir of his travels—as Kevin occasionally did. Was something wrong at Thornhill Park? Before she speculated further, the object of her concern was ushered into the room.

"Sean, what an unexpected surprise." Mina kissed her eldest brother on the cheek. "All is well with you?"

"Fine," he responded, sounding suspiciously like Genie that afternoon at the Arcade.

" 'Tis good to see you. You look wonderful." Indeed, her brother was dressed like a veritable dandy. Sean, who had always preferred simple country tweeds, was garbed in beige pantaloons, a striped marseilles waistcoast in brilliant peacock blue, and an astoundingly intricate cravat which was so high that he could hardly see over it and so stiffly starched that he could barely turn his head. Despite this fantastic outfit, there was the mud of Kent on his Wellington boots, and Mina imagined she smelled the scent of moist earth after a gentle shower.

"Oh, Sean," she said again, " 'Tis good to see you! I've missed you. What brings you to Town?"

"Kevin and Michael went off to Antrim to visit our Irish cousins," he began, and Mina nodded, recalling what Liam had told her about the O'Maras. They bred race horses and had two lovely daughters, and Liam had often asked the twins whether 'twas the lassies or the cattle that struck their fancy.

"Anyway, 'twas rather lonely at Thornhill Park." He shifted his weight from one Wellingtoned foot to another. "So I thought I'd see how you were doing."

This did not sound like Sean. He was seldom at a loss for something to do and someone with whom to do it. She arched one fine brow and pinned an examining gaze on him.

The confident swagger was gone from his stride, she observed as he accompanied her to the settee by the window.

He lowered his bulky frame to the seat across from Mina. "Saw Liam in Knightsbridge. Said Brierly's planning a ball for you." He cast a glance about the morning parlor. Its golden splendor surpassed even the finest room at Thornhill Park.

"Yes. A May Fair. Would you like to come? I'm sure it would be—"

"No," he interrupted, looking uncomfortable. "No need to invite me. Wouldn't want to ruin your visit seeing as how the earl don't like us O'Kieffe men."

"Nonsense. You're welcome here and to attend my ball," she declared, although she was not truly certain how the earl would react if her brother chose to attend. She added, "Liam would be welcome, too, if it wasn't for Catherine and her rackety ways."

"The girl's a wild one, eh?"

"A bit headstrong, 'tis all."

"Ah." The conversation drifted into silence for a few moments. "Not too wild for Liam, is she?"

"Not at all," Mina replied. Then she added, "Sean O'Kieffe, I've never heard you talk like that before. You sound ever so much like a parent!"

He shifted his weight on the settee, leaned forward, and rested his elbows on his knees. "I know I've never been much of a brother to you. Don't think I would have cared about you the way the earl has about his sister. Not that I don't love you, but I never really thought overmuch about family."

"Have you ever thought of having your own family?"

"Well, that's what I was wondering. Don't suppose you've seen Genie Grevey, have you? She ain't the kind to keep company with the likes of Brierly, so it's unlikely. But she's a nice sort, honest. A real actress, too, not a tart." His ruddy complexion deepened and he coughed. "Didn't mean to insult you."

Mina gaped, wide-eyed, at her brother. Her faith in love was restored. Gone was the careless, uncouth oaf, and in his place sat a very humble, quite lonely, and none-too-confident man who was desperately in love.

"I've seen her," Mina said.

"Genie?"

"Yes. Several times. She's a true friend, Sean. I like her very much and was sad to learn she'd left the Park."

He shrugged and splayed his beefy hands in the air as if to say "What's done is done."

"Perhaps it's not too late," she suggested.

"That's what I was wondering. Maybe you could arrange for me to see Genie. I know where her flat is and all, but I'm afraid she won't talk to me. Thought maybe if you approached her, then she'd see me. You don't have to, if you don't want to. I'll understand."

"Of course I will," was her response without the briefest hesitation. "In fact"—Mina checked the cloisonné time-piece pinned to the bodice of her ecru gown—"'tis almost noon. Genie strolls through the Arcade each day at half past the hour. Come, we've not a minute to spare if we hope to see her this morning."

"This is swell of you, Mina." He offered his sister an arm, and the siblings exited Cavendish House looking as if they had always been as close as they were at that moment.

Brother and sister had been waiting at the entrance to the Arcade for less than five minutes when Sean said, "Look over there. It's Genie in the purple hat. Ain't she a wonder to behold?"

Mina repressed a giggle, for Genie was indeed a sight. She had outdone herself in a two-piece walking suit of violet, the spencer and dress both trimmed with lace. Her hat, as Sean so simply called it, was a masterpiece of dark purple silk with two ostrich feathers placed in front to fall contrary ways and an enormous bow of white edged with purple in the middle. There were matching bows on her shoes and reticule and at the collar of her spencer. It was a new outfit tailored to fit her trimmer figure, and as she strolled along the concourse, she was attracting a great deal of male attention.

Genie did not see Sean, for he was assuredly the last soul she expected to encounter that afternoon. She went directly to Mina's side, giving her a hug. "Hello, lambie."

"Hello, Genie," Sean said in a quiet and very tentative voice. "You look fair beautiful."

"Sean?" Genie stiffened perceptively.

"Yes, it's me." He grinned a rather stupid grin, as if he had lost all control of his facial muscles.

"Oh." Genie glanced about the concourse in such a manner that Mina feared she was about to bolt. She had the look of a treed fox, but Mina averted disaster. In a matter of seconds, she took Genie's package, instructed her brother to carry it, and then hooked her arm through Genie's.

"Sean!" Genie said again, and he repeated her name, then told her how beautiful she was in her purple plumed hat.

"We were on our way back to Berkeley Square," Mina fibbed. "We plan to stop in Gunter's for an ice. Won't you join us?"

Sean picked this up eagerly. "Yes, please come." The sincerity in his voice made Mina want to cry, and she noticed that Genie looked as if she might start wailing at any moment.

"Don't start blubbering, Genie Grevey," Sean teased. "Can't take you anywhere if you start spouting like a watering pot."

Genie essayed a nonchalant smile. "Must have been a speck of dust."

"Let me check." He stepped closer to inspect her eyes. "Looks fine to me. Must be gone. So how about it, Genie, will you come with us?"

Mina was nodding her head yes, but Genie did not need any encouragement. She accepted, and the three rode in Sean's hired chaise to Gunter's, where Signor Vitelli found them a table for two in the window and brought a third chair for Mina.

"Swell place," Sean remarked. "Come here a lot, do you?" He addressed this question to his sister, for Genie appeared robbed of all ability to speak. She merely stared at Sean as if he were an apparition.

"A few times." In an attempt to bring Genie into the conversation Mina said, "I've seen London's different faces, thanks to Genie."

"Hmmm," Sean uttered, but he was not really listening. He was gazing quite intently at his lady fair.

"The earl took me on a walking tour of Mayfair," Mina continued, "but Genie showed me the Strand and Covent Garden and the Exeter Exchange."

"Hmmm," he uttered again, still staring at Genie, who was blushing like a schoolgirl. Her hazel eyes were sparkling and a shy smile was turning up at the corners of her mouth.

They needed little help. Soon they were engaged in an intimate conversation that excluded Mina entirely. Tea was served, and they made a brief stab to include her in their conversation; but halfway through, they once again forgot that Mina was there. Indeed, they were so fish-eyed they would not have noticed if the room caught fire.

Oh, how divine it would be if the earl ever favored her with a look such as the one Sean was bestowing on Genie, Mina thought, idly stirring her ice into raspberry soup. How perfectly perfect it would be if the earl held her hand and gazed into her eyes as if she were the most beautiful woman on the face of the earth, as if he might burst apart with wanting and love and tenderness.

"Good afternoon, Miss O'Kieffe." It was Percival Barcroft. "Saw you as I was passing by. Hope you don't mind that I came in?"

"No, not at all, Mr. Barcroft. Allow me to introduce my brother Mr. Sean O'Kieffe and his friend Miss Eugenia Grevey."

"A pleasure. Mr. O'Kieffe. Miss Grevey," said Percival. Then, ascertaining that Mina had become *de trop*, he invited her to join him at the neighboring table which had become available. Mina readily accepted.

"I say, Miss O'Kieffe, I've some splendid news," confided Percival. "Do you recall my mentioning Margaret Hamilton, the young lady in Oxford whose father wouldn't have me? He's changed his mind. He's posting the banns week after next.''

''That's marvelous. My felicitations to you and Miss Hamilton. Wasn't I right? Dreams are worth waiting for. You shall have a seat at Oxford and Miss Hamilton, and you'll make your papa happy at the same time.''

''Yes. You were right, but I can scarcely believe 'tis true. Thank you for your good wishes and friendship, Miss O'Kieffe. You made this Season an enjoyable one.'' In an impulsive move, he reached across the table to lay his hand across hers. ''I hope we'll remain friends.''

''Of course.'' Mina smiled. ''And I trust you and Miss Hamilton will visit me in Kent.'' Out of the corner of her eye, she noticed the earl on the sidewalk outside. He was staring directly at the spot on the wrought-iron table where Mina's hand rested beneath Percival's pale one. For the first time in several days she observed a scowl marking the earl's countenance.

Remembering her lessons about jealousy and flirtation, Mina waited until the earl glanced up. When their eyes met, she nodded, then leaned nearer to Percival and whispered in his ear.

It was a very brief whisper, barely long enough to point out that his cousin Elizabeth, seated on the other side of Gunter's with Sir Thomas, was exchanging flirtatious glances with an exceedingly handsome young lord. When next she looked out the window, the earl was gone.

The earl glanced up from the document he was studying, and an unexpected nervousness assailed him as Mina entered the library. ''To what do I owe this interview?'' he asked.

'' 'Tis a matter of personal concern I wish to discuss with you,'' Mina said, taking two steps towards the desk. She had decided to approach the earl about Catherine and Liam. The May Fair presented the ideal opportunity to broach the issue in a tenable fashion, and she intended to ask him if Liam could attend. If he said yes, Mina reasoned, then it would be simple for Liam to return to Cavendish House for visits with Catherine; from there a normal courtship could ensue.

This interview was all-important, for if she failed there would be scant hope of a second chance. Lately, the earl had been in such a fine mood that Mina did not anticipate failure. Tonight, though, he was different. He appeared very forbidding behind the massive desk. His fingers were laced across his chest and his smile was cool, more like the earl of the orchard stream than the way he had been these past weeks.

"If this isn't a convenient time, I can return later," Mina said, hoping to smooth any ruffled feelings she might have unwittingly aroused.

The seriousness of Mina's voice was not comforting. Its tone indicated that something of vast import was afoot. The earl stood up and concentrated on the bookshelf beyond her shoulder. This was the moment he had been dreading since seeing her with Barcroft at Gunter's. Since then he had been expecting an offer. And an offer from Barcroft would be devastating. The earl had no qualms about turning down von Ruttiger. But he could not be so glib if an offer came from Barcroft. There was genuine affection between the serious young man and Mina, and the earl was loath to stand in the way of Mina's happiness. He did not think he could refuse her if she wanted Barcroft.

Until the moment he had spotted them in the bow window, the earl had thought his plans were progressing well. Daily, his confidence had grown, along with his assurance that Miss O'Kieffe was coming to hold him in better regard and that he would discover the truth at the May Fair. He had been content to wait until the gala, for he readily admitted to cowardice at the prospect of simply telling Miss O'Kieffe of his change of heart. It seemed a safer course to wait and let her come to him. That way he would not risk rejection. Now that course seemed to be in vain. If Barcroft wished to marry Miss O'Kieffe, there would be no chance for the earl at all, and the prospect of losing Mina before he discovered whether she was his forest nymph was unthinkable.

He coughed and then dared to ask, "Coming to tell me to expect another offer for your hand?"

"No. Not an offer," Mina answered, unable to detect the false levity in his question. "This has to do with the ball."

A great weight lifted from his shoulders, and he allowed his gaze to meet hers. "The plans are going smoothly, I trust."

"Yes."

"Then what seems to be the problem?"

" 'Tis not a problem exactly," Mina hedged. "I have a favor to ask." It was her turn to glance away, and she did so, biting her lower lip. She took a deep breath, shifted her weight, and grasped her hands tightly behind her back. Mina's question tumbled out. "Could my brother Liam attend? He's in Town—I know you've seen him—and it would mean a great deal to me and—there's no use denying it—to Catherine as well."

The earl frowned. Preoccupied with his own concerns about Mina, he had not thought overmuch about his sister or O'Kieffe. Of late he had quite forgotten them, but Mina's request brought it all back. It made him realize a few unexpected truths about himself and that episode in Catherine's life. It was not really O'Kieffe or his family background that he had objected to. Verily, it had never been the man who had driven the earl to entertain his ill-conceived revenge in the orchard stream. It had been his sister's reckless betrayal of his authority that had prompted him to forbid her contact with O'Kieffe.

"Are you suggesting that I forget Catherine's betrayal of my authority?" he asked, feeling that he could not yet forgive his sister. His pride was still wounded.

"Noooo." She searched for the correct response. "But I know she's very sorry."

"Sometimes being sorry is not enough," he said slowly, stricken with the realization that this interview was going to be more difficult than he had thought. He and Miss O'Kieffe had long been at odds over their divergent views of marriage and love. And although the earl did not think he shared Miss O'Kieffe's views, he no longer scorned them, nor did he wish them to be a barrier between them. He desperately wanted Miss O'Kieffe to understand what he had done and why. He threaded those long, lean fingers through his hair and, looking Mina straight in the eye, he said, "I'm going to confess something to you, Miss O'Kieffe. Something that I did not realize until this very moment. I used your brother to punish my sister."

There was a deadly pause.

"I don't understand," said Mina.

The earl continued, "It wasn't your brother who caused the trouble between Catherine and myself. We hadn't been getting along before she encountered Liam at the peace celebrations. When Catherine left the schoolroom, I expected a certain mode of conduct from her. 'Twas the same standard I'd set for my other sisters, but Catherine isn't like them. They obeyed, while Catherine defied me at every opportunity. 'Tis unpleasant to admit, but when I forbade Catherine to see your brother, I was punishing, not protecting her."

"If you admit that, then what possible reason could remain to keep them apart?"

"Ah, problems exist nonetheless. First, as I said, sorry is not always enough. Even though Catherine may regret her rebelliousness, that doesn't erase it."

Mina sprang to Catherine's defense. "But I don't think she could help herself, nor that she really ever thought about what she did. You know Catherine."

"Yes, I know Catherine," he admitted. "But knowing Catherine does not automatically forgive her, nor does it temper my anger. I've always considered myself a reasonable and forgiving man. But with Catherine it hasn't been so. The betrayal I've felt as a result of her ill-mannered behavior has festered. Forgiving and forgetting were never choices where she was concerned."

"Oh." Mina could think of nothing else to say. His words made her see that the world was not black and white. She also realized that she had considered the earl from a distinctly personal point of view, a perspective from which she never wondered how he might have felt when Catherine taunted him and went against his wishes. It had never occurred to Mina that the earl might have suffered for it. Now Mina could see that no one was any more to blame than anyone else; wrong had to be shared equally between the earl and Catherine.

"Furthermore," finished the earl, "although my reasons may not have been of the noblest caliber, my logic remains impeccable: ladies should not marry beneath their rank."

"Do you mean that even if Catherine hadn't defied you, you wouldn't have allowed her to see my brother because he isn't of the aristocracy?"

"To be honest, I don't know. At one time my unequivocable reply would have been yes, for I believe if a lady marries a man of lesser social standing, she may suffer. Such a marriage could be devastating: gone would be the acceptance of Society enjoyed since birth; one might even be cut by the *ton*. I wouldn't want that for my sister. But now, I don't know how to answer."

There was such infinite weariness in his voice that Mina was moved to offer him an encouraging smile. Her own soft words were laden with emotion, for her love swelled hopeful at the earl's uncertainty. "I think that you aren't such a poor creature, after all, my lord."

His heart leapt in his chest. Hope suffused his eyes, and his voice took on a husky quality. "Thank you, Miss O'Kieffe." His lips curved into a lopsided grin. Suddenly he felt damned silly, and he quite forgot what he and Miss O'Kieffe had been talking about in the first place.

Softly, she suggested, "Perhaps you might even come to accept that love doesn't need permission to thrive? The proof is in Catherine and Liam. For although you endeavored to quell their affection, it survives nonetheless."

This was undeniable, and the earl shifted his glance to the floor to hide his mounting confusion. This was, he recognized, a turning point of monumental significance in his life. Mina's question was a test of his newfound belief in love. Whatever he said would have a profound effect on his future. Grandmère had been correct when she called him a dolt, and he would be a hypocrite, too, if he denied Mina's request. Zounds! He had been a fool to believe that he could disallow a relationship between Catherine and Liam. For he had neither the right to allow, nor the power to control, the course of love.

"Well?" Mina prodded and cast him an irresistible elfin-sweet smile. "My brother will neither disgrace nor hurt your sister. He's an honorable man who wants nothing more than to manage the estates at Thornhill Park and provide a home for Catherine. He loves her very much. Won't you let him come to the May Fair, please?"

"Yes," came the only answer he could give in good conscience.

"Oh, thank you," Mina cried, her face alight with pleasure.

"With one provision," the earl interrupted her ebullient thanks. "Liam may attend the gala and he may even see Catherine in the future, pending my approval of their en-counters, but there must be no secret meetings. You must remind Catherine; I'll not tolerate deception. I'm quite in earnest. The consequences would be dire, I assure you."

For an instant Mina's throat was dry. She swallowed hard and spoke in sort of a squeak. "Of course, I agree. No secret meetings. And I'll convey your wishes to Catherine. She'll be as thrilled as I that Liam can attend." With that, Mina lifted her skirts to dash upstairs and spread the good news.

The earl grinned like a Cheshire cat. He had put that radiant smile on her face and was extremely pleased. Except for a few bumpy moments, his plans were back on course. In fact, Miss O'Kieffe and he were not so different any-more, he decided as he hummed a few bars of "Cherry Ripe." He was looking forward to the May Fair, especially the costumes. His grin widened as he thought about those costumes. The only thing he wished was that he might be a spider on the wall in Mina's chamber when she received her box from Madame Rabelais.

Later that evening Mina had even more cause to rejoice. Shortly before retiring, an envelope was delivered to Cavendish House. It was addressed to Mina, and inside was a note from Genie.

"Thank you, lambie," Genie had written. "Sean and I will always remember how you helped us the other day. He was right. I would have shut the door in his face if he'd come to Adelphi Terrace. And I'd probably have run off if you hadn't grabbed my arm in the Arcade. Thank you. What a wonderful sister you'll be! Yes, my dreams of a family and home of my own are coming true. Sean and I are off to Gretna Green. We couldn't wait for a family wedding and hope you'll forgive us for not including you. I'll be thinking of you when Sean slips the ring on my finger. Fondly, Genie."

At the bottom was scrawled in Sean's heavy hand, "I never would have believed it myself. You've helped make a miracle. Your brother, Sean."

Mina sniffled a little, read the letter twice more, and smiled. It gave her a good feeling to know that Genie and Sean had found each other and their love would be fulfilled. Genie would bring boundless happiness to Thornhill Park, and perhaps next summer there would be a baby with hazel eyes playing in the field of daffodils beside the lake. She fell asleep thinking of all the little copper-haired children Sean and Genie's love would bring to the old manor house.

The next morning when Jenny entered Mina's bedchamber, she carried a large green-and-gold-striped box. The attached card indicated it was from Madame Rabelais, and Mina tore off the twine to look inside. When she lifted off the tissue paper to reveal the first costume, she experienced a stab of disappointment. It was an elaborate shepherdess outfit. Granted, the bright yellow would be lovely on her, but like Catherine, Mina wanted to wear something special. Reluctantly, she peered beneath the next layer of tissue, and when she saw the second costume she gasped. There, nestled at the bottom of the box, was a near identical copy of the gossamer green gown.

Stroking the layered skirt, she wondered what this meant. Was it possible that the earl had so admired the woman from

Vauxhall that the notion of dressing Mina in the same costume was amusing to him? Perhaps this meant that the earl wanted Mina to reveal herself to him? Or was this a ruse to entrap Mina and punish her for the masquerade? He had said that he loathed deception; was he laying a trap?

Mina was far too optimistic to dwell on the dismal prospects. She preferred to look on the sunny side, and so she dismissed the worst of her fears. This dress was not a trap, nor was it the earl's idea of a joke. She was left with only the best prospect: the possibility that the earl loved her. Mina decided that he suspected she was the woman in green, and clearly he was reluctant simply to ask her about it. That much made sense. What did not make sense was why he had orchestrated such an elaborate ruse when it would have been easier to confront her.

Mina believed that a man who loved a woman gave that woman choices. He did not force her hand or corner her into a situation that might not be to her liking. And that was why the earl did not confront Mina. He was giving her the chance to make a choice: whether or not to reveal herself to him.

The green gown was the most thoroughly romantic notion Mina had ever imagined. It was all the proof she needed of the earl's love. Only a man in love could conceive such a plan, and her heart swelled at the knowledge of how he had been transformed these past weeks. His kinder, gentler nature was triumphing over his darker self; the stern, cold-faced man was becoming a part of the past.

Unhesitatingly, she would wear the green gown, for she did not doubt the direction of the earl's heart, and to make certain that he did not misunderstand her declaration, she would carry a green domino. She wanted no mistaking the direction of her heart.

Chapter Thirteen

Hughes stood sentinel outside Cavendish House as carriages circled Berkeley Square and lined up down Mount Street to discharge passengers. Lights blazed from the top to the bottom of the mansion. Inside, footmen wearing formal livery ushered guests through the rotunda, maids scurried between the cloakrooms set aside for ladies and gentlemen, and a veritable army of second cooks garnished platters of food destined for refreshment tables. The night of Mina's May Fair had arrived, and upstairs she was readying for the ball.

During the past twenty-four hours, butterflies had taken up residence in her stomach. The tiny creatures batted their wings in a renewed frenzy as she slipped on the green gown. She took a deep breath, and while Jenny began doing up the buttons, Mina gazed at her reflection in the full-length pier glass. The girl who stared back was wide-eyed with anticipation, and there was a natural flush in her cheeks. Her hair had been brushed four hundred strokes; shining tendrils tumbled over her ears. In the glass there was no hint of the little wings fluttering madly within her. She radiated confidence and a certainty that the future held naught but good.

Everything was perfect. Sean and Genie were man and wife, Liam was going to court Catherine in a proper fashion, and her dreams would come true. Yes, it was going to be perfectly perfect.

At the sound of crinolines swishing into the room Mina turned. She smiled at Catherine, who was stunning in a regal costume of scarlet velveteen. Black hair arranged in short ringlets and powdered as was fashionable eighty years before, she wore a decorative beauty patch on her right cheek.

"You look ever so lovely," said Mina. Jenny finished fastening the tiny buttons that ran up the back of the gown, and Mina stepped into the center of the room. "I'm so glad you picked that costume instead of being Joan of Arc. Who would want to dress up like a martyr? Whatever was your brother thinking? 'Tis far merrier as you are. Why, you look like a queen."

"Gracious!" Catherine ignored the fulsome compliment. She cried, "You're wearing the sprite costume!"

"I am, aren't I?" was Mina's composed rejoinder.

"No wonder you wouldn't tell me what you were going to wear! I can't believe it. Surely that wasn't one of the costumes Compton consigned from Madame Rabelais!"

"It isn't too bold, is it? Too revealing?" asked Mina. She glanced back at the mirror and adjusted the scooped bodice.

"No, 'tis far more modest than the real one. Not half as décolleté, and the fabric is heavier. You look positively as lovely as you did in the other, but that's not the point. How can you be so calm? Egad, if you were worried about the domino, what do you think Compton will do when he sees you in that!" It never occurred to Catherine that her brother might have given her the costume on purpose.

"Oh, don't fret," Mina said mysteriously. "I'm quite certain I should wear it. In truth, I was hoping it might elicit a proposal," she said with a confident grin.

Catherine was taken aback. There could be only one explanation. "Have you been spending time with my brother all this while?"

"No," replied Mina.

"Then I don't understand."

Mina merely smiled.

Catherine shook her head. "Can't say I'd be so brave. But this is your party." Eager to join Liam, she dismissed her curiosity and scurried towards the door. She called over her shoulder, "See you downstairs."

Before going downstairs Mina went to Nanny's room, where the elderly woman was seated on the balcony, observing the proceedings in the garden. An orange sun was dipping below the horizon, the sky was darkening, and footmen were lighting paper lanterns in the trees and along the walkways. The terrace was awash with flowers, and music echoed from the ballroom.

"You're a lovely sight, Miss Mina. Quite as lovely as your mama ever looked." Her wrinkled old face brightened.

"Thank you, Nanny dearest. Won't you join the party?"

"Can see the goings-on perfectly well from here. Don't need to get crushed like a peppercorn. Flat as a tuppence I'd be if I ventured down there, surely to be squashed between a bosky highwayman and a giggling shepherdess. Not my idea of a ball. Whatever happened to old-fashioned come-outs?" She shook her head. "Would like some destiny cake."

"I'll have Hughes send some up," Mina promised. "With a spot of sherry. You'd like a spot of sherry, wouldn't you, Nanny dearest?"

"Hmmm. Very kind of you." Nanny rested her head against the back of the chair, and Mina got a cushion to prop behind her. "Liam's a sight," she remarked, and Mina glanced below.

Catherine and Liam was standing on the terrace. He was dressed as a Cavalier in a short-waisted doublet, a collar of rich Vandyke lace at his throat, and his lady in red velvet looked as if she too had stepped out of King Charles's court.

The old woman continued, "All my chickens going to roost. Sean and his Genie. Liam and Catherine. Maybe next year it shall be time for the twins. And you. Oh, yes, you can't fool me, Miss Mina. You'll be betrothed before the hops are harvested in Kent." The words faded into the gathering night sky. She yawned and closed her eyes.

Zounds! Where was the girl?

In the rotunda the earl stopped pacing between the orange trees and glanced up the circular staircase. It had been twenty minutes since Catherine bounced down the stairs and said Mina was behind her. What was going on up there? He balled his hand into a fist and attempted to shove it in a pocket that did not exist. His hand rubbed against the metallic weave of chain mail.

Would she wear the green dress? And what if she didn't? He had not considered that possibility. He had been so sure that she was the enchanting girl from Vauxhall. So sure that she would reveal herself, so sure that she must harbor the same love for him as he cherished for her. He did not question the how and why of it. His heart ruled his senses, and he concentrated only on what he wished to be true.

He removed his helmet, held it beneath an arm to thread trembling fingers through his hair. When he looked up, he saw Mina. She was a vision in green. A smile curved her rosebud lips, and a green domino was dangling from one hand. Even her hair was as he remembered from Vauxhall; the gold-burnished curls were caught at the nape of her neck.

At the sight awaiting her in the rotunda Mina's heart fluttered wildly. Everything was going to be perfectly perfect. Tears misted her eyes. She gripped the banister and blinked twice to clear her view. It was a sight she would always cherish in the soul of her heart. The earl was dressed as the knight of his boyhood daydream.

"Good evening, my lord," she said when she reached the bottom step.

His response came huskily, "Not 'my lord.' 'Tis Compton. Say it. I wish to hear you say my Christian name."

"Compton," she whispered, hearing her voice peculiarly muffled by the thumping of her heart. "You look very dashing this evening, sir knight."

"And you, darling forest nymph, are magnificent." His silky words fell on her like an intimate caress.

"You like my costume?" She flirted, tilting her head to the side and peering at him from beneath her lashes.

"I wouldn't have made any other choice. 'Tis perfect." His eyes raked over her heatedly, moving from her face to her creamy shoulders and then back up. Their gazes fused. They saw only each other. Forgotten were their interested onlookers, the guests entering Cavendish House and servitors who gawked from behind marble pilasters. He stepped forward, placed his hands on her shoulders, and drew her to him. He kissed her tenderly, once on the forehead, then on the tip of her nose.

"I hope that before the night is out we shall speak in private." There was promise in that, and Mina answered with a misty smile, a look so laden with love that the earl experienced a stab of fierce longing. For an instant he wanted to forget propriety, to take her in his arms and kiss her soundly, fully on those inviting lips. Instead he took a deep breath and returned her smile with a wobbly one of his own. Then, as if it were the most natural thing in the world, he slipped his arm about Mina's waist, and they walked to the balcony where the countess was awaiting them.

"You look lovely, my dear. Come meet some of your guests," the countess, resplendent in silver as Marie Antoinette, welcomed Mina. Then she turned to her grandson and, observing the adoration that glazed his face, grinned delightedly. If she was not mistaken, tonight her hopes for Mina and Compton would reach fruition.

During the next twenty minutes, Mina and the earl remained by the countess's side to receive Mina's guests. Percival Barcroft and Sir Thomas were there, as were Lady Jersey and several other Almack's hostesses. Afterwards the countess and Compton escorted Mina to the ballroom. Catherine was dancing with Liam, and when the music stopped, they spotted Mina and her companions. Aglow with happiness, Catherine fairly dragged Liam towards them. There was caution, however, in Liam's eyes. The earl too held back.

Mina glanced between her brother and Compton. She saw a muscle in Compton's jaw twitch; Liam's hand clenched at his side. Neither man spoke. Catherine, tittering to her grandmother about the roundabout, was oblivious to the tension. The older woman held her breath, eyes darting between the players.

"It's good to see you, Liam," said Mina.

"Evening, puss," he responded, and taking in the sight of her green outfit, he gave a conspiratorial wink.

Her eyes widened. Quickly, she glanced to the right to see if Compton had noticed this, but it was impossible to tell what was on his mind when he extended his hand to Liam.

"Good evening, O'Kieffe," was his reserved greeting.

"Evening, Brierly. Generous of you to include me in the

festivities. Can't thank you enough for all you've done for my sister.''

"Our pleasure.'' Warmth infused this statement. Then he looked at his own sister and remarked, ''A Cavalier's lady. Glad you chose that costume. Thought scarlet would become you, Catherine, but wasn't sure whether you'd rather have been Joan of Arc. O'Kieffe, mind if I dance with my sister?'' Grinning broadly, he excused himself. ''Until later,'' he whispered to Mina.

Liam, in turn, asked *his* sister to dance. ''How about it, puss?'' He winked again.

She wanted to stomp her foot and tell him to stop winking. This was not a prank. Her heart, her future, her very life were at stake, and she did not want anything to ruin her progress with Compton. What would he think if he supected Liam was making light of him? She knew Compton had been wounded by Catherine's deception, and she did not want to hurt him in any way. ''Stop that right now!'' she hissed as she accepted his arm.

''Got a lot of nerve, puss,'' he said. ''Catherine told me you were wearing a sprite costume, but I thought she was bamming. The earl will put two and two together and realize you're the woman he met at Vauxhall!''

She frowned. ''You know about that?''

With a wry grin, he said, ''My darling angel is hardly the soul of discretion.''

''What else did Catherine tell you?''

''Likely all of it, but then I usually listen to only half of what she says.'' His attempt to soften Mina's scowl failed. He added, ''Well, how about it? What do you plan to do when the august Earl of Brierly realizes who you are?''

''He already has. In fact, this costume was his idea.''

''Oh ho, you don't say? Something in the wind?''

''I hope as much,'' she confessed. ''Oh, Liam, I know you'll think me mad, but I love him dearly and had quite despaired of ever winning his love. There were hints here and there: a thawing of his icy demeanor, his assent when I asked if you might attend tonight. But I was never certain. Then the box from Madame Rabelais arrived, and I knew

I'd been given a chance to declare myself. He's done so himself. His costume means something very special.''

''Can't say this ain't a great surprise. Catherine hinted something was up, but I thought 'twas nothing more than silliness. Never can tell with her, you know.''

'' 'Tis no silliness,'' was all that Mina could say before the dance steps separated them. While she was partnered with Major MacFarland, Liam studied her intently. Then she parted from the major and returned to Liam's side.

He asked, ''The earl's made an offer?''

''Not yet.''

''If it don't happen, come to me, puss. I'll set him straight. If this is what you want, you'll have it. I'll see to that.''

''No! No, thank you. I know you mean well, but I don't want anyone interfering. Can you understand?'' She wrinkled her nose at her brother, and he laughed.

''Perfectly. We'd start with a round of fisticuffs and no telling what muddle might evolve. I shan't interfere, but you must promise to invite me to the wedding.''

''I promise.''

''Excellent.''

They separated once more and the dance ended.

The evening passed in a whirl. Mina danced until she thought she might drop, rode the roundabout and swings, had her fortune told by a gypsy—who insisted a tall, dark stranger loomed in her future—and by midnight she was exhausted. Thus she was delighted when Percival Barcroft asked her simply to sit with him. He brought her a plate of delicacies, and they rested on a marble bench in the rose garden. A yew hedge sheltered them from the lively crowd gathered about the rides. It was quiet and private and a welcome relief from the party.

''It's ever so nice to get away for a few moments. Thank you, Mr. Barcroft.''

''Please call me Percival. If you and I and my Margaret are to be friends, we can hardly go about so formally.''

On the other side of the bushes, the earl was watching the

riders. Beside him the countess tilted backwards a tad to better listen to the couple behind her.

"And you must call me Mina." After a bite of curried beef, she queried, "How is Miss Hamil—I mean, how is Margaret?"

"Very well, thank you. Quite busy these days with wedding preparations. I plan to leave soon to join her. We'll be married at the university, first week in September. Might you join us? My mother and father would be pleased to have you at Hallcroft Manor as their guest."

On the other side of the hedge the roundabout halted. The riders disembarked and drifted towards the refreshment tables for champagne punch and destiny cake. The crowd quieted. Mina's lilting brogue floated over the shrubbery.

"An excellent notion, Percival; of course I'll be there. I wouldn't miss it for the world. Thank you for asking me."

The earl turned towards the hedge; a tightening in his jaw indicated he heard Mina's every word.

"Your thanks are misplaced. 'Tis I who must thank you, Mina," said Barcroft. The earl peered between the leaves. He watched the other gentleman raise Mina's hand to plant a solemn kiss upon it. "It will be a marriage made in heaven," finished the pale young man.

It could not be possible. Were Mina and Barcroft talking of marriage? Perhaps the earl had misunderstood the gist of what Barcroft was saying. Or, worse yet, perhaps he had misunderstood why Mina had worn the green gown. Confusion in his expression, the earl met his grandmother's keen gaze.

"Compton, did you hear that? I believe that's Miss O'Kieffe with Barcroft," said the countess.

"If you're thinking what I am, Grandmère, let me hasten to say that no good comes of eavesdropping. It's likely we've misunderstood."

"Like to believe that, would you?" she needled. "Still think that he's not right for her?"

"Yes."

"Going to do something about it?"

"Yes," was his firm response. She was his forest nymph, by damn, and no one, especially not Percival Barcroft, was going to have her.

* * *

It was three in the morning before the last of the guests had left. Mina and Compton stood together on the terrace outside the library. The light from paper lanterns bathed her in golden warmth. Shyly, she smiled. Compton extended his hand, and without hesitation she gave him hers. Ripples of delight danced from his fingertips into hers; they raced up her arm. For a moment they remained silent, looking self-consciously at each other. They had come this far, but they were new to love and did not quite know what to say.

Finally, she said, "Thank you. I'll remember this night for eternity. But why, Compton? Why did you do this for me?"

The reason was a simple one. He loved her and would do anything to make her happy. But, foolish though it might be, he could not say it straight out. He was intensely vulnerable and having overheard her and Barcroft, he was more unsure than ever. He felt hurt, his emotions exposed like a raw wound onto which salt was about to be poured. He may have gotten the hang of the frivolous part of love, but he was not accustomed to the constant turmoil in his heart, the uncertainty and ever-hovering threat of rejection. What had been happening in the garden? He had to know before he bared his soul to her.

On a quick breath, he spoke, "Saw you with Barcroft. Nothing between you, is there?" It was a clumsy, ill-phrased question. What he really meant to ask was "Do you plan to marry Barcroft?"

"Our relationship is as it's always been, and as I expect it shall be for many years to come."

Zounds! What did that mean? His raised his free hand and drew a slender finger across his jaw. "Well?" he asked.

"Well, what?"

He cleared his throat and started again. "What I really meant to ask, Miss O'Kieffe . . . Mina . . ." His voice lightened to a caress when he said her name. "What I really meant to ask is . . ." He paused for another breath. This was damned harder than he had thought it would be.

"Yes?" Her emerald eyes warmed with knowing affection. It was painfully clear that Compton's poise had suffered a blow of some kind. The sight of him grasping for words and shifting his weight from foot to foot reminded her of Sean. "Go on, Compton. You were about to say—" she encouraged and boldly gave his hand a slight squeeze.

At that instant, Catherine exited the house. She was spinning whimsically about the balcony, skirts rising like clouds. Her voice was exceedingly merry, and she fairly sang, "This was a glorious night. A marvelous night."

She skipped gay circles about them while Compton tapped his foot on the stone, looking terribly impatient and more than a little angry at his sister's interruption. Two more skips and she bounded up to Mina to give her a hug.

"Oh, thank you for finally asking him. I know you promised from the start you'd do anything to make him see your way, and sometimes I thought it might never happen. I should have trusted you. You're a wonderful friend. Everything is exactly as you said it would be." Turning to her brother, she added, "Good thing Mina talked you into letting Liam come. 'Twas dreadful confining our visits to Lane's."

Compton's face sobered; he dropped Mina's hand and cast his sister such a quelling look that she froze with dread. Mina saw this and recoiled.

"Have you been defying me all along?" Bitterness sharpened his question. All he could think was that Catherine was up to her old tricks—she had played him for a fool. It did not occur to the earl that Mina's masquerade also constituted a deception. Nor that he was about to repeat the same mistake as before: to let his anger and pride rule his reaction to his skittlebrained sibling. All he could think about was his blasted sister haring off on some other escapade.

Catherine blanched. She mumbled something incoherent in a voice so tiny that he could not catch it. Sharply, he instructed her to speak up. Her face was white as she hastened to reply, "It was not precisely like that."

"Not precisely like what? The answer is either yes or no. Have you been sneaking about behind my back? That's the long and the short of it it. Isn't it?"

Both girls were growing alarmed by the vehemence in his

voice. Neither could formulate a response before he went on with increasing anger.

"Have you fallen so low, Catherine? A Cavendish reduced to conducting flirtations on the sly?" he goaded, thinking of little else save the wound that Catherine had reopened. "It appears I trusted you for naught, Catherine. And you, Mina? Have I misplaced my trust in you as well?"

Mina's voice faltered. She understood the depth of his reaction—his pride had been wounded anew. And she recognized that same tremble of trepidation she had experienced when he first said he would not tolerate deception.

"You needn't scruple to deny it," he said to Catherine through tight lips. "I see quite clearly what's been going on. Mina, excuse us, please. I'd like to speak privately with my sister."

"Certainly." Mina forced the word to her lips. A cold lump settled over her heart at the knowledge of what had been destroyed in a few easy words. The differences between herself and the earl had been great, and it seemed a miracle that the chasm had been spanned at all. A fragile bond of trust and understanding had only begun to grow between them, and now it was destroyed. *Oh, Catherine, you fool. What have you done*? she wondered, realizing in the next thought that she could not blame Catherine. The secret meetings between Liam and Catherine had been wrong, and, undeniably, Mina had to share the blame. She had been girlish and foolish and yes, far too romantic for her own good or Catherine's. Nanny was right. One could not have storybook endings; real life was not that easy.

Chapter
Fourteen

"He ordered me to return to Brierly," Catherine said between sniffles. "He's positively enraged. Worse than before. He's actually going to White's to see if my name's in the books!"

"Hmmm," murmured Mina. She was thinking about everything that had happened last night. Everything that had gone wrong. It boiled down to one thing. Deception. And in Mina's case she had been deceiving herself with the notion that the earl might change.

How wrong she had been. Mina and the earl were still at square one in the stream at Brierly. Only one thing had altered. One dreadful, horrible, and implausible thing had happened to unbalance the equation. She was in love with Compton. And despite the changes that she thought she had seen in him—his willingness to please her, to give her the May Fair and enact his daydream—he had not changed.

Obedience, duty, responsibility, and reputation mattered most. He had not changed enough to shrug indulgently at the discovery of Catherine's and Liam's ongoing secret romance.

Too late, Mina realized the folly of her plan to aid Catherine. She should have known that deception would come to no good. She should have known how hurt and angry any man would be to learn his family had been acting behind his back. Most important, she should have been honest with the earl. But she had not been, and her chance for happiness was gone. It was over and done. She would, however, do the right thing this time. She would apologize to Compton. That was the least she could do, but she did not think it would make any difference.

She merely wished, on a long, sad sigh, that things might have turned out otherwise. Last night they had been so close. She was certain of the look in his eyes when she called him by his Christian name, so certain of the words he was about to speak when they stood on the terrace those final moments before the dream had shattered.

"Can you ever forgive me?" Catherine implored.

"There's nothing to forgive. You didn't intend for this to happen," Mina answered sadly. "We're all to blame in some way. You, me, and Compton. Perhaps love between Compton and myself wasn't meant to be. Better to discover that now rather than later." Her words sounded very brave, but the tears in her eyes and the pinched expression about her mouth gave away her true feelings. She was not so brave or stoic as it would seem. She was devastated and frightened by the decades of loneliness that spanned ahead of her. Her love for Compton was true. It would be her only love, a lasting love, a love never to be fulfilled.

"What will you do? Will you come back to Kent with me?" asked Catherine.

Mina gave an indifferent shrug. "Whatever reason could there be to remain here? I vowed to help you and Liam. Having failed, I think I'd like to go home."

Likewise Catherine remembered her promise to Mina on the journey to London. "And I vowed to help you find a beau." Silence filled the space between them. Footsteps echoed in the corridor. "I'm sorry, Mina. Truly sorry."

Jenny entered the bedchamber and went to work closing trunks and gathering up bandboxes. She was followed by several footmen, who began to carry the luggage out of the room.

Next the earl appeared at the door. His jaw muscle flexed erratically, but Mina did not observe his discomfort, for she resolutely directed her gaze at a needlepoint pillow. They were speaking, Catherine and Compton, but Mina did not hear them. She was thinking very hard. This was her chance, perhaps her only chance, to apologize. Compton was here, and she could not let him leave without saying what had to be said. She forced herself to look up from the pillow just as Compton concluded.

"I want no further arguments. I've said you'll return to Brierly, and you'll do so first thing in the morning." He pivoted, and his eyes traveled over Mina, but he did not acknowledge her, merely proceeded through the door.

Mina took a deep breath and followed him into the corridor. "Please wait, my lord. I've something I must say to you."

Her voice stopped him cold. He clenched his fist at the hope that quickened within him and steeled himself to face Mina. He had wanted to avoid her until matters with Catherine were settled and his anger abated, for he did not want to say something he might regret. Thoughts in turmoil, he slowly turned to her.

"Yes?" There was not a trace of encouragement in his voice. He held himself in check, cool and aloof as he had been that first day in the orchard stream. But inside he was seething with emotions. Disappointment. Vulnerability. Anger. Hurt. Again he felt betrayed. This time, though, it was not Catherine's fault. His dreams had betrayed him. He had dared to dream of a future with Mina, and where had it gotten him? Nowhere, or so it appeared. "What is it? I'm off to my club."

"I wish to apologize."

His eyes widened and then narrowed. He stared intently at her pale, upturned face. "An apology is not always enough. It doesn't erase what's been done. You *do* recall our conversation in the library, don't you, Miss O'Kieffe?"

"Yes, and I know how terribly wrong and blind and utterly childish I've been. I should have told you what we'd been doing. We were wrong, and I, for one, shall never be so foolish again. And I'll do my utmost to make certain Catherine understands the reason for your anger." Was that a gentling about his eyes? Had he relaxed? Had he even understood? wondered Mina, stricken by the fact that Compton gave not the slightest sign he cared. In desperation, she continued, "She doesn't understand your feelings in this—

which is unfortunate. But I do. And, if nothing else ever passes between us, I hope you'll believe I never intended to affront you. And I pray you'll not allow this incident to color your perspective in the future.''

The earl was stunned. He did not know what to say. There was a positively awkward burning sensation in his throat. Damned if he didn't feel like crying. What was he to do? This was too much for him to consider. He knew that he could forgive Mina. She had proven by her very words that she understood him, that she cared for him and was no flighty girl. She was a woman, with a woman's sensibilities. But he was uncertain whether he could ever expose his inner emotions to her. He needed time to think and so he said, ''Should you wish to talk when I return from my club, I'll be at your disposal, Miss O'Kieffe.''

That was proof enough that Compton no longer cared. Tears coursed down Mina's cheeks as she watched his retreating back. His love, if it had ever existed, was not true enough. He had no further interest in her. His club was more important.

On returning to the bedchamber, Mina surrendered to wrenching sobs, and Catherine rushed forward to embrace her friend. They looked like lost kittens, near drowned in the river by a rotten lad and pulled from a sinking burlap bag by a fisherman. Faces moist with tears, eyes and noses reddened, and their hair rumpled, they were not a pretty sight, but a touching one for the manner in which they comforted each other. Arms wrapped about each other, they sat in the embrasure that overlooked the garden.

''When we get back to Kent, Liam and I plan to leave England,'' Catherine confessed quietly. ''We talked about this in Bath and decided that if Compton didn't allow us to marry in England we'd go to America, to Philadelphia or Boston, perhaps.''

''Oh, no! Don't do anything rash, I beg of you. I couldn't bear to lose both you and Liam. When would I ever see you again?'' implored Mina.

''It's not so far away. You and Liam have often told me how Sean and the twins travel freely across the Atlantic.

Besides, there's another reason why we'll leave. I don't think Compton is really upset with you, Mina. He's angry, but not so angry he'll forget his true affections. Liam and I stand in your way. If we're gone, there'll be no reason why Compton can't marry you.''

''Oh, Catherine,'' Mina whispered ever so sadly. She was deeply moved. ''I wish it were that simple. You and Liam don't stand in our way.'' She raised a trembling hand affectionately to brush a strand of hair from Catherine's eyes. ''Just now I apologized, but he didn't utter a word of acceptance. He dismissed me. I don't know if he even heard what I said.''

For once Catherine was speechless.

Silently, they watched the scene in the garden below. A crew of footmen removed the last of the May Fair refreshment tables. The pretty orange trees were carried out the gate to wagons which would transport them back to Brierly. Pieces of the disassembled roundabout were stacked in three piles beside the wall. Soon all vestiges of Mina's daydream would be gone.

''Too much sun in here,'' Nanny grumbled.

The dowager countess looked up from the gold inlaid escritoire. '' 'Tis the way I prefer it, Miss Saltmarsh.'' The countess did not desire company at this precise moment. There were pressing matters to which she must attend, and she could not afford distractions. In a distant but nonetheless polite tone, she said, ''There's a pot of tea on the caddy, if you care to enjoy some. But don't close the curtains, if you please.''

Nanny grumbled, adjusted the mobcap that was sliding down the right side of her head, and walked over to inspect the tea tray. She selected a scone and took a seat on the settee nearest the writing table.

''Got themselves in a pack of trouble,'' she said between bites. ''And didn't I warn them!''

''Yes, you did, indeed,'' the countess answered. She turned back to the blank piece of paper before her. On it she drew four circles and put one of the following names into each: Catherine, Mina, Liam, Compton. From Mina to

Compton she drew an arrow, and over the arrow she drew a large question mark.

"Attending to correspondence?" Nanny muttered something about Lady Elaine's stationer on Bond Street, then yawned and closed her eyes for a catnap.

The countess cast a thankful gaze heavenward. *Silence at last,* she thought, turning to the business at hand.

Beneath her breath she whispered, "What a muddle they've made of the simplest matter. Never seen such a catastrophe. I shall simply have to set it straight. *Alors,* 'tis what I should have done in the first place!" She considered the problem some more, glancing alternately between the names in the circles and out the window at the vestiges of the May Fair. She tapped her fingers on the leather-topped table and took out another piece of paper, two quills, a bottle of black ink, and a bottle of brown ink.

"Dear Compton," she began to compose aloud. "Goodbye. I have decided to . . ."

Oh no, that wouldn't do at all. Not the right approach. Mina would not write a letter to Compton, the countess was certain of that. She concentrated. She had to formulate an alternative ploy. What would make Compton follow Mina anywhere she might go and demand that she marry him immediately?

Then she had the answer and commenced to pen a note in the brown ink. She wrote very carefully, very legibly, making certain that each letter was rigid and upright, as her own hand was recognizable by its impossible slant to the right. Next, using the black ink, she wrote a second note in large circular cursive, to which she added an assortment of feminine flourishes at the end of each word. A third letter was addressed to Charles Boswell, the curate in Tilbury, a small village east of London where the Thames widened to meet the sea; a fourth and last letter was penned, in her own hand, to the bishop.

When she was done, she reread the missives and sanded them. Once they were dry, she sealed one in the envelope on which she wrote "Mina." The second letter did not go into an envelope. It was merely folded and unfolded a number of

times, lending it the appearance of having been read. The
countess put that letter in the top drawer of the escritoire,
which she locked with a tiny key. The envelope addressed to
Mina was discreetly pushed up the sleeve of her gown.
Finally, the third letter was dispatched posthaste to Reverend
Boswell, as was the bishop's letter, into which she placed
two one hundred pound notes.

By seven o'clock the next morning, the countess had
finished her toilette. She entered Catherine's bedchamber,
roused an extremely grumpy girl, and told her that she
might say a final good-bye to Liam. He would be at
Dawson's in an hour. Catherine sprang from her bed and
began to dress.

It was approaching seven-thirty when the countess entered
Mina's room quiet as a churchmouse and placed the envelope on the dressing table where Mina would be bound to
see it first thing.

Then she repaired to the morning parlor, where she sat
down at the writing table. She summoned Jenny.

"Miss Mina has asked that you deliver a message to her
brother Mr. Liam O'Kieffe at his lodgings in Knightsbridge.
She wishes to see him straightaway."

Jenny was a tad perplexed that the countess and not Mina
would relay such a message to her, but she executed a
curtsy. "Yes, ma'am," she said and went out the door on
her mission.

Then the countess ordered a hired chaise sent round to the
front door. Next she unlocked the desk drawer, retrieved the
twice-folded letter, and proceeded to the dining room.

As she passed through the rotunda, she spotted a girl with
golden brown curls dashing out the front door, and she
smiled.

The scheme had been launched.

Chapter
Fifteen

As the carriage wheels rolled over cobblestone streets, Mina anxiously glanced out the window. The coachman followed the Thames out of London, passing the West India Docks on the Isle of Dogs, then Blackwell and the East India Docks. They went past glimpses of a widening river on the right, the sky composed of rigging and masts, and although Mina mused for a fleeting instant about the cotton, rice, tea, and spices those three-masted ships brought upriver, her thoughts quickly returned to the letter she had found on her dressing table. As the city disappeared behind the carriage, she reread it.

"My Dearest Friend, I hope you'll not be too angry with me, but Liam and I couldn't bear another separation. He has obtained a special license, and we shall be married this noon. Of a certainty you'll not approve, but I hope you'll find it in your heart to join us in Tilbury for the ceremony. A carriage has been hired and will be waiting outside the house for your convenience. It will deliver you to the Tilbury coaching inn. Wait for us in the private parlor. Please come. With All My Love and Sisterly Affection, Catherine."

Egad! She was doing it again, absconding with Liam and perhaps even planning to board a boat for America this very day! Mina's reactions were ambivalent. On the one hand, she believed this was no way to start a marriage—in open defiance of one's brother, as Catherine was determined to do. Mina did not want them to marry in such a cloak-and-dagger style, but she could not naysay their plans. There was nothing she could say or do, short of sending a message to the earl—and she certainly would never betray her own brother in that fashion, no matter how wrong he might be.

On the other hand, although this marriage made her angry, it also made her glad. It did not make the slightest bit of sense that she could feel good and bad at once, but she did. She leaned back against the musty cushions of the rented chaise and closed her eyes. At least one ounce of joy might survive this debacle; this day in Tilbury would be the one bright memory out of her first and only Season. She would watch Catherine and Liam launched into matrimony, and through the years ahead she would cling to the memory of their happiness. With or without Mina, a wedding was going to take place, and she wanted to be there. She hoped she would reach Tilbury in time.

"Jenkins, I don't see the black-currant preserves any-where on the table, and my grandson is prodigious fond of black currants. Please check with Cook," the countess instructed the footman, who then left the dining room in the direction of the kitchen.

There was no time to spare.

The countess hurried to the sideboard, where she prepared a second plate. She returned to the table, set the plate at her place, and put her plate of half-eaten food at the place next to the earl's. She exchanged her empty cup of chocolate for the clean cup at this place, ripped a croissant in two, and laid a piece on the empty plate. Lastly, she set the letter that had been locked in the escritoire between the mock setting and the earl's before returning to her chair.

The earl entered the dining room at the same time Jenkins returned from the kitchen with black-currant preserves.

"Good morning, Grandmère." Compton crossed the room and gave his grandmother a kiss on the forehead.

"Hmmph," she muttered. "Good morning, yourself."

"Mad at me, are you? Well, what was I to do?" He strolled to his seat.

No response was forthcoming from the countess. She

sipped at the fresh cup of chocolate and pretended to concentrate on the morning news. In truth, she was peering from beneath half-lowered lids at her grandson as he peeled an orange.

He finished the fruit and wiped his sticky fingers on a napkin, then glanced down the table towards his grandmother, his eyes passing over the empty place where someone, Mina likely, had already eaten. Grandmère was reading the paper, clearly in high dudgeon that he intended to send Catherine back to Brierly this morning. *Let her stew,* he decided. There was no point in trying to reason with her, for she would only argue, he was certain.

His glance went back to the empty seat, and he wondered what Mina was doing. He intended to search her out this morning. He realized how curt he had been with her. She should never have suffered the backlash of his ire at Catherine, and he should not have been such a coward. He would find her, accept her apology, tender his own, and then propose.

Coming out of this meditation, his eyes caught sight of a piece of paper. It was lying next to Mina's place, but near enough that he could see it was addressed to Mina.

It was signed, "Your Loving Servant for Life, Percival."

Instinctively, he focused on the letter, reading every word. A deep line appeared across his brow. His countenance darkened considerably.

At the other end of the table the countess hid a satisfied smile behind a napkin as she daubed her lips in a ladylike fashion. She recalled the letter she had penned in rigidly upright brown letters.

"My Darling Girl," it began. "Has there ever been a man as blessed as I this bright summer morn? The other night I could scarce believe my ears when you returned my sentiments. Perhaps 'twas merely the excitement of your ball, my dearest girl, and you shall feel differently as time passes. As for my heart, it is steadfast. My love for you shall never waver.

"Do you know your heart, my darling girl? Is your love as radiant in the light of the sun as it was beneath the silvery moon? If your answer is yes, then meet me in Tilbury this noon. A special license has been procured; the curate will unite us in holy wedlock. I've arranged for a carriage to convey you to Tilbury. Should you not come, I will understand, though my heart shall ache. Your Loving Servant for Life, Percival.''

"Where's Mina?"

"Eh?" The countess glanced up in feigned confusion.

"Mina? Where's the girl?" He shot the question down the table, words resounding through the room like the retort of a pistol.

"I believe I saw her leaving," the countess said in an offhand manner.

"Leaving? Good Lord, where to?" He jumped up from his seat.

"I hardly know, Compton. Thought you were riding roughshod on the girls these days."

"So you simply let her leave the house!"

"Whyever not? She's a good gel. Never caused me a moment's worry. Probably gone to see her brother."

"Not hardly," he raged, his voice rising to a bellow. "Hughes!" he thundered, then tossed the letter towards his grandmother. "Take a gander at that!"

"Yes, my lord?" Hughes stood on the threshold.

"Did Miss O'Kieffe leave the house this morning?"

"Yes, my lord. A hired carriage arrived at eight-thirty. Driver said he'd been instructed to wait for Miss O'Kieffe."

"Did he also volunteer his destination?"

"Tilbury, my lord."

The earl prowled across the polished wood floor, long fingers running through his hair. What had gone wrong? He thought they would talk the matter out between them, but she had not sought him out last night. Why not? Had he driven her to Barcroft? Not a minute passed before he declared, "I'm leaving."

"What do you intend to do?" the countess blinked at him as though surprised.

"You've read the letter. I have no choice. I intend to stop her."

"*Mais non*, Compton. If this is what the gel wants,

you must not interfere." She tested the strength of his determination.

"Rubbish! Don't care what the chit wants. Clearly she's not thinking straight. She's not marrying Barcroft. Not so long as she's under my roof. Until she returns to Kent, I retain authority over her, and I say *she's not marrying Barcroft*!" With that, he stomped from the dining room, calling as he went, "Hughes! Have my horse brought 'round in five minutes."

The countess hopped up from her seat and followed him into the rotunda. They entered at the same instant Liam O'Kieffe walked through the front door with Jenny in his wake.

"Hell and damnation! What are *you* doing here, O'Kieffe?" the earl demanded without preface.

"Come to see my sister," was the defensive response.

"Not likely unless you plan to witness a wedding."

Liam stopped in his tracks. "What?"

The earl strode to his grandmother's side, yanked the letter from her, and thrust it at Liam. "Take a look at that."

Quickly, Liam scanned the letter. "Good Lord! She can't marry Barcroft!"

"Precisely my sentiments."

Liam looked at the earl and observed the muscle ticking in his jaw. "Do you intend to stop her?"

"Yes," was the immediate and definite response.

"I'll accompany you, my lord. Can't let her hare off and marry Barcroft. He's not the man for her."

The countess, who had observed this in silence, cast a nervous glance over her shoulder. She could not allow the men to leave quite so soon. She rushed forward. "Don't be hasty, gentlemen," she cautioned. "What do you know of affairs of the *coeur*, Compton? And you, Mr. O'Kieffe, how dare you naysay your sister's elopement when you planned the very same with my granddaughter?"

Liam looked abashed, and for an instant he did not speak. Then he said, "Your pardon, my lady. 'Tis not the elopement. 'Tis Barcroft of whom I disapprove. I would not stop her if I believed she was marrying for love, but I believe her motives are ill-founded." He directed his gaze on the earl and said in a serious voice, "She doesn't love Barcroft, my lord. Surely you know that."

The earl returned Liam's gaze. "I pray you're correct, O'Kieffe," he said. "Will you help me stop her?"

"Need you ask?"

And as the two men sped out the door, the countess sighed. This was unfolding far better than she had envisioned. It could not be more perfect had she written a script for her players.

Exactly seven minutes later Catherine burst into the morning parlor where the countess sat at the escritoire.

"I declare! Whoever gave you that message, Grandmère, had windmills in his head. There was no one at Dawson's. I waited a full hour, and if Liam intended to be there, he would have come or sent me a message." She tossed her gloves onto a settee and collapsed beside them. "What a lot of rushing around for so early in the day. 'Tis positively exhausting." She yawned. "Saw the queerest thing as I was crossing the square."

"Yes?"

"I know 'twas not possible. Thought I saw Compton and Liam riding towards Regent Street."

"*Mais oui*, Catherine, 'twas quite impossible," said the countess in such haste the Catherine peered closely at her grandmother, who appeared to be avoiding her gaze at all cost.

Suspicious, Catherine queried, "What is it, Grandmère?"

"Nothing. *De rien. De rien.*" The countess shuffled some papers, glanced at the floor, then out the window, and again at the floor.

"What is it?" repeated Catherine. Her grandmother was behaving prodigious odd. She was nervous and even appeared a trifle guilty about something. Impossible. Her grandmother was never discomposed, and she had certainly never been guilty about anything. Clearly, she was hiding something. "Well, Grandmère, out with it," Catherine demanded.

"I did not want to tell you this," the countess began and

then halted, again alternating her attention between the floor and window.

"Grandmère, you shall make me crazy if you don't tell me!"

"Very well." She looked at Catherine, her expression rigid with apprehension. "You did not imagine seeing Compton and Liam. They were together."

"Why? Don't stop now, Grandmère. The whole story, if you please."

"They argued, my dear. A dreadful argument, and your brother challenged Liam."

"A duel!" Catherine gasped and jumped to her feet. "Mercy, no! Where?"

Again the countess appeared reluctant to answer. Catherine repeated the question. "Where were they headed? Grandmère! Where are they going!"

"Tilbury."

"I must stop them!" she declared on her way out the door, never pausing to consider that this was hardly the normal fashion in which two gentlemen went about a duel. The only thing she could think was that her worst nightmare was about to come true.

The door slammed behind Catherine, and once more the countess smiled.

The two gentlemen on horseback wound their way through the congested streets. They too followed the docks out of London, and as the day lengthened traffic became heavier. They were forced to pause as an enormous wagon laden with barrels exited one of the warehouses.

Liam cleared his throat, and the earl glanced his way. "About your sister, my lord. I know we've gone about this all wrong from the start, and perhaps you still believe I'm not good enough for Catherine, but with or without your consent I intend to make her my wife."

Three months ago those same words would have outraged Compton. This morning he understood and nodded solemnly. "You have my consent and blessing, O'Kieffe. As I told your sister, I was acting out of bitterness before and I don't intend to do so again. I've learned the hard way that love is infinitely fragile and precious. One is exceedingly foolish to do less than cling to it as tenaciously as you and my sister have done, sir.''

"Thank you, my lord."

"Nay, 'tis Compton, if we're to be brothers." With a merry twinkle in his eye, he teased, "Are you certain you want her? She'll take ten years off your life, I warrant."

Liam chuckled. "Yes, Catherine is enough to try even the holiest of saints."

"Hah! You admit it. Think you're man enough to handle her?"

"I believe so. We've achieved a sort of balance between us. And although she likes to challenge me, she likes to please me better."

"Yes, 'tis the way with love, I believe." They rode in silence for the next quarter mile. Then Compton asked, "What did you mean when you said that Mina did not love Barcroft?"

Reining in his mount, Liam shot a sideways glance at Compton, who was none too successfully endeavoring to hide his apprehension. "Precisely that. Her affections are already engaged. And 'tis not conjecture, 'tis fact, for she told me so the night of the May Fair. She loves you."

Uncertainty gave way to boyish delight and Compton said, "Thank you for your honesty."

"What are your intentions, my lord?" Liam sounded very fatherly.

"I would marry your sister myself," was his sincere statement. Silently, he said, *If she'll have me.* For although hope bloomed within his chest, the earl would not be at ease until he had heard the truth from Mina herself.

"I'd like that above all else," said Liam; all animosity between the two men vanished.

"Let's pray we're not too late," Compton replied. Tilbury was twenty-six miles below London Bridge. It was passing eleven, and they had yet to reach Greenwich.

Setting spur to his horse, Liam cried, *"S'rioghal mo dhream."*

Compton cantered alongside Liam and gave him a questioning glance.

"'Tis a Celtic battle cry. Passed from father to son. From one brother to another. 'Our blood is royal. We shall triumph!'" Liam repeated the phrase. Compton tried it, his tongue tripping over the unfamiliar words. Then the earl said it a second time, only louder and with more force.

"*S'rioghal mo dhream!*" Both men, brothers in heart now, bellowed the cry in unison the third time, and following the Thames they urged their horses to a punishing pace towards the ancient riverbank hamlet of Tilbury.

Chapter Sixteen

No one was waiting for Mina when she arrived in Tilbury a few minutes before eleven o'clock. The innkeeper's wife escorted her to the private parlor overlooking the vegetable patch and the Thames beyond. A serving girl brought a pot of tea and day-old scones, and after removing her bonnet and gloves, Mina settled down before the open window. An assortment of crafts were sailing downriver with the tide; a ferry crossed between Tilbury and Gravesend, where brown warehouses clustered about a steeple. She sighed. A crude clock above the hearth ticked off the minutes. Outside a dog barked. Mina hurried to the door, but neither Catherine nor Liam entered the common room.

Where were they? she wondered. Surely Compton had not discovered their plan. That would mean disaster, for Mina did not doubt Catherine would fight him tooth and nail. Of a sudden, Mina was exceedingly weary of this. She wanted it over and done with once and for all. She wanted Catherine and Liam settled. She wanted to go home.

At a few minutes past noon, the door burst open. It banged against the wall, and Mina jumped from her seat. Compton, followed by Liam, marched into the parlor, both of them behaving as if they were in pursuit of a band of deadly cutthroats.

"Where is he?" demanded Compton, searching the tiny room for Percival Barcroft.

But Mina had not heard the question. She was too intent on putting forth one of her own. Turning to Liam, she asked, "Where's Catherine?"

And Liam, for his part, did not hear his sister's question. He was far too intrigued by the possibilities this situation presented. They had arrived in time. There was no ring on Mina's left hand. Liam grinned, and wondering how the earl was going to manage a proposal under such circumstances, he leaned negligently against the wall.

"Where is she?" she asked again, assuming that Catherine had already been confined to the earl's carriage. It did not matter that she was in the wrong; she needed a friend. *Oh, how bereaved she must be*, Mina thought as she tried to hurry out the door.

The earl observed Mina's quick movement. *Oh no, she's not going to run off*, he thought as he stepped in front of her. "You're not going anywhere."

"Let me pass, my lord. You have no business with me," she said in as bold a voice as she could muster, for her heart was racing at the sight of him.

"That is strictly a matter of opinion," he drawled. "And what business have you here, pray tell?"

Indignant, her eyes flashed. Was he accusing her of abetting this latest fiasco? How dare he think so low of her! "Ooooh!" she said and stamped her foot. "Let me pass! I'll not stay here another minute and tolerate one of your royal setdowns!"

"Have something to confess, have you?" he said in what was cutting close to a tease.

"I've nothing to confess," she huffed and stared up at his

implacable countenance. Little did she realize it required every ounce of strength the earl could employ to prevent his mirth from spreading. All she saw were the thin lines about his mouth, the scowl forming between his eyes. "Oh, what's the use in going on? I had no part in it. In truth, I cautioned Catherine, and I know you'll never believe me—for you didn't believe my apology—but 'tis the truth."

By this time the earl had a fairly good notion of what Mina was babbling about with such fervor.

"Hush, my love, I believe no such thing," he said to Mina.

"What did you say?"

"I don't believe that you had anything to—"

"No, the other." Her heart seemed to be trying to get out of her chest as Mina repeated his words. "My love."

His voice was harsh with emotion. "Yes, my love. My own love." When she did not speak but stared spellbound at him, he assured, "Truly." He offered her a loving smile and stepped towards her. "Don't you think 'tis high time we put a stop to this charade, Mina? I didn't ride this distance at breakneck speed to prevent Catherine marrying your brother. I did so to stop your marrying Barcroft."

"Barcroft?"

A low chuckle rumbled from his chest. "Yes, Barcroft, or so I'd been led to believe." Responding to Mina's puzzled expression, he added, "If I don't miss my mark, we're the witless pawns in some rather heavy-handed machinations."

She felt a flicker of hope. "You would have stopped me marrying Barcroft?"

"Of course. I couldn't permit anyone else to have you when I love you so much myself."

"You do?"

" 'Tis precisely what I intended to tell you the other evening until we were so rudely interrupted by my peagoose of a sister." He crossed the final feet that separated them and took one of Mina's hands; his other hand tipped her chin to better meet his gaze. "I had hoped you might have come to feel some affection for me these past weeks. Was I wrong?"

The light in his eyes brightened while he searched deeply into her green ones. The world came to a grinding halt. The single second that passed between his question and Mina's answer seemed an eternity.

Breathless, she responded, "No, Compton, you weren't wrong."

"Won't you say it?" he urged on a husky whisper.

"I love you, Compton."

It was a humbling moment, loving her beyond all reason and knowing she returned that love, and he thought his chest would burst with emotion. It was as if a dam had opened. Giving a laugh of sheer joy, he threw his arms about her, crushing her to him, while planting tiny kisses across her brow and cheeks.

"Ahem. Excuse me." It was Liam, an arm wrapped about a rather wild-faced Catherine.

The lovers glanced up.

"What are you doing here, dear peagoose?" Compton asked in so jolly a voice that Catherine's eye widened like saucers.

"I came to stop the duel," she responded, to which Compton threw back his head and broke into peals of uninhibited laughter.

"Don't tell me," he managed between guffaws, his deep blue eyes dancing with delight at the absurdity of the situation and the inevitability of its conclusion. "Grandmère told you Liam and I had gone to Tilbury to duel."

"Yes, she did." She slowly glanced about the room, eyes moving from her brother embracing Mina and back to Liam, who was far too at ease for a man about to face death. "You're not dueling. Are you?"

Liam, beginning to comprehend what had occurred, retained his mirth long enough to say, " 'Twas a grand hoax, my angel."

"You aren't getting married today?" Mina asked Liam and Catherine. They shook their heads in denial. She pulled the letter from her reticule. "Then who wrote this?"

"Grandmère!" Catherine and Compton declared in one

voice. The four of them began talking at once, Catherine about her trip to Dawson's, Liam about his summons to Cavendish House, the earl about the letter, and Mina about the mischief of it all.

They were interrupted when the door opened and the innkeeper announced the arrival of the Tilbury vicar, Reverend Boswell.

"My-my lord Brierly?" the reverend stuttered.

"Yes?" The earl moved forward to greet the balding curate. "Brierly at your service, sir. What may I do for you?"

The earl's queston perplexed the curate, who glanced about the room. "I—I had been led to understand you were expecting me, my lord. Was an old friend of your grandfather's, you see, and when the countess wrote and requested my services in your behalf, I was more than happy to oblige."

"And what request was that?"

The curate blushed furiously, then bumbled, "Not the usual sort of request, to be sure. And on such short notice, too. Good thing she wrote the bishop. Took some doing, but I obtained them precisely as she asked. Owed a favor to your grandfather and was mighty glad to repay him after all these years." He cleared his throat as if making an announcement and handed an envelope to the earl.

Compton looked inside and smiled. *Ah, Grandmère, bless you.* He took out two pieces of paper, handed one to Mina, the other to Liam.

"A marriage license!" Mina whispered in surprise.

"Let me see that." Catherine snatched the other paper from Liam and perused it. "Egad. This has our names on it!" She looked at her brother to see if he were about to steal away this precious document, but his attention was directed at Mina.

"I can perform the services here or at the chapel— 'tis only a stone's throw through the village," said the reverend.

"Which will it be?" Compton asked Mina.

"Are you suggesting we marry in what would amount to

little more than an elopement?'' Mina scarce believed her ears.

"I believe it would behoove us to do just that. My grandmother has gone to a great deal of trouble to arrange this. Likely more trouble than a fashionable wedding at the Grosvenor Chapel would have entailed.''

After some consideration, Mina remarked, ''You're right. And Lord knows what she might do if we returned to Town unwed!''

"Spare us her further interference!'' added Liam.

They were reduced to gales of laughter—all of them except the vicar, who stared at the young people as if he had found Bedlam.

Catherine composed herself long enough to turn to Compton. "You would let me marry Liam?''

"Can't think of any other man better suited to keep you in line. *I* certainly failed. He's welcome to you, my scapegrace of a sister,'' he teased on a roguish laugh, followed by a kiss to her forehead. His eyes twinkled as he added, "And I wish you years of happiness.'' Catherine squealed and threw her arms about his neck, fair strangling him with exuberance. He choked out in jest, ''Do something, O'Kieffe. Save me, man.''

Catherine returned to Liam's side, and Compton returned to Mina. "Have you decided? Where is our wedding to be, my love? Here or in the chapel?''

"I would like to be married in the chapel, if you please.'' The delicate blush of a bride fanned her complexion.

"Anything, my love,'' he said as his lips trailed across her cheek. Between shockingly playful nibbles, he whispered in her ear, ''Anything, my darling forest nymph.''

On the way to the chapel, they passed a flower cart and without any prompting Compton and Liam each purchased a bouquet of flowers for their respective brides. Mina carried deep purple violets mixed with sprigs of heather and white roses, while Catherine carried crimson tulips and white irises.

"Once we're wed, Grandmère shall be out of mischief.''

"Yes, but only for a while.''

"Heh?"

"Soon she'll want great-grandchildren, and there's no telling to what lengths she might go to achieve that goal!"

Their laughter rang through the narrow street, echoing off the walls of the old stone fortress. The chapel was in sight, and they quickened their pace.

Bringing up the rear of the jovial wedding procession was the Reverend Boswell. He frowned at the spirited couples he was about to join in holy matrimony and paused on the threshold of the chapel to watch as they proceeded up the aisle. He cast a dubious glance heavenward and then shrugged as he retrieved his Book of Common Prayer from a pew. Their laughter died down when they reached the altar, and the curate sighed. A smile replaced his frown. It was a bright, broad smile, for Reverend Boswell loved weddings.

Author's Note:
THE MAYFAIR SEASON

Readers who are familiar with seventeenth- and eighteenth-century English history will note the literary license I have employed regarding the confectioner's Gunter's and the artwork of William Hogarth.

Gunter's, located at Number 7, Berkeley Square, beneath the sign of the pineapple, was founded in 1757 by an Italian pastrycook whose business partner was Gunter. The famous confectioner's was known for its delicious ices, elaborately decorated wedding cakes, and turtle soup. The description of a tearoom within the establishment is mine alone and, I hope, will not offend readers more knowledgeable than I.

Among Hogarth's works there is no etching entitled *Execution of a Fencing Master*—the name of the etching that Mina and the earl observe in the Dog and Ducks Tavern. His well-known picture of the *Apprentice's Execution At Tyburn,* coupled with the fact that an execution of one Thomas Cook for inciting a May Fair fracas in 1702 did occur, served as inspiration in the writing of *The Mayfair Season.* The real Thomas Cook was not, however, a fencing master; an Irishman, Mr. Cook was a butcher and prize-fighter found guilty and hanged for the murder of a constable, John Cooper. My fictionalized account of an *Execution of a Fencing Master* is true to the spirit of Hogarth's work; it is the sort of scene that Hogarth loved to capture in his art.